PRAISE FOR JULIA GABRIEL

"Julia Gabriel does an amazing job with this devastatingly, heartbreaking love story." —*RT Book Reviews, Top Pick* for *Hearts on Fire*

"A compelling romance supported by nuanced characters ... heartbreaking and sensitively drawn ... a well-crafted contemporary romance." —*Kirkus Reviews* on *Hearts on Fire*

"A heart-wrenching and emotional read, with a sweet payoff that will leave readers smiling" —*InD'Tale Magazine* on *Hearts on Fire*

"A bittersweet story about perseverance and adversity. Julia Gabriel does an amazing job of conveying the characters' feelings. The writing style is flawless, and the characters are both multifaceted and dynamic." —*RT Book Reviews, Top Pick* for *Next to You*

"The second novel in the Phlox Beauty series, *Back to Us* is an intimate look at an unforgettable, albeit imperfect, love.

Ms. Gabriel's deeply moving storytelling evokes every facet of emotion from the reader. Not only does this book have standout characters, the city of New York shines in this tale. All in all, between the beautiful settings and the sweet and satisfying ending, this book is a winner!" —*InD'Tale Magazine* for *Back to Us*

"*Back to Us* is a unique romance about falling in love all over again. Colt is a great character that readers will be rooting for throughout the book." —*RT Book Reviews*

THIS REMINDS ME OF US

JULIA GABRIEL

SERIF BOOKS

THIS REMINDS ME OF US

CHAPTER 1

'm dead.
        And I don't know why.

Serena Wolfe blinked hard. She was surrounded by harsh light, light that was so white and pure it could mean only one thing. She had died. She closed her eyes again to contemplate this unexpected turn of events. A moment ago, she was alive.

Right?

She was at her cousin's wedding on the eastern shore of Maryland, a welcome weekend break from her job on Capitol Hill. She'd been working as a legislative assistant for one of New York's senators since graduation. "Since graduation" meant all of a month and already she was bored out of her mind.

"It will get better once you've settled in, learned the ropes, and met some people," her mother said. Her father had said nothing. As far as he was concerned, there was nothing to be said. She had graduated from Princeton in May, now she was working on the Hill, in a year or two she would head off to law school some-where. Columbia or Harvard—those were the only two options in his worldview.

Her life had been mapped out for her since before she was

born. Boarding school in Connecticut, summer internships in Europe, the Ivy League and a respectable career until she married a nice young man, preferably one who worked in finance like her father. They would buy a co-op on a nice street on the Upper East Side, just like the one she had grown up on. Then she would pop out a few babies and join her mother on as many charitable boards as there were hours in the day.

Never mind that her mother had been utterly miserable for as long as Serena could remember. Her father was happier, but only because he distracted himself with alcohol and affairs. Not necessarily in that order.

So spending a weekend in some tiny waterfront town for the wedding of a cousin too minor for her parents to attend? Hell to the yeah. Serena RSVP-ed to that invite so fast she practically chased down the mail carrier before he got to the end of her tree-lined block in DC.

And so far it had been one glorious weekend off the radar of her usual life. She hadn't felt this alive since … well, since never. So she couldn't be dead!

I just met the most hot damn gorgeous man on the face of the earth. No way am I dying yet!

Oliver Wolfe was one long cool drink of tall hot fireman. And right before she had opened her eyes to that infernal light, he was rolling his eyes at her lame attempt to win a stuffed animal at the tiny town's fireman's carnival.

Yet … it felt like such a long time ago, too. She tried to move her arm. Then her leg. Neither moved. She tried the other arm and leg. Nada. She opened her eyes just a hair. Yup. That awful bright light was still out there. She scrunched her eyes shut as tight as she could. *Don't go toward the light.* Even though a snarky voice was telling her she was obviously already at the light. She tried moving again—and again, nothing.

So she really was dead. Maybe that part where Oliver Wolfe was rolling his eyes at her had been her life doing the proverbial last moment drive by. In that case, she was going to ignore the light for as long as she could and let herself sink back into the life she was enjoying a moment ago. Because Oliver Wolfe … mmm, mmm, mmm …

She turned to Kayleigh, standing next to her. Kayleigh was another distant cousin and one of the bridesmaids from yesterday's wedding. She and Serena had hit it off at the reception. Plus, Kayleigh had been up for a night on the town.

"Do you have any more tickets?" Serena asked.

She didn't care about winning some silly stuffed animal. She was almost twenty-two years old, way past that stage of life. And if she hadn't managed to loop a plastic ring over one of the painted wooden stakes by now, a few more tickets weren't going to make much of a difference. But she didn't quite want to leave the presence of the hunky fireman manning the booth just yet. There was something just so … earthy and … primal about him. Unlike the guys she had gone to boarding school and college with, guys whose idea of dressing down was sporting Gucci loafers with bare feet. She couldn't see what Hot Damn Firefighter was wearing on his feet, but it certainly wasn't a pair of suede slip-on shoes. She'd bet the absolute last dollar in her promised trust fund on it.

"Here." Kayleigh thrust her last strip of tickets at her. "This is how gambling problems start," she laughed.

Serena was in a betting mood tonight. She peeled off three tickets. "Give me three more," she said to the firefighter.

Hot Damn Firefighter took the tickets from her outstretched fingers and gave her three plastic rings in return. The skin on the back of his hands was a map of tiny scars, but his nails were neat. Not manicured and buffed like her father's, but simply clean and precisely trimmed.

She twirled the rings on her fingers as she stared down the landscape of wooden stakes. Most of them had already rejected her advances. She narrowed her eyes, zeroing in on a target.

"Wax on, wax off," Kayleigh bantered next to her.

"Oh hush. I am not leaving this town without a prize."

She flicked her wrist and watched as the first plastic ring sailed over the stakes and … bounced onto the grass just like all its compadres that had gone before.

"And her first shot goes wide," Kayleigh mimicked a golf announcer's low, ponderous voice.

"*First* shot?" Then Hot Damn Firefighter pointed to a faded red stake. "I would try for that one."

Serena coolly lifted one eyebrow at him. "You would, eh?"

"Yes, ma'am, I would."

She zinged the second ring toward the red stake. It too bounced off and onto the ground.

"She has one more shot," Kayleigh murmured.

The third ring sailed smoothly over the stakes but Serena immediately realized she had put too much spin on it. She'd be lucky if it hit any rings at all before sailing off into the sunset, so to speak. At the last minute, though, Hot Damn Fireman's hand rose up and gently bumped the ring. It fell neatly onto the red stake. He looked across at Serena and winked.

"You didn't see that," he said.

"The crowd goes wild," Kayleigh said in her golf monotone.

"But I get to pick the prize," he added.

He turned to the pegboard behind him and scanned the colorful array of stuffed animals. His gaze settled on a row of white and black dalmatians near the top. As he stretched an arm up to grab one, his black fire department tee shirt rode up his back, revealing a slice of hard tanned back. Serena felt an overwhelming urge to lick his skin.

By the time he turned around, she had retrieved a pen from her purse and scribbled her room number on the back of a gas station receipt. She slipped it into the palm of his hand as he gave her the stuffed dalmatian. He glanced down at the receipt, then at her.

"Chesapeake Inn," she said quietly.

"I'm stuck here until eleven."

"I'll wait up." She smiled as he stuffed the crinkly slip of paper into his pants pocket.

"Did you just give him your room number?" Kayleigh asked as they walked away from the game.

"I did. Why not? He's hot, don't you think?"

"You think he'll show?"

Serena shrugged. "Probably not."

They wandered around the carnival for awhile, gorging on funnel cake and rating the hotness of the many firefighters working the game booths and rides. It looked like every last person in the tiny town was there, like it was *the* social event of the year. It was charming, in a way. And certainly more fun than the social events her parents went to in New York. Fundraisers for the private schools she and her brother had attended, museum galas for big money donors, dinner parties with people who looked like they slept in black tie.

Ugh. That lifestyle held no appeal for her, even as she knew her parents would probably be successful in roping her into it. They were successful in everything they did.

"Let's get on the ferris wheel," Kayleigh suggested. "I haven't ridden one of those since I was a kid."

"I haven't ridden one of those since ... never."

Kayleigh's head swiveled toward her, a look of disbelief on her face. "Never?"

Serena shook her head. "I'm not real crazy about heights."

"Oh." Kayleigh's face fell.

"But I'll get on it." Serena looked up at the top of the ride. "This one doesn't look that high."

They bought another strip of tickets and boarded the metal car. As it slowly rose into the night air, Serena began to doubt the wisdom of her choice. But hey, she was off the grid for a weekend. If ever there were a time and a place to do wild and crazy things, this was it. Monday morning, she'd be back in her office, behind a desk, pushing paper while breathing in recycled air.

She took a deep inhale as the car reached the top of the wheel and they began going backward. The ferris wheel was a good bit higher than it had looked from the ground. But she refused to close her eyes, even as a prickly ball of panic started to take shape in her chest. She squeezed the stuffed dalmatian tighter. She could handle this. Besides, it was for a good cause. The carnival was raising money for … well, for something. The fire department, probably.

As they rounded the wheel a third time, the ride slowed and they stopped at the very top. The car swung gently back and forth. It was quieter up here. The shrieks and screams from the other rides sounded more distant. The tinny music playing from speakers hung up on poles around the carnival was fainter. She looked out over the miles of earth around them, marveling at the way she could see where the lights of the town ended and the black of the countryside began.

It was never completely dark in New York. She didn't realize that until she went to Princeton. She took another deep inhale. The air here was clean—no toxic perfume of car exhaust and garbage. No noise pollution either—no sirens and car horns blaring all night long—unless you counted the squawking of birds first thing in the morning. Which she didn't.

After another moment, the ferris wheel stuttered to life and their car began its slow descent.

"Well, that wasn't too bad," Serena admitted as they walked away from the ride, although her legs felt a little wobbly.

"How did you grow up in a city where every building is a skyscraper?"

"It was rough." Serena laughed. "I always took it as a sign that I wasn't meant to be a New Yorker."

Up ahead, a small crowd was gathered around a dunk tank,

jeering and catcalling the unfortunate fellow inside. As they got closer, Serena saw that it was Hot Damn Firefighter.

"Oh I am so doing this," she said. "How many tickets do I need?"

"The sign says three."

"Perfect. I have three left. Must be a sign." She handed the stuffed animal off to Kayleigh and got in line. In the thick of the crowd, she was too short to see him get dunked every time. But over and over, she heard the splash of water, followed by loud cheering and shouts. His name was Ollie, apparently.

He didn't look like an Ollie. What he looked like was the most gorgeous man she'd ever seen. Tall. Dark. Handsome. And when he had smiled and winked at her, her insides damn near melted.

At last, she made it to the head of the line and handed off her last three tickets to the teenaged attendant. The crowd quieted down, as she hefted the first softball in her palm. There was no way she could dunk him. She couldn't throw a ball to save her life. She had just wanted to see him again.

Sure enough, her first throw sailed wide. Way wide. Her cheeks grew hot with embarrassment. At least at the other game, there wasn't an audience beyond Kayleigh. But she couldn't back out now. The teenaged boy handed her the second ball.

Wide again.

She took the third ball, keeping her eyes on the round metal target attached to the lever that should—in theory—dunk Hot Damn Firefighter in the water. She felt his gaze on her, felt its intensity flicker over her skin. There was no chance he was going to turn up at her hotel room that evening—not after this pathetic incident. Just as well anyway. It wasn't like she was in the habit of picking up random strangers and engaging in one-night stands.

The crowd was growing restless. Conversations that had stopped were now resumed. She wiped her sweaty palm against her plaid Bermuda shorts, then cocked her arm and hurled the ball with all her might. To her surprise—no, to her complete and utter shock—the ball clipped the edge of the metal target. But not enough to trigger whatever mechanism governed the lever.

She stole an embarrassed glance at Hot Damn Firefighter just in time to see his arm reach behind the narrow seat he was perched on. A second later, he dropped into the water with a splash.

CHAPTER 2

*O*liver Wolfe leaned his forehead against the cool blonde wood of the hospital door and took a deep breath. His heart physically hurt in his chest. There had been false alarms in the past—the hospital calling to say his wife might be waking up. Ollie would jump in his SUV, leave the boys with his dad or his brothers, and hightail it to Baltimore like a bat out of hell ... only to get to this very spot, the cool blonde wood door to her room, and discover that she was still asleep.

Asleep. That's what he told the boys. *Mommy's asleep.* Even five-year-old Cam wasn't buying that anymore. Serena had been "asleep" for almost four months now. The day of the accident had changed all their lives, and Oliver was nearly beyond hope that things would ever go back to normal.

He took another deep breath, trying to get the stinging in his eyes under control. *I don't know if I can do this again. Push open this door and be disappointed another time.* He had to be strong for the boys, but that left no strength for himself.

Maybe the idea of a life with Serena had been too good to be true. What business did he, a small town firefighter, have with a woman like her? He had already cost her the trust fund she was supposed to inherit when she turned twenty-five. She maintained that she didn't care about that, but how could a person not? There had to have been days when she thought about alternatives to the life she had in St. Caroline. Days when one of the boys was colicky or teething or not sleeping through the night and he had been on shift at the station, not home to help. Alternatives she could easily have had. A nanny. A husband with regular hours.

It was a fireman's life—the odd hours, the buzzing pager that interrupted dinner or bath time or … more intimate times. And not a day had gone by since the accident when he hadn't wondered whether she had fallen asleep at the wheel, exhausted, or been distracted by her never-ending list of things to do. Or distracted by more existential matters—regret, resentment, roads not taken—all the things that wear away at a marriage.

He lifted his forehead from the cool wood and dropped his hand to the door's handle. It was also cool to the touch. Everything in the hospital was cool, sterile, a blank slate for a person's fears and worries. Serena was the opposite of that—warm and outgoing, the sort of person who took on other people's problems and fixed them right up.

Oliver gave a tiny shake of his head. And to think how charmed he had been by her ineptness at carnival games the night they met. He had never believed in love at first sight until he took his first look at Serena. She was everything he had never thought to want in a woman—short of stature, wildly curvy, not an athletic bone in her body. And that hair … it nearly defied description. Black as night and curly as all get-out. A shiver ran down his spine as a sudden memory hit him—the feel of her hair on his shoulder, against his neck and cheek, as they made love. The sweet vanilla scent of her shampoo.

He swayed, unsteady on his feet, and pressed a palm to the door. Wasn't this where it had all started? At a door he'd never expected to be at. Eight years ago, he had done the most un-

Oliver Wolfe thing: go to the hotel room of a woman he had just met. He was certain his younger brother, Matt, did that sort of thing all the time. But Oliver was the eldest son in the family and, as such, had always felt visible ... watched. First kids grow up under a microscope, their parents marveling anew at every "first." First smile, first laugh, first steps, first day at school, first driver's license. It was why he hadn't wanted too many years between Mason and Cam—he didn't want Mason bearing the brunt of all that parental obsession.

Love at first sight. Who would have predicted it of Oliver Wolfe? When the carnival shut down for the evening and he had changed back into dry clothes, he pulled from his pocket the receipt on which she had written her room number. Room 222. Was there some meaning in the symmetry of the numbers? Some fated destiny? He didn't know. All he knew was that if he didn't knock on that door, he would never see her again.

So he had knocked. She opened the door, still dressed in the plaid shorts and wrinkled white shirt she'd had on at the carnival. Her feet were bare. That was the only difference, and he was surprised to see that her toenails were unpainted—bare shells on tiny tanned feet. At that moment, he had never wanted anything as much as he wanted to pick up her curvaceous body, carry her over to the plush hotel bed, and make those tiny toes curl with pleasure.

But instead, he had said, "Care to go for a walk?"

He took a deep breath and pushed down on the cold handle of the hospital door. Whatever lay on the other side had to be faced, and he might as well get it over with.

SHE HEARD a door wheeze open on its hinges. Were there doors in heaven? Or hell, for that matter? Who was she to presume she'd gone to the better place? Hers had not been a terribly religious family and so Serena couldn't say what to expect from either place. *Hot as Hades.* Her grandfather used to say that when she was a child. He'd been gone for many years now, though. Probably enjoying the heat in Hades, if Serena had to guess.

She heard the soft thud of the door closing. It was an oddly familiar sound and suddenly she felt as though she'd been hearing it all the time.

"Babe."

The word hung in the air like a hummingbird, not moving yet not still either. *Babe.* That was Ollie's pet name for her, his favored term of endearment. But was that Ollie's voice? The suddenness of the word's arrival caught her off guard.

"Say it again." She felt her lips moving, but it was hard to tell whether any sound was coming out. Her jaw felt stiff—rigor mortis?

"Babe."

Then she felt a strange rush of air being pushed toward her, and she forgot the need to keep her eyes shut against the white light. But she opened them too quickly and had to immediately close her lids again. There was too much light for her pupils to handle.

"Serena. Baby."

It *was* Ollie. She was certain of it. Maybe she wasn't dead after all?

"Can you lower the lights?" she said softly.

A moment later, his voice returned. "There. I turned it off. The only light now is from the window, but it's not too bad."

She heard a scraping noise. A chair being dragged across a floor? Where was she? She became aware of a mattress beneath her body, a pillow cradling her head. She was in a bed. But why? She wasn't at home. She could tell that. This place didn't smell like home. Then something touched her forehead. Skin. A hand.

"Here. I'll shield your eyes while you open them so you can get used to the light."

Yes, it was definitely Oliver. Her husband. He was kind that way. Thoughtful. Wasn't that what had attracted her to him in the first place? He'd given her a stuffed animal even though she sucked at that silly game. When he came to her hotel room later that night, he never even set foot inside. He invited her on a walk through the sultry summer night. They walked to the little beach and when she stripped off her clothes to skinny-dip, he still managed to be the perfect gentleman.

She felt her lips curve into a smile. Wherever she was, Oliver was here with her so how bad could it be? She fluttered her eyelids open and his calloused palm was right there, blocking the light from her tender eyes. She blinked a few times to help them adjust, then moved his hand away with her own. Her arms were working!

I think I'm still alive.

But Ollie wasn't looking so hot at the moment. Even in the dim light, she could see the shadows beneath his eyes. His hair badly needed a trim, which was completely unlike him, and his cheekbones seemed more pronounced.

"You look like hell," she said.

"I'LL TAKE THAT AS A COMPLIMENT." He smiled a wary smile. He'd rehearsed a thousand things to say for when this moment finally came and now he couldn't remember a single damn one of them.

She looked around at the room, taking it in. "I'm in a hospital," she said. She locked eyes with him. "I didn't lose the baby, did I?"

Ah damn. He had hoped to avoid this particular conversation right off the bat.

"Yes," he answered quietly. "We did. But we can try again."

She closed her eyes for a moment. When she reopened them,

they were full of sadness. "But we'll never have another chance at a honeymoon baby."

He threaded his fingers through hers, gave them a gentle reassuring squeeze. "Well, no." He was puzzled by her comment. "But we already have our honeymoon baby." Another reassuring squeeze.

"I thought you just said that we lost the baby."

Oliver leaned toward the bed and brought their clasped hands to his lips. He kissed her knuckles, trying to collect his thoughts and arrange them into some order that made sense here.

"We lost the new baby. But Mason and Cam weren't in the car with you, sweetheart. They're at home right now, safe and sound. Mattie is watching them."

"I'm not talking about those kids. I'm talking about *our* baby. We got pregnant on our honeymoon. Accidentally, but still …" Her eyes brimmed with tears. "Don't you remember?"

He felt the earth begin to shift beneath him, the bottom starting to drop out of what was left of his life, of what he had come to regard as his *normal* life.

He scooted the chair he was sitting in as close to the bed as he could get it. "You were in a car accident, love. Almost four months ago. You just woke up."

"I was out … for … four months?"

He nodded.

"But we haven't been married much longer than that."

"We've been married eight years. Mason is seven and Cam was born five years ago."

She shook her head back and forth on the wrinkled pillow. "No. That's not—"

"They can't wait to come see you. They miss you. I've missed you, too."

In her dark eyes, he saw a spark of fear ignite. It matched the spark of fear in his gut. *She just woke up. That's all. She's a little disoriented.*

"Four months ago?" She shook her head. "I don't remember being here that long ... I don't remember being here at all." The fear in her eyes was more than a spark now.

"You've been in a coma all this time." Oliver stood over the bed and gently cupped her face in his palms. "Baby, I am so glad you're awake." *I was beginning to think it wasn't going to happen.*

He leaned down and kissed her, tentatively at first but then deeper, fueled by the desperation and fear that should have disappeared with her waking. He forced himself to break the kiss before the desperation and fear became obvious. He looked into her eyes. Months in the hospital had not been kind to her. She was thinner than he'd ever seen her. Her glossy black hair was dull and matted about her head. But she was beautiful to him. Their life together had been beautiful. Their family together was beautiful. Until the day of the accident, Oliver Wolfe had nary a complaint in the world.

CHAPTER 3

*O*liver waited in the hall while the doctor and nurses tended to Serena. He checked his phone for messages, then called Matt.

"How are the boys?" he asked.

"Asleep. At last," Matt answered, chuckling. "All in one bed, too."

"Yeah, Cam usually ends up in Mason's bed these days. I'm hoping that'll stop when Serena gets home."

"How is she?"

"Groggy, but awake. The doctor is in with her now." Groggy, that was it. Who wouldn't be groggy after almost four months in a coma? "I'm not sure when I'll be home. What's your schedule like tomorrow?"

"Evening shift."

"Okay. I'll call around to find someone to relieve you if I'm not home by noon. Does that work?"

"Don't worry about it, Ollie. I'm sure I can get Jack or Becca or someone to come over for a few hours."

Oliver ended the call, then stared at his phone as a light bulb lit up in his brain. He thumb-tapped the photo icon and swiped until he found a photo of the boys. *Seeing them will jog her memory.*

He anxiously paced the hospital's squeaky linoleum floor until the doctor emerged from Serena's room ten minutes later.

"How is she?" he asked. The doctor was at least as old as Oliver's father, with a bushy grey mustache.

"She's doing well. Physically, she's in good shape these days. Which we knew, of course."

"She seems a little confused." *Groggy.*

The doctor nodded. "Perfectly normal in these situations. That will likely settle down in the coming days."

"Is there any chance she'll slip back ..." Oliver couldn't bring himself to even say the words.

"I don't think so. We've been seeing signs that she was waking for the past several days. We didn't want to notify you until we were more certain."

If Oliver had learned anything these past months it was that doctors and nurses weren't perfectly transparent—in the name of sparing patients' families from disappointment or worry. As a certified EMT, Oliver understood the impulse. How many times had he sugarcoated what was speeding away in an ambulance? Losing your shit never helped any situation.

Oliver had totally lost his shit at the scene of Serena's accident. It had taken three people—his father and both brothers—to restrain him. Thank god the boys weren't in the car with her. He didn't know what he would have done in that event.

"Can I go back in?" he asked the doctor.

"For a few minutes, son. She needs her rest. It's best not to overwhelm her with everything she's missed in the past months. Plenty of time for that later."

Oliver nodded his understanding. She had missed a lot since the accident. His mother passing away. The whole situation with his brother and Becca Trevor. No one saw *that* coming.

The doctor clapped a big hand on Oliver's shoulder. "I think we're out of the woods now."

Oliver slowly pushed open the door to her room and was greeted with a smile from his wife. *Well, at least she remembers me.* If she hadn't … there was no one else for her to go home with. Her parents hadn't spoken to her since before their wedding.

"Hey there," he said, dropping into the chair next to her bed. He patted the cold metal arm of the chair. "I'm not sure I can sleep in a bed anymore," he joked.

"I love you, Ollie."

The look on her face was soft and open, making her look like the old Serena despite the weight loss. He reached out and clasped her small hand in his, threading his fingers between hers.

"I love you too, Serena."

He pulled back his hand and retrieved his phone from his pants pocket. He tapped the photo icon and turned the screen around for her to see. "That's Mason on the left and Cam on the right."

She lifted the phone from his hand to put it more directly in her line of vision. He held his breath while she studied the pictures, but there was no flash of recognition in her eyes. She wiggled her thumb in front of the screen.

"May I?"

He nodded and watched as she scrolled through the photos. At last, she stopped at one and stared at it for a good three minutes before speaking.

"This is us." She turned the phone around for him to see. It was a picture of the four of them on the boat, over a year ago now.

"Do you remember that day?" he asked.

She was quiet as she studied the picture. Then she shook her head. "Is that our boat?"

"Yes."

"And you said Cam is the older one?"

18

"No, Cam is five and Mason is seven."

"What month are we in?"

"November."

"So Cam just started kindergarten."

Hope flickered in his chest. She was starting to remember.

"Is Cam short for 'Cameron?'"

Or maybe not.

"Are those family names? Cameron and Mason?"

"No. We just liked them. We were going to name Mason 'Austin' but then two days before you went into labor, we changed our minds."

She nodded and handed the phone back to him. "Either name would have been nice."

The tiny flicker of hope was now an icicle, short and sharp as a dagger, and aiming in an uppercut straight for his heart. He held his breath, sitting on the edge of the hard hospital chair. *This can't be happening.*

"Serena," he whispered.

Her eyes filled with tears. "I can see that we're a family. I just don't remember it."

SHE HAD NEVER SEEN fear in Oliver's eyes before, but that was unmistakably what she was seeing now. That rattled her almost as much as the discovery that she had a life, large chunks of which she apparently couldn't remember.

She had children.

She was older than she realized.

She'd been in a car accident.

How could she not remember any of that?

"How old are we now?" she asked him.

"We both turned thirty this year."

Thirty! How'd we get so old? But she kept that thought to herself.

"March eleventh. That's my birthday, right?"

He nodded.

"And yours is July seventh?"

He nodded again, but the fear remained stuck in his eyes. "You were my older woman."

She appreciated his attempt at humor and mustered a smile for him.

"Mason's birthday is July seventh, too."

"Really?"

His lips broke into a small smile. "I don't know how you pulled that off. But thank you."

"And Cam's?"

"March twenty-fourth."

"What are their favorite flavors of ice cream?" Ice cream might seem like a trivial matter at the moment, but if she could make Oliver feel useful—feel in control—it might chase away some of the fear in his eyes. Ollie hated being out of control and if she had been in a coma these past several months … she couldn't even imagine how he had coped.

"Cam is cookies and cream all the way. He's a one-flavor man. Mason, on the other hand, likes everything. Cam is usually finished with his cone by the time Mason whittles his choices down to three or four."

"I'm sorry, Ollie," she whispered.

He shook his head slowly, sadly. "It's not your fault, sweetheart."

"What caused the accident?"

"We don't know."

"So it might have been my fault."

"You're a careful driver," he countered.

"The boys weren't in the car?"

"No. You dropped them off with Charlotte Trevor, for some reason."

For some reason. Maybe she was imagining it, but she thought she heard a note of accusation in those words.

"I'm guessing Charlotte's not a teenager anymore."

"You remember her?"

"Yes, vaguely." From the expression on his face, she could tell that he wanted to ask her to tell him everything she remembered. But just then, the door to her room opened and a woman's head appeared. A nurse.

"Mrs. Wolfe? It's time for your physical therapy."

She wiggled her legs beneath the hospital's scratchy sheet. "I feel pretty weak."

The nurse pushed the door aside and completely entered the room. "Well, that's what we're going to ascertain today. The PT has been working with you every day but now that you're awake, we can better gauge where you are."

She could tell Oliver wanted to stay, but she didn't want him to see her fall flat on her face. Or ass.

"Go talk to the doctor," she said to him. "Ask him how long my ... problem will last."

CHAPTER 4

*O*liver knew he was dreaming. He had always been one of those people who swore he never remembered his dreams. Probably because, as a firefighter, he never let himself fully fall asleep. His brain was always ready for the phone call, the alarm, the heavy clatter of boots on the station floor, the dispatcher's steady voice. Even as a child, he had slept with one ear open for the sounds of his father getting up in the wee hours of the morning to respond to a call.

By the age of four, he knew his mother was Santa Claus.

But his father put him on leave from the St. Caroline fire department the day of Serena's accident. Since then, he had been sleeping like the proverbial baby. And dreaming—in vivid Technicolor-Imax-Surround Sound detail. In fact, he had an entire catalog of dreams he could practically revisit at will, and he was having exactly the dream he wanted to be having tonight. The one where he and Serena had gone skinny-dipping the night they met.

The minute the lights went down on the carnival, he had hopped in his truck and headed for the Chesapeake Inn. He strode right through the lobby, past the front desk and the girl working there—a girl he'd gone to high school with—and skipped the elevator for the short flight of stairs to the second floor. He figured there'd be gossip the next morning (*Ollie Wolfe was at the Inn late—and not at the bar, either!*) but he didn't care. All he could think of was seeing that woman again, a woman whose name he hadn't even thought to ask for. If he stopped, even for a moment, to worry about gossip or that she might have fallen asleep already or would just plain ignore his knock, the normal Oliver Wolfe would catch up to him and put a stop to this crazy idea.

He hurried down the carpeted hall to room 222 and knocked on the wooden door, quietly enough not to wake other guests but firmly enough that she would definitely hear. The crazy idea was multiplying into more crazy ideas. What if she answered the door in sexy lingerie? Or a towel? Or ... nothing at all?

When she answered the door in the same clothes she'd had on at the carnival, Normal Oliver slammed into him so hard it knocked the words right out of his mouth: "Care to go for a walk?"

By the time they reached Secret Beach, normal Oliver Wolfe had been left behind again. "There's a little cove around that bend," he said. "Sometimes people skinny-dip there."

"Think anyone's there now?" she asked.

"We can go check."

The cove was empty. Was that a sign from above or what? He tugged his SCFD tee shirt from the waistband of his jeans and pulled it over his head. By the time he dropped it onto the sand, she was completely undressed and jogging toward the black water of the bay.

It was all he could do to remember how a zipper worked. They had exchanged names and basic details on the walk over, all of which he'd left with Normal Oliver for safekeeping.

It was early in the summer and the bay was still chilly, but he didn't notice. He cut through the water until it was up to his chest and he had reached the spot where she floated on her back, the round tops of her breasts bobbing pale and wet in the moonlight. Her dark hair lay on the surface of the water like seaweed, and she smiled at him.

"I would have thought firefighters could get undressed faster than that," she said.

"We're generally fully dressed beneath our turnout gear."

She rolled her eyes at him. "Well, there goes that fantasy."

She flipped onto her stomach and began to swim away from him. He dove into the water and followed, coming up right behind her, so close he could feel the heat of her body through the cool black water. She turned and wrapped her arms around his waist, an open invitation if ever he'd seen one. He leaned down to kiss her. He could slip his hands beneath her lovely bottom, hike her up an inch or two, and he'd be inside her. And damn damn damn, if that wasn't exactly where he wanted to be.

Her lips were salty from the bay and he tasted them over and over, until there was nothing but sweetness left. He wanted her and she wanted him, and the opportunity was right there for both of them. They'd never see each other again. He wasn't her type for anything beyond a roll in the hay—or surf or sand—anyway. That fact alone would have been all some guys needed—a secluded beach, one night of satisfaction, wham bam thank you ma'am. And Oliver wasn't saying that he wasn't that kind of guy. He'd partaken of offered pleasures in similar situations while on vacations with friends or weekends at the shore.

This felt different, somehow. And while he was pondering why that might be, Normal Oliver snuck up on him from behind. The guy could walk on water, apparently.

If you have sex with her tonight, you'll want her again and again and again.

The pleasure of holding this woman in his arms was exquisite. But Normal Oliver was right. If he indulged in it—just this once —no other pleasure would ever be enough. He knew it made no sense—and a certain appendage was vociferously arguing its case otherwise—but enough of his brain cells were still functioning for him to know it was true. Could he spend the rest of his life knowing that he'd never have it this good again? On the other hand, if he abstained tonight, he could talk himself into the idea that she wouldn't have been that good anyway.

Sometimes it's better not to know, man? You know what I mean?

That was the start of his life with Serena, a running battle between two Olivers, between the man he was and the man he wanted to be—for her. The war was won—or lost, depending on how you looked at it—the day of her accident. Since then, it was only Normal Oliver and the dreams of his other, better half.

"Ollie?"

Serena's voice wasn't part of his current dream. He knew that instantly. He had all these dreams memorized, after all, and he brooked no deviation. His waking life was so out of control, he needed to count on consistency and predictability when he slept.

Her voice came again. "Who responded to the call?"

He swallowed, then bit down hard on his lip to keep it from trembling. The sharp taste of blood kissed his tongue. He kept his eyes closed. Maybe she'd assume he was asleep and go back to sleep herself.

"Ollie. Please tell me it wasn't you."

He swallowed the blood. "The police got there first."

"They usually do."

He knew Serena well enough to recognize the subtext in her words. *You're not answering my question.* It wasn't that he didn't want to answer her question. He didn't want to remember the answer.

"Jack got there first." And then the words spilled out. "He called dispatch to tell me not to come. But Mattie and I were already on the way." *Don't cry. Do not let her see you cry.* But he could feel the tears clinging to his eyelashes. "It took all three of them to hold me back."

"Come here."

He opened his eyes and saw her struggling weakly to pull back the covers.

"Get in bed with me."

"I'm probably not supposed—"

"Break a rule for once, Ollie. For me?"

He rose from the chair, blinking his eyes hard to shake off the tears. He could never say no to Serena. She knew that. She was his weakness, his Achilles heel, his kryptonite. *You can't afford to be weak anymore.* He'd thought her waking up would be the end of this road. Now he realized they still had a long ways to go. If they were to get there as a family, he had to be strong enough to carry them there.

"I'll go get a nurse," he said.

CHAPTER 5

*S*erena plastered a bright smile on her face until the door closed behind the exiting physical therapist. Then her face fell as she collapsed back onto the pillow, exhausted. She'd been awake for a week and already she was sick of the hospital. She wanted to go home. Even though "home" wasn't the small two-bedroom apartment she remembered. Apparently, she and Oliver had bought a house two years ago—the apartment had gotten too small for two rambunctious boys.

Her rambunctious boys.

How did she give birth to two children and not remember it? She closed her eyes. The doctor said she might regain her memory. Or not. Or regain some memories and not others.

And she'd been pregnant when the accident happened. She'd give anything to rewind time to before that awful day.

She opened her eyes and peered over at the clock on the wall. She hoped Ollie would wait until after lunch to visit. The doctor had started her on solid food two days ago and … it wasn't going well, to say the least. Oliver saw worse on the job all the time, but still. She looked bad enough as it was—her hair several months overdue for a cut, her face breaking out like a teenager's. She'd rather not vomit up soup and gelatin in front of him on top of that.

Even worse, she feared being a burden on him when she went home. The doctor assured her that she wouldn't be released until she could keep solid food down consistently and had recovered her muscle strength. Right now, just walking down the hall exhausted her.

But damn, she wanted to go home, even to a home she couldn't remember. Any place would be better than a hospital.

Lunch came and, true to form, she couldn't keep any of it down. Oliver walked in right as one of the nurses was helping her into the tiny shower.

"Let me do it," he said, kicking off his shoes and rolling up his pants legs and shirt sleeves.

"I don't want you to see me this way."

"Naked?" he answered quietly, smiling.

She watched helplessly as the nurse retreated and disappeared.

"I'd rather see you this way than the way I've been seeing you for the past several months." He calmly reached over and turned on the water, keeping his hand in the stream until it was warm enough. "The doctor says this is all normal, love."

"Not being able to eat. Atrophied muscles. *Fine.* But not being able to remember my own kids is not *normal.*"

He helped her sit down on the narrow tiled bench. "You'll remember them. It's just temporary. They're clamoring to come see you."

It's just temporary. That's what she kept telling herself. But with each passing day, it grew harder to have faith in wishful thinking. She took a deep breath.

"I'm sorry. I don't want you to pull them out of school to come all the way to Baltimore."

"Thanksgiving is next week. How about I bring them and

we'll have Thanksgiving dinner here together? Dad offered to come with me."

She took a deep breath, ignoring the way moving her lungs made her feel like she'd been punched in the stomach. She scooted along the bench until she was beneath the water, where Oliver's soapy hands began to wash her shoulders and back. The feel of his hands on her skin relaxed her. A little bit, anyway. She let the water run over her skin, imagining it washing away every worry and care.

"Did anyone call my parents?" The question popped into her head suddenly. Oliver turned off the water.

"I did."

Of course, he did. Even though they had always treated him like dirt, Oliver would do the right thing.

"They did come visit twice," he added.

"Oh. Good." She felt him drying her skin with a scratchy hospital towel. "Were they …" *Any nicer?* She couldn't force the words from her mouth. But Oliver knew what they were.

"No." He wrapped the towel around her shoulders. "Are you okay sitting here while I go get you a clean robe?"

She nodded and pulled the towel tighter.

"CAN I sit in the chair for awhile?" Serena asked as Oliver helped her back from the shower.

"Sure."

She gave a little yelp as he sat in the chair and pulled her down onto his lap. He stretched toward the bed and yanked off the blanket, wrapping it around her. He felt a moment of protest hover in the air, then she let it go and leaned back into his chest.

"You going to cop a feel?" she said.

He pressed a kiss into her shower-damp cheek. "Sounds like a good idea to me." He slipped his hands beneath the blanket and the thin fabric of the hospital robe. He spread his palms over her stomach and just rested them there. Her stomach was so completely flat now he could feel the points of her hip bones pressing into his wrists.

Serena had never been stick-thin, and even less so after two pregnancies. He had liked the soft roundness of her belly, the way the curve of her hips melted into the curve of her thigh. That intense physical attraction he'd felt the night they met? It had yet to diminish. Not even a tiny bit.

Case in point: the part of his body that was lengthening beneath the warm weight of her bottom.

"You're incorrigible, Oliver Wolfe." But she smiled as she said it.

"I can't help it. Raised by Wolves, you know. Plus you're just so damn sexy."

"Right. In this very sexy gown."

He pressed a kiss into the base of her neck, inhaled the scent of soap and skin. "I kinda' like the way it's completely open in the back." He rocked his hips under her. His erection was now long *and* hard.

He ran his hands up her ribs, which were too prominent beneath his fingertips, and cupped the underside of her breasts. That was all the further his hands went. He wasn't trying to be overtly sexual, other than a certain appendage he had little to no control over. He suspected she just needed to be touched, after all these months, in a way that wasn't clinical. Touched by someone who cared about her. Who loved her. Lord knew, he needed to be touched.

He slid his palms back down her ribs and over her thighs. As he skimmed his hands across her skin, he felt her body relax against his.

"Maybe you can ask the doctor when we can resume," Serena paused for effect, "marital relations."

Her laughter caused her body to jostle against his. He groaned into her back. "If you don't hold still, we're going to be resuming in about ten seconds."

She carefully spun herself around on his lap, ending up straddled across his thighs. She caught his eyes as she unzipped his grey cotton pants.

"Serena," he whispered. Her hands were soft where he was hard. "I'm not going to last."

"That's okay. I know you need this."

"I do. I need you back in our bed, just the two of us."

She was stroking him a little harder now.

"It's okay ... you know ... if ..." She stared at his shirt as her hand continued to move. "You probably thought I was never waking up."

Oliver covered her hand with his and stilled her motion.

"I'd understand if you did," she added, quietly.

A tear dropped onto the back of his rough and scarred hand. Just like that, his arousal went soft. He hated to give voice to what he thought she was giving him retroactive permission for. But he needed her to be crystal clear on this.

"Are you asking if I was with another woman while my wife lay unconscious in the hospital?"

"You had needs. I'd understand, Ollie, really."

He put himself back into his pants, pulled up the zipper. Then he lifted her teary face to meet his gaze. "I never—*never*—even *considered* being unfaithful to you." He cupped her jaw in his palms. "I've been on leave from the fire department. These past four months, I've either been here with you or at home with the boys." His thumb brushed away a tear from her cheek. "The only people who have been in *our* bed with me have been the boys. Right after the accident, we all slept in the same bed for awhile."

"Were they afraid to sleep alone?"

He pulled her head into his chest and nestled it there. "No. I was."

CHAPTER 6

The crayon and marker drawings were spread out across Serena's lap. Fortunately, the boys had signed each one. In Mason's drawings were burning buildings, boats on the water, and fireworks. The pictures of fireworks seemed especially carefully drawn. Cam's drawings were all variations on a theme: four stick figures clearly meant to resemble their family in different settings. At the beach. On a boat. (Oliver had mentioned they owned a small boat—she remembered that.) In front of a house with oversized tulips off to one side.

The boys had made dozens of drawings and her heart ached at the thought of two little boys without their mother for months on end. She was certain they had been well cared for. The Wolfe family was tight-knit. When Serena's parents disowned her over the marriage, Angela Wolfe had been a surrogate mother to her.

Her vision blurred over. Oliver said Angie had died of cancer not long after the accident. She rubbed at her eyes with the back of her hand. She didn't remember Angie even being sick—which, as Oliver pointed out, was probably a good thing. "I think she would have preferred that everyone remember her as healthy."

She neatly stacked the drawings and set them aside. She

reached beneath the blanket and pulled out a small notepad, flipping it open. She was taking notes on everything Oliver told her about the boys. Tomorrow was Thanksgiving and they were coming to visit.

Mason's favorite subjects in school were gym and recess. Cam was in kindergarten but liked reading so far. Cam had a growth spurt last month and was now almost as tall as his older brother. Both boys were fanatic about Legos. Mason was a pumpkin pie man. Cam preferred apple. Favorite foods were pizza for Cam and cheeseburgers for Mason.

She read through the pages, stopping now and then to quiz herself, to test her memory. She had no trouble remembering what happened yesterday or who said what. So why couldn't she remember the rest?

Her heart began to race, as it did every time she thought about the fact that years of her life were completely unknown to her right now. What had she done in those years? Nothing terrible, she was sure, but to not know was terrifying.

She slipped the notepad back beneath the blanket and closed her eyes to sleep. Her boys were coming to visit tomorrow. She prayed she could fake it well enough to fool a five-year-old and a seven-year-old.

OLIVER PAUSED OUTSIDE THE BOYS' bedroom, listening. Between the prospect of the long Thanksgiving weekend away from school and the news that they were going to see their mom tomorrow, they had been wired and hyper all day. They were excited.

Oliver, on the other hand, was cautiously optimistic.

Or trying to be, anyway.

He padded barefoot down the hall to the master bedroom, where it was considerably harder to maintain anything resembling optimism. He brushed his teeth, swapped his jeans and tee shirt for flannel pajama pants, and crawled into bed. Outside, the wind had picked up and a branch from the oak tree in the yard was tapping the side of the house like a metronome.

He rolled onto his side and wondered whether he should trim back the tree. Then he wondered why that particular project hadn't occurred to him until now. He had occupied his time and thoughts with home project after home project these past few months. Replaced the carpet in the upstairs hallway. Repainted the cabinets in the laundry room. Installed a heated towel rack in their bathroom and towel hooks shaped like sharks in the boys'. Planted a row of hydrangeas along the side yard and put in nearly two hundred tulip bulbs in the front—as a surprise for Serena next spring.

But what if she didn't remember that hydrangeas and tulips were her favorite flowers?

They're just flowers.

When the doctor mentioned that the head injury might cause memory loss, Oliver had assumed that meant she might not remember certain events, a day or a week here and there. But years? Not remember the boys? That idea never even crossed his mind.

And what if she never remembers? What then?

You'll figure it out from there.

But what if he didn't? He rolled onto his stomach and buried his face in the pillow. When she saw the boys tomorrow, she'd remember. How could she not? Two humans she had birthed from her own body—there had to be some primal connection between a mother and her children, right?

He was drifting into sleep when another errant thought woke him back up: she thought he might have cheated on her while she was in a coma? The old Serena would never have said such a thing. Was their marriage perfect? No. Nobody's is. But it was solid. Oliver didn't even lust in his heart after other women. Since the day he met her, Serena had been his be-all and end-all. He loved being a family man—a husband and father. His parents had been extraordinary role models. Their example hadn't rubbed off quite as much on his younger brothers, but Oliver had exactly what he wanted inside the four walls of this house. Not once had he ever felt the need to look elsewhere.

If he were more awake, he would have been able to fight off the next thought hurtling toward him. It wasn't like him to go looking for trouble where none likely existed, but he was too utterly exhausted from the past four months to prevent the thought from crashing right into him.

Had *she* cheated on *him?*

Is that why the idea occurred to her? Granted, he wasn't the most exciting guy in the world—a small-town firefighter who worked for his dad and wanted to send his kids to the same schools he'd gone to. But if it's not broke, why fix it?

But ... Serena wasn't from St. Caroline and, while she had loved it at first, maybe she was getting bored here.

You're letting your imagination run away with you.

But was he? After all, Oliver wasn't the most imaginative guy in the world—in addition to not being the world's most exciting. He was steady, reliable, a good provider. He always did the things she liked in bed. Unless ... no, he would have known if she was faking it.

Oliver!

Sheesh. He was yelling at himself. In his mother's voice, no less.

He reached over and pulled his laptop off the nightstand. He kept it there to give himself something to do besides stare at shadows on the ceiling when he couldn't sleep. He flipped open the screen and began to scroll through the dozens of sites he had bookmarked over the past week, even though he knew he would find no new information on head injuries.

Memory loss was a common aftereffect. It could go away on its own. Or not go away. No one at the hospital could say.

Time will tell.

He was so flipping tired of hearing that phrase. He had a life to live *now*, kids to raise *now*. He didn't have the luxury of waiting for time to tell him anything.

Stay hopeful. Things will work out.

He shut the laptop and closed his eyes. In twelve hours, he was taking the boys to see her and they would be reunited as a family. Would things work out? Maybe tomorrow would tell.

CHAPTER 7

*S*erena was running through her mental list of all the things she needed to remember today when the door to her room vibrated with a series of scattered soft knocks like the pounding of tiny fists. Oliver was here. With the boys.

Her boys.

She took a deep breath. The door swung open slowly, then what happened next happened in a blur. Two human projectiles launched themselves onto the bed. Serena could almost swear their feet didn't touch the floor on the way. She struggled to get her arms around them, worried that one or both might tumble off the narrow hospital bed and onto the floor.

"Guys! Guys!" Oliver was shouting. "Careful!"

There were arms around her neck and cheeks pressed up against her own. Dark hair and the scent of soap tickled her nose. She couldn't tell who was who.

Then her father-in-law, Tim, peeled one of the boys off her chest—Mason, she saw—and set him gently on his feet on the floor. Tim leaned in to plant a kiss on the top of her head.

"Welcome back," he said.

Cam tightened his grip on her neck.

"Are you okay?" Oliver mouthed.

She nodded and tugged Cam loose. "Hey there." She ran a hand through his dark curls and the look of sheer unconditional love on his face took her breath away. His blue eyes brimmed with tears, his love for her about to overwhelm his emotions. She pulled his head back down to her neck. Over Cam's shoulder, she saw his brother standing patiently next to the bed, waiting his turn.

Her heart broke at the thought of these two boys—*children*—waiting for months to see their mother. And already she could see the differences between the two. Cam with his emotions right on the surface, clung to her like his life depended on it. Mason, on the other hand, had Oliver's dark, inscrutable eyes. He had rushed the bed with his brother, but now he seemed to have regained his composure. He watched her closely, almost as if he wasn't sure she really was his mother. She gave him a smile, but his expression remained unchanged.

With her free hand, she patted the mattress. "Sit up here, sweetie."

Oliver lifted Mason up so he was perched stiffly on the edge of the bed.

"You've both grown so much," she said.

Her words seemed to relax Cam and he released his death grip on her neck. She knew about Cam's recent growth spurt but what about Mason? Had he grown in the past four months? At their age, it seemed likely. *Right?* But she watched as a thin film of skepticism shaded Mason's expression. *Maybe not.*

"I'm in kindergarten now," Cam announced.

"I know you are." She smoothed a dark curl from his forehead. "You're a big kid now. And you'll have to tell me all about it." She glanced at Mason. "And I want to hear all about second grade, too." She remembered that his favorite subjects were "recess and gym." "How's recess this year?"

Mason frowned. "Every day is a giant four-square tournament. I don't like it."

"Why not?" She reached over and folded her hand around his.

"The girls are better at four-square," Cam answered the question for his brother.

"Oh." She kept her gaze on Mason. "Well, I'm a girl. Maybe I can give you some pointers when I get home. Okay?"

Mason gave a grudging shrug of the shoulders.

"Are you coming home today?" Cam continued.

She switched her gaze to Cam's hopeful face. He was like an open book, his thoughts translated without hesitation into words. *He takes after me.* Mason on the other hand clearly was more like Oliver, a man who kept his own counsel and played his emotions close to the vest. She and Ollie were the classic "opposites attract" couple.

"No, sweetie, I can't come home today." His face fell. "The doctor wants to make sure I'm strong enough to take care of you two."

"Uncle Matt's been helping to take care of us," Mason said.

"And Aunt Becca!" Cam's voice was suddenly excited, and Serena felt a twinge of jealousy.

And who exactly was Aunt Becca? Neither of Oliver's brothers were married. Were they? She shot a *help me out here* look towards Oliver. But his back was turned as he spoke quietly to a nurse who had entered the room. She wracked her brain, trying to come up with a person in St. Caroline named Becca. Rebekah Trevor? Dr. Trevor's adopted daughter? But no way she and Matt were married. If someone had gotten Matt Wolfe to settle down, she'd definitely remember *that.*

"And Jackie's coming for Christmas!" Cam added.

"Jackie ...?"

There was a puzzled frown on Cam's face. "Jackie. You know. Uncle Jack and Aunt Becca's daughter. *Our cousin.*" The note of pride in his voice was unmistakable.

A wave of disorientation started to lap at her feet. Jack was married? And for long enough to have a child? She and Oliver had spent the bulk of their study sessions preparing her for the boys. They'd spent less time on other family members because she remembered them. Or thought she did, anyway.

She glanced helplessly over at Oliver, who was still deep in conversation with the nurse, when Tim Wolfe rescued her.

"Who's ready for some turkey?" he boomed, reaching out to lift Cam off the bed. "Guys, why don't we go down to the cafeteria and find a table while daddy helps mommy get ready?"

After Tim and the boys left, the nurse returned with a wheelchair. Serena swung her legs over the edge of the bed, then walked cautiously and deliberately toward it. Her stamina was improving, but slowly. Oliver steadied her as she sat down.

Can we leave the wheelchair outside the cafeteria?" she asked. "I don't want the boys to see me in it. I think I can walk that far."

"Understood."

She felt him release the brake with his foot as the nurse held open the door. The hallway outside was bright and busy, as usual. Nurses and orderlies scurried back and forth. The elevators at the end of the hall opened and closed, disgorging visitors.

She wanted to leave the hospital. Every day since she'd awakened, her homesickness became more acute. She struggled not to indulge it, since the two-bedroom apartment she was homesick for was apparently not her home anymore. But anyplace would be homier than a hospital.

Oliver pushed the wheelchair onto an empty elevator. When the doors opened three floors down, she could push herself up and out of the wheelchair and make a run for it. She longed to be outside—she hadn't been outside in months—feel the warmth of the sun on her face, or the coolness of a breeze skim her arms.

But when the doors opened, she didn't make a run for it. She knew that the odds of her making it all the way outside without falling were low. And then she'd be stuck here even longer.

Tomorrow, she was scheduled to be moved to the rehabilitation wing, to transition her to home.

Oliver pushed the wheelchair off the elevator and the aroma of food hit her nose immediately.

"Are you hungry?" he asked as he wheeled her down the hall.

"I'm too nervous to be hungry."

"You're doing fine."

The question hung, unasked, in the air. She answered it anyway.

"I'll remember them, Ollie. It'll happen. I know it." *I love kids.* She always had. She'd even nannied for a family in Switzerland the summer between her freshman and sophomore years of college, much to her parents' chagrin. Her father had lined up an internship for her at a bank in Brussels, but by then she was certain she had no interest in banking.

"So you didn't … when you saw them …"

"It'll happen," she repeated, with more conviction this time. She was their mother—at some point, the memories would come flooding back. How could they not? *And I adore kids.* Of that, she was certain.

"What if you don't?"

He slowed the wheelchair to a spot next to the wall outside the cafeteria, engaged the brake. She took his outstretched hand and pulled herself up to standing. She lifted her eyes from the plaid flannel of his shirt to his face.

"Then we go from there. I'll get to know them all over again. I mean, what choice do we have?"

She saw his head start to shake, but then he caught himself. His head dipped forward and caught her lips in a kiss. He murmured words into her mouth.

"We'll fake it until we make it."

Another thing she was certain of—"fake it until you make it" was the most un-Oliver Wolfe sentiment she could imagine.

~

THE HOSPITAL'S cafeteria was surprisingly crowded and it took Oliver a moment to spot his father and the boys.

"They're over there, about halfway across." Serena pointed.

She leaned on him as they threaded their way slowly through the cafeteria tables, dodging people carrying trays laden with slices of turkey, mashed potatoes, and cranberry sauce. It didn't take long before Serena's breathing grew labored, punctuated by sharp intakes of breath. He slowed to a stop.

"Do you need to rest?"

She took several deep inhales. "No. I'm good."

"I can go get the wheelchair."

"No." Her words were more forceful this time. "I don't want them to see me that way."

They moved forward again, even slower this time. He was thankful that she was moving to the rehabilitation wing the next day. A more intensive physical therapy regimen was waiting for her there. The doctor was hopeful that she'd be ready to go home in a couple of weeks—in plenty of time for Christmas.

Fingers crossed. Oliver wasn't sure he could pull off Christmas on his own. Definitely didn't *want* to do Christmas without her.

He looked across the sea of tables. His father and the boys were waiting patiently for them. That's when it hit him. This was their first Thanksgiving without his mother. The first of many holidays without her. He thought back to a year ago, when she was newly diagnosed and they were all so irrationally optimistic. His breath caught in his throat at the memory of their hopeful innocence. They told themselves that she would beat the odds. They would get through this, together. Life would go back to normal.

It didn't work out that way.

This is your new normal.

The toe of his boot bumped the heel of Serena's slip-on shoe and they both stumbled. He caught her, his hand holding tight to her waist.

"I'm okay," she said.

"I'm sorry. I got distracted there for a moment."

"Your mom," she said quietly. "I thought it, too, as soon as we walked in here."

"Yeah."

She wrapped her arm around his lower back and pulled herself into him.

"I'm sure she's watching over all of you."

That would be nice. *We could all use the help.* But he left those words unspoken. He'd been holding up well these past months, as far as the boys were concerned. He did his best not to let them see how worried he was. When he got too close to the edge, he called someone to come stay with the boys and then drove out into the countryside or took the boat out alone until he felt centered again. He had to be strong enough for all three of them —and when he couldn't be, he had to fake it until the moment passed.

He was relieved when they reached the table with no further incident. "I'm going to carry you back," he whispered into her ear as he helped her into the chair next to Cam.

The table was small and square. His father had commandeered a fifth chair from an adjacent table. Three half empty water glasses sat in wet rings on the tabletop.

Oliver remained standing. "Grandpa and I will go get the food, okay?" He locked eyes with Serena for a split second. If she was nervous about being left alone with the boys, she didn't show it.

It took two trips to bring back plates for all five of them, heavy on the mashed potatoes for Mason, no gravy for Cam. Cam chattered away nonstop about school and television shows, and for once Oliver allowed it. The point of the day was for them to be together, as a family. Going with the flow was not really Oliver's style, but he knew he had to endure it today.

"Uncle Mattie said there's going to be live fire training soon," Mason piped up when his brother slowed for air.

"Week after next," Tim confirmed.

"Can I come watch?"

"Bud, that won't be safe," Oliver said.

"I promise I won't be underfoot."

"It's against the rules, Mason," Tim said.

"But you're the chief, Paps. You make up the rules."

"And it's against my rules. It would be against any fire department's rules."

Mason's lower lip jutted out into a pout. Mason was already showing signs of following his grandfather, father, and uncles into firefighting. Oddly enough, Oliver understood his mother's desire for Jack, his youngest brother, not to go into the "family business." As much as he loved being a firefighter, the thought of his kids doing it filled him with abject terror.

You don't know true fear until you have kids.

His mother had said those words to him the day Mason was born. *You were right, mom.* Racing into a burning building was nothing compared to the thought of Mason driving someday, falling and breaking an arm, getting his heart broken for the first time … all the things parents can't protect their kids from.

"Can Aunt Becca watch us?" Cam asked.

"We'll see," Oliver answered, then turned to his dad. "You want me there, too?"

"I need you back at the station soon."

Oliver shot a quick glance at Serena.

"You don't need to come here everyday," she said. "I can't imagine what you've been doing if you haven't been going in to the station."

"He painted our room," Cam said.

"He painted everything," Mason muttered before putting another forkful of mashed potatoes into his mouth.

Serena reached over to touch his arm. "You don't need to be here every single day," she reiterated. "I'm going to be exhausted from all the physical therapy anyway."

"I won't send you out on calls until Serena comes home," Tim added. "But I need an extra set of hands around the station."

"I know you do. I know we're short-staffed."

Oliver also knew that if Serena hadn't pulled through, he would have had to leave the fire department entirely and find a safer career—for the sake of his sons.

Tim Wolfe pushed back his chair and patted his belly. "Who has room for pie?"

The boys' arms shot into the air.

"Alright then, you two can help me carry these trays over to the conveyor belt. Then we'll go check out the pie selections."

Oliver started to stand up, intent on helping, but Serena tugged him back down. "They'll be fine. Kids that age like being helpers, having some responsibility."

"They've had plenty of responsibility recently. Although Mason still bristles at having to put away his laundry."

There was a long moment of silence before Serena spoke. "Are you saying I used to spoil them?"

"All three of us were spoiled."

Oliver wasn't a man who didn't understand—let alone appreciate—all that his wife did for the household. On the contrary, he now felt a little guilty that—knowing firsthand what she did—he hadn't pitched in more at home. But Serena always seemed to like being a stay-at-home mom. She never had much good to say of her job on Capitol Hill. And the job she had in St. Caroline? No way she missed that. Then she got pregnant with Mason on their honeymoon, and they were both thrust quickly into parenthood.

"They're seven and five, Ollie. You can't expect them to put away their laundry *and* enjoy it."

"I know that." He took a deep breath. "I'm just being ..."

"You're just being Oliver Wolfe."

True, that. He was wound too tight. No secret there. Everyone in St. Caroline knew it.

You were born wound too tight.

It worked for him, though. *If I weren't wound this tight, I wouldn't be half the firefighter I am.* He looked up to see his father and Mason carrying trays of pie back to the table, Cam clutching a fistful of forks and napkins in each hand.

"We'll get through this, Ollie. We will. I just need a little time to recover." She covered his hand with hers.

He flipped her hand over, threaded his fingers into hers, and lifted it to his lips. The scent of her skin triggered all sorts of memories that he knew it was safer not to indulge right now.

"I know we will. It's just that I expected things to go back to normal and ..." He watched as his dad and the boys got closer. Soon they'd be in earshot of the table.

"And it hasn't. I'm sorry."

Under the table, she pressed her thigh against his. She used to do that all the time when they were dating, a discreet promise of what was in store once they left the restaurant.

"It's not your fault, baby." He kissed her hand again before lowering it back to the table. The pie-gatherers were nearly upon them. "You know me. Patience is not my strong suit."

She nudged his thigh again. "I do seem to remember that, love."

CHAPTER 8

"Mom's different," Mason declared as he looked around the main bay of the fire station. The school bus had dropped him and Cam off here after school. It was quiet right now, but he had his fingers crossed for a call to come in. Then the bay would explode into action. The guys would jump into their turnout gear, the engines would rumble in the trucks, the bay doors would lift, the sirens would wind up. He loved everything about the station.

"Oh yeah? How so?" His Uncle Mattie was keeping an eye on him and Cam until their dad was done talking to their grandfather.

Mason was proud that Paps was the fire chief. It was a family thing, working for the St. Caroline fire department. Paps, Dad, Uncle Matt, Uncle Jack. A few other family members in the past too was Mason's understanding. Some of the other boys at school wanted to be firefighters when they grew up, but Mason knew he actually would be.

"Like, she doesn't remember who my teacher was last year." This had been on his mind since their Thanksgiving day visit to the hospital last week.

"Well. Huh. Does it matter if she doesn't remember that?"

Great. Uncle Matt was just like Dad and Paps.

Does it matter if ...

We have to be patient ...

It's not that important ...

But some of it was important! *Important to me!*

"I didn't have a teacher last year," Cam chimed in.

Well, duh.

"Your mom was in an accident, bud. She bumped her head. She might have trouble remembering things for a little bit. Be patient, okay? Help her out when she's forgetting something."

"Yeah. We know." Well, Cam didn't really seem to know but he was only five. What could you expect?

Mason glanced toward Paps' office. His dad was inside. The door was closed. Dad said he was going back to work soon, which Mason was happy about. Dad didn't do things around the house the way Mom did. Not in a bad way, just different. Mason didn't like different. Too many things were different these days. Second grade was harder than first, for starters. And Nana was gone. Sometimes he woke up in the middle of the night because he thought he smelled her perfume—oranges and flowers. And then he had trouble falling back to sleep. He didn't like that.

Different was definitely not good.

Serena tried to ignore the throbbing ache in her right leg. The doctor wasn't kidding when he said that physical therapy in the rehabilitation wing would be intense. Her muscles felt like jelly after each session and she hadn't slept through the night once since she was transferred. On the other hand, it did keep her too tired to dwell on bigger picture issues.

Such as who am I?

What kind of mother forgets her own kids? Oliver had

brought the boys to see her twice since Thanksgiving. Try as she might, she couldn't even picture their bedroom at home. She looked at their outfits and knew she must have gone shopping for those clothes, but they were completely foreign to her.

She was staring at a spot on the ceiling, trying to picture the boys' closets at home, when the door to her room slowly swung open. A pile of brightly colored fabric appeared, followed by a middle-aged woman with greying blonde hair and brown eyes. Serena recognized her immediately, which had her inwardly breathing a sigh of relief. It was Michelle Trevor, one of Angie Wolfe's closest friends.

"Hi there," Michelle said, a broad toothy smile accompanying her greeting. "I'm glad I caught you awake."

Serena smiled back. "They keep me pretty busy here."

"I'm Michelle Trevor ..."

Serena nodded. "I know." The door fell closed behind the other woman.

"Wasn't sure you would remember me."

"I haven't forgotten everything." She tried to picture Michelle's daughters. She knew it was a family of all girls, but all she could come up with was a generic picture of blonde and tan, athletically beachy.

"No no, I know. Oliver filled me in."

Serena wondered how many people had been "filled in" on her condition. Michelle was a close family friend of the Wolfes, so no surprise there that she was up to date. But it was also entirely possible that the entire town of St. Caroline knew that she had memory loss. *That I can't remember my own kids.* A hot flush of shame washed over her. How much detail was Ollie going into when he spoke to people?

Michelle began unfolding the bundle of fabric in her arms. It was a quilt. Michelle Trevor owned a quilt shop in town, Quilt Therapy. She remembered Tim Wolfe always joking that when he didn't know where his wife was, he could just assume she was at Quilt Therapy.

"Tim asked me to bring this by," Michelle explained. "He thought it might help make the room a little homier."

"Thank you." Serena pulled the edge of the quilt closer. It was white with multi-colored stars. "Is this one that Angie made?"

"It is. Ohio Star quilts were a favorite of hers."

"She made a quilt for me and Ollie as a wedding present. Not this design, though. It was so beautiful that we never put it on our bed. We didn't want to wear it out." She traced her finger along a line of stitching.

"Oh honey, she would want you to use it all the time. A quilt like that takes hundreds of hours to make. It's a shame to keep it put away."

Serena squinted at the tiny white stitches outlining the pattern. "Maybe I'll put it on our bed when I get home then." She exhaled. "You're right. Seems silly to save things instead of using them."

Especially now, after what had happened to her. It took awhile, but Ollie had finally filled her in on some of the details of the accident. The cause was still undetermined, but she was lucky to be alive. And lucky that the boys weren't in the car with her.

"Did I quilt?" She looked over at Michelle Trevor.

"No. Angie always wanted to teach you, but you and Oliver started a family right away so you had your hands full."

Serena couldn't remember ever wanting to quilt but now … tears welled in her eyes. Maybe she should have let Angie teach her. Sure, with two kids, she would have been busy but … now the opportunity was lost for good. She swiped her cheek.

"It's not real to me," she said, "that she's gone. I don't remember her even being sick."

The expression on Michelle's face tightened and then softened as she got her own emotions under control. "It's not real to me, either. Maybe not real to anyone who knew her."

"How long was she …" She pulled the quilt up to her chest. "I didn't want to ask Ollie for all the details. Talking about that kind of stuff isn't his strong suit, to begin with."

"In my experience, it's not the strong suit for most men. If you're asking how long was she sick, it was about ten months. My husband—Dr. Trevor, he's your boys' pediatrician—said that's not uncommon with ovarian cancer. By the time it's found, it's often spread too far to be treated. The very end was pretty quick, though. Mercifully."

"I can imagine she had everything organized and in order by then."

"She did. You and Angie were close."

Serena nodded. "I do remember that."

"She considered you to be the daughter she never had."

Tears spilled over her lashes and cut a path down her cheeks. "She was the mother I never had. A mother who had time for me. I'm not sure anyone would even call me if my real mother were sick." The tears were a torrent now. "Sorry. I just can't believe I woke up and she's gone."

Michelle set a box of tissues on the bed next to her. It took a moment, but Serena got herself under control again. Everyone in St. Caroline thought she was a free-spirited wild child. Next to Oliver, everyone looked wild but Serena liked to feel in control, too. She and Ollie were alike in that way. It was maybe the only way. She took a long, deep inhale.

"Can I ask you something?"

Michelle nodded.

"I don't like asking Oliver too many questions. It worries him. And I'm sure I'll remember everything sooner or later, but …" Maybe she shouldn't ask this of Michelle either. With the words right on the tip of her tongue, the idea sounded rather pathetic. But she plunged in anyway. "Could you maybe fill me in on things? But not tell anyone we had this conversation?"

Michelle made a zipping motion across her lips. "Of course. Mum's the word. Ask away."

"The boys were talking about Uncle Jack and Aunt Becca. And a cousin?" Serena shrugged her shoulders in bewilderment. "Has Jack really been married long enough to have a child? It just doesn't seem possible."

Michelle made a noise that might have been a sound of amusement … or might not. Serena couldn't tell and she hoped she hadn't just asked the wrong question right off the bat. But Jack was her brother-in-law. She needed to know what was happening in the Wolfe family.

"Well, they're not married yet."

From the look on the older woman's face, Serena wasn't sure if she was going to tell her the story.

"But the Becca everyone is referring to is your daughter, right?"

Michelle nodded. "She was living in Ohio for a number of years. She moved there a few months before Mason was born, I believe. You probably didn't know her well."

"And Jack moved back home after college?"

"Beginning of last summer. That's when Becca moved back, too. It's a long story but I have the time if you do." Michelle smiled at her.

"All I have is time right now, so lay it on me. And whatever else you think I should know before I go home."

CHAPTER 9

*A*fter just five minutes on his hands and knees, Oliver felt the stiffness wrapping around his legs like a vise. The training building was dark with thick black smoke, and hot. It felt hotter than he remembered but then again, it had been six or seven months since he took part in a live burn training exercise.

Oliver felt along the floor with his gloved hands, searching for the end to the corridor he was crawling through with three other firefighters. His brother, Matt, was in the lead position. The training facility was configured like a house with two main levels plus an attic and basement. Somewhere in the building were gas burners—the simulated fire Oliver's team had to find and put out. Another team was searching for victims.

Earlier in the day, Matt had suggested that they needed to find a training facility that could be configured into the layout of a much larger home. Every year brought the construction of more summer homes—some could even be called estates—on what used to be the farmland surrounding St Caroline. And every year, those homes seemed to get bigger and bigger, with rooms sprawled every which way. Sunrooms, morning rooms, his and hers offices, dressing rooms, butler's pantries ... but a firefighter only had so much air in his tank. A building had to be searched and victims found before the air ran out. Oliver agreed with Matt—it would be helpful to train in a larger layout.

The stiffness in his legs wasn't dissipating. His physical fitness was not as good as he had assumed. Nor should he even be thinking about that right now. He forced his attention back to the matter at hand—finding the fire.

The air temperature in the corridor was growing noticeably hotter. They must be getting close to the burners. His hand hit the boot of the man in front of him. He paused and waited, blind in the darkness, calculating how long they'd been inside. He knew his brother up ahead was determining which way to go.

Normally, following Mattie was not a good idea. His life choices were, in Oliver's estimation, not the best. But in an emergency, there was no one Oliver would rather be behind than Matt. His brother had an almost preternatural ability to navigate unfamiliar environments without the aid of most of one's senses.

"Left up ahead." His brother's voice sounded in his earpiece.

They began to move again, slowly feeling their way along the floor and wall, until the glow of the fire came into view. They stood as they entered the room, pulling the hose with them. It was a simulated bed fire, the gas burners engulfing the fake bed in raging flames. Oliver spotted the mannequin on the floor immediately.

Son of a gun. They weren't messing around with this exercise. Matt radioed command with the news that they had a victim while Oliver pulled the "body" away from the burning bed. No way this guy would have survived. If this had been one of those new mansions on the other side of town, they definitely would not have gotten to him in time.

OLIVER PULLED his shoes and jacket from his locker at the station.

He was exhausted. The live burn exercise had gone well, but his day was far from over. He still had to get home and relieve Becca of her babysitting duties. He slipped his hand into the jacket's pocket and wrapped his fingers around his cell phone. He'd give Becca a quick call to let her know he was on the way.

When the screen lit up he saw a voice mail notification. He recognized the number immediately. The hospital. Without even giving himself a chance to think, he tapped the screen to listen. He closed his eyes as the nurse's voice bore into his brain. When the message was over, he hung up and shoved the phone into his pants pocket.

"What happened?"

He looked up to see Matt, a worried expression on his face.

"That was the hospital. Serena had a fall."

"Is she okay?"

Oliver gave an ambiguous nod. "She's bruised and shaken. But nothing broken."

"That's good. Could have been worse."

It could have been, but Oliver was too numb to feel anything resembling relief at this point. Just when he thought things might be getting better, the proverbial rug got pulled out from beneath him again.

"I'll go to your house. I can stay with the boys tonight, if you need to get to Baltimore."

"Thanks, man." Oliver clapped his brother lightly on the back. "I'll make all this up to you somehow."

"No worries. You'd do the same for me."

CHAPTER 10

*S*erena opened her eyes. Yup, the ceiling was still doing that wavy, woozy thing. *I'm high.* The last time she was high like this was in college. Then she had gone and married a man who had smoked pot exactly one time and never had the desire to try it again. *That was Oliver for you.*

She glanced down at her arms to see whether she was hooked up to an I.V. *Nope.* She let her eyelids drift shut again, hoping the pain meds wore off soon. The fall yesterday could have been worse. Nothing broken. Nowadays "nothing broken" qualified as good news. Her hip was bruised, along with her ego. She was making progress in physical therapy—just not as much progress as she thought, apparently.

The bad news was that the doctor wanted to keep her another week now.

"Just to make sure."

But Christmas was now only a week away. Serena knew the boys would be disappointed if she weren't home for the big day. Ollie had managed to get all the shopping done, but she'd been hoping she could at least help him wrap gifts. Especially since he and the boys would have decorated the tree by now.

Decorating the tree was her favorite part of Christmas, bar none. She hadn't known people actually decorated their own trees until that first Christmas with Ollie. Growing up, her mother's interior decorator had always done the family's trees. One for the marble foyer, one for the living room that was over the top glitzy for guests, and one in the family room, which was where Serena and her brother's gifts appeared on Christmas morning. Her friends' families had done the same.

She felt her cheeks warm with embarrassment at the memory. How awful that she didn't even realize until she met Oliver Wolfe that most people put up only one Christmas tree and that they hung it with ornaments themselves. But that first Christmas with Ollie when they were newlyweds and she'd been pregnant with their honeymoon baby was hands down the best Christmas of her life.

It was also the only Christmas with Ollie that she could remember, even though there were two young boys who remembered more.

She pulled Angie's quilt up to her chin. Since Michelle Trevor's first visit, her mind was consumed with thoughts of what her life apparently was in St. Caroline. She was a stay-at-home mom. No outside job. Her closest friend in St. Caroline was Ashley Wardman.

Michelle came back yesterday morning for another visit and to answer more of her questions. It was becoming depressingly obvious that getting released from the hospital wasn't going to be the end of the accident. Going home was going to be like moving to St. Caroline all over again. How many people would she pass on the street and not recognize? How many times would she get lost going to places she'd gone to hundreds of times? Not that they were going to let her drive for a few more months.

And how many times would she stick her foot in her mouth with people because she couldn't remember important things about them? Michelle couldn't give her the entire history of St.

Caroline in a few visits. On top of that, there were things Michelle clearly wasn't comfortable discussing.

Like Ben Wardman.

Ben was Ashley's husband. Apparently, Serena had been friends with the Wardmans since they moved to St. Caroline five years ago. Ben was a science teacher and soccer coach at the high school. Ashley was a photographer, which was how Serena and Ashley met. Cam had just been born and Ashley's very first job in St. Caroline was a portrait of Mason and his new baby brother.

At yesterday's visit, Michelle asked if Ashley had been to visit.

"No. Just family," Serena replied.

Michelle's head moved back and forth, sadly. "Well. She's going through … a time right now."

Serena had waited for her to elaborate. When she didn't, she said, "Mrs. Trevor, you can't put something like that out there and then not say anything more."

"Michelle. You can call me 'Michelle.'"

"Okay. Michelle."

"Ben has been sick."

Given the look on Michelle's face, Serena was reluctant to probe for more information. But she needed to know, especially if she and Ashley Wardman were friends. "How sick?"

Michelle took a deep breath. "Very sick. Cancer."

Serena felt like she'd been punched in the kidney. "First Angie and now Ben, too?"

She opened her eyes and took a deep breath, willing away the nausea. The news of Ben's illness was why she'd fallen during physical therapy that morning. She was walking on the treadmill and thinking about, well, everything when an image of Ben Wardman popped into her mind. It was clear as day—Ben running along one of the quiet country roads outside of town, the hem of his tee shirt flapping, his ginger hair plastered to his scalp with sweat. He ran gracefully, almost as though his feet weren't touching the ground. He didn't shuffle and lumber along like some people did when they ran.

The image—the memory!—so startled her that she stumbled on the moving track and fell. But through the pain, she was elated. She had remembered something! That had to be a good sign, right? Not just for her, but for Ben too. She wasn't into any of that woo-woo, mystical stuff—you couldn't be when you were married to Mr. Practicality—but a memory of Ben running, of being so *alive* had to be a good omen. After all, he was thirty years old. Far too young to die.

Just as a sharp pain shot through her hip, the door to the hospital room swung open and jolted her out of the memory. The nurse, probably, with more pain meds. Instead, a large bouquet of flowers entered the room, followed by Oliver. The words were out of her mouth before she had a chance to reconsider.

"Why didn't you tell me Ben was sick? Who else in town has cancer? You can't leave me in the dark here, Ollie! What am I going home to?"

Oliver had the classic deer-in-the-headlights look in his eyes. Then his chest slowly rose and fell as he took a deep breath and let it out. He laid the cellophane-wrapped flowers at the foot of the bed.

"Who told you about Ben?"

"Michelle Trevor. But it should have been you. We're friends with them!" Serena could hear the register in her voice rising.

Oliver leaned over, resting his elbows on the mattress right next to her shoulders. "It didn't seem like you remembered them." He paused to gather more of his thoughts. "So I didn't want to worry you *right now* about someone you might not have any memory of at the moment. The doctor's instructions were to not try and fill you in on everything all at once. I wish Michelle had checked with me first."

"I remembered Ben this morning! Because I knew! That's why

I fell on the treadmill. I had this picture of Ben running ..." A thought occurred to her. "Is he here, in this hospital?"

"No. He was in a hospice facility closer to home."

Hospice ... that wasn't good news. But she had remembered Ben running! Alive and healthy—that was a sign. It had to be. And yet ... Ollie was biting his bottom lip. It was the classic Oliver tell. She looked down as his warm hands wrapped around hers and pulled them into his chest.

"Baby. Ben Wardman passed this morning."

OLIVER SAT on the floor in his parents' living room. Would there come a day when he didn't think of it that way—as his "parents' house"? He supposed it was just his father's house now.

It's your childhood home.

Yeah. But now that his mother was gone, the house didn't feel the same anymore. Like it was less familiar somehow. He didn't know how to describe it. He was awful at putting words to that kind of stuff. Serena was much better at that sort of thing.

He unrolled a tube of wrapping paper and spread it out on the floor. He needed to get the boys' Christmas gifts wrapped. His parents' house had always been a good place to hide presents, but Mason and Cam were spending more time here with one or another family member as babysitter. Oliver wasn't sure how closely Matt supervised them. Mason no longer believed in Santa —wasn't seven too young for that?—but Cam definitely still did. The last thing he needed *this Christmas* was for Cam to discover that Santa was fiction.

He laid the big pair of scissors on the edge of the paper to hold it flat. Then he surveyed the piles of boxes scattered around him, trying to decide which to wrap first. There were Lego sets for both boys. A remote-controlled helicopter for Mason and a remote-controlled race car for Cam. He picked up one of the larger boxes, a chemistry kit. He thought Mason was too young for it, but Jack swore that it was the thing Mason most wanted.

He centered the box on the paper. How was it that Jack knew how Mason had prioritized his wish list and he didn't? *Hell, I was the person who drove "Santa" into town for the winter festival. On my boat!*

He adjusted the centering another time, sliced through the wrapping paper with the scissors, looked around for the dispenser of tape.

What could he have done differently yesterday? *How was I supposed to know that she'd remember someone? And Ben Wardman, of all people? On the day he dies?*

The visit went from bad to worse. No, it went all the way to disastrous. Serena had gotten hysterical at the news that Ben was gone. Nurses came running at the sound of her screaming.

"Do you want us to sedate her?" one of the nurses had asked.

Of course, he didn't want Serena to be sedated. But it seemed like she had gone out of her mind, was out of control.

The nurse asked again. "Do you want us to sedate her?"

Again, he had hesitated. But when she swung her legs over the side of the bed and started to get out, he gave his consent. She had already fallen once that day, making the doctor decide to keep her in rehab awhile longer. He didn't want her to fall again. That would not have helped matters, either.

He tore off a length of tape and folded the wrapping paper over the chemistry kit.

But maybe he had made the wrong decision in not telling her Ben was dying. Ashley Wardman had asked several times if he thought she should go see Serena. Oliver had asked her to wait until she came home. Getting visitors she couldn't remember would either upset or confuse her.

At least she asked. Unlike Michelle Trevor. Yeah, he remembered that his father had asked Michelle to take that quilt to Serena. He hadn't expected her to keep going back, however.

He spun the box around and folded the ends of the paper into crisp points. His mother had taught him how to wrap gifts. And cook, a little. Do laundry without turning everything pink. *I'm not saddling some poor woman with a son who's helpless around the house.* He could still hear his mother saying that, clear as a bell.

He could use her advice right about now. Maybe she wouldn't know what to do. Maybe no one knew what to do in a situation like this. But she'd brew a pot of coffee and sit with him at the table and try to puzzle it out. She'd tell him straight up whether he was a total jackass for allowing his wife to be sedated.

Tough call.

That's probably what his dad would say. He'd waffle and equivocate, hem and haw. Chief Wolfe was as decisive as could be in the station but outside it? He would neither blame Oliver nor let him off the hook.

Makes terrible coffee, to boot.

Oliver found himself chuckling at that last thought. *Dad does make terrible coffee. Close to undrinkable.*

He rubbed the last piece of tape into place and set that gift aside. One down ... he looked around. Only a few dozen to go! He sighed. Normally, Christmas was his favorite holiday but this year he felt positively Grinchy. Nothing had put him into the mood, not the lights around town or the holly wreaths on the lamp posts on Main Street. Not the town's first Winter Festival, which hadn't been a complete catastrophe despite his brother Matt co-chairing the event.

And now Serena might not be home for Christmas, thanks to the fall. The doctor said he'd try to have her out by then, but that he couldn't make any promises. Oliver centered another gift on the wrapping paper. He was seriously pissed at Michelle Trevor. *I'm her husband! No one should be going around me to see my wife.* Not that he was Serena's gatekeeper, but he was responsible for her well-being. Who else did she have? Her parents had visited the hospital twice, but had given no indication that they were going to become part of her life again. *Just as well.*

He cut the wrapping paper and folded it around the gift. He just wanted Serena home as soon as possible. Things were not going to be easy, but he wanted to just get it over with so they could all begin to move on. The boys had been without their mother long enough. He didn't need town busybodies interfering.

She meant well.

That's what his mother would say about her friend. But Oliver didn't care about Michelle Trevor's intentions. The road to hell and all that. He taped down the wrapping paper and moved on to the next present. He needed his wife to come home, for a whole host of reasons. But also so he wouldn't be alone with his own thoughts all the time. When the house was busy with the noise and activity of a family, it was easier to shush up the thoughts he didn't want to think about.

Like why was Ben Wardman the first thing that Serena remembered?

CHAPTER 11

They look dumb, Mason thought as the nurse held out two small lumpy Christmas stockings.

"One for you and one for your brother."

His father was shooting a meaningful glare his way.

"Thank you," Mason dutifully said. "He didn't want to come today."

"Well, that's a shame."

Something was up—and not just the fact that it was Christmas Day. All of the nurses at the hospital were wearing red Santa hats and grinning weird, awful grins. Something was definitely up.

"Don't you just look adorable?" another nurse said. She looked about as old as his nana had been.

He glanced down at the horrific red and green monstrosity covering his tee shirt. Even seven-year-olds knew about ugly Christmas sweaters, and he was most definitely wearing one. They were gifts from Jackie's other grandparents in Ohio. His dad had made him wear it. Cam had actually *wanted* to wear his. In his mind, Mason was rolling his eyes.

"That sweater is just precious," the older nurse added. "So cute."

He bit the urge to say that goofy thing Cam had taken to saying lately. *I'm not cute. I'm dangerous!* It had to be said while gritting your teeth for full effect.

The Christmas sweater was not cute or adorable or precious. Uncle Mattie would say it was "ugly with a capital U." One thing Mason had learned since his mother's accident was that grownups lied to you, often while smiling nicely at the same time. They said you were cute when you were not. They said things were going to be okay when any blind fool (Uncle Mattie again) could see that they weren't.

Worst of all, he found himself lying to Cam in the exact same way. At night, when his little brother crawled into Mason's bed with his pillow and that dirty old stuffed stegosaurus he slept with, Mason lied to him and said that mom was okay. Mom would be home soon. Even though Mason had no idea if any of that were true. He had no idea what to believe anymore.

But he didn't want Cam to worry.

It wasn't like all of the grownups' lies had caused him to worry any less. In fact, it was just the opposite. If there wasn't anything to worry about, there'd be no reason to lie. Grownups thought kids were so stupid.

"Thank you," he said again to the creepy grinning nurses. If you said "thank you" and "you're welcome," sometimes grownups would be satisfied and go away.

"Ready, bud?"

His dad had one hand on the door to his mother's room His other arm cradled two wrapped gifts—one from him and one from Mason and Cam. Mason had wrapped it himself. Well, with a little help from Aunt Becca.

His dad pushed open the door and Mason ducked beneath his arm to go in first. His eyes landed first on the bed, which was empty. For a split second, he thought he was going to hurl. But the waffles and bacon he'd eaten at Paps' house earlier stayed in a heavy lump in his stomach. Then he saw his mother sitting in a wheelchair by the window, dressed in normal clothes, her hair also brushed to look normal.

"Merry Christmas, sweetie." She smiled at him, a smile only slightly less weird than the nurses' grins had been.

He walked around the bed to get to the wheelchair, where she leaned forward to hug him. The lumpy stockings got mashed between her and Mason's stomach.

"Baby, you're up," he heard his dad say. (Uncle Mattie said never to call a girl "baby," but his father did it all the time.)

His mom loosened her hug and leaned back into the chair. "Where's Cammy? Is he out flirting with the nurses?"

"We left him with Jack and Becca." His dad shrugged, a thing he always did when he knew he'd made a mistake.

"That's okay," his mom said. "He's probably having too much fun with his presents."

It wasn't that, Mason knew. Uncle Jack and Aunt Becca had taken Cam and Jackie to the Trevor house. Cam didn't take any presents with him. It was because Cam had lost hope that their mother was ever leaving the hospital. He wasn't buying Mason's lies anymore.

"Mason? Want to come get this?" His dad nodded down at the presents in the crook of his arm.

Mason carefully lifted the gift he had wrapped and turned to hand it to his mother. "Merry Christmas, mom. This is from me and Cammy." The box held a bubble bath set that matched her favorite perfume. From France, his dad had said. Mason wasn't sure why that mattered but whatever.

She smiled at him and, for a moment, he forgot that this whole thing—his family—was messed up "six ways to Sunday" (Aunt Becca). Sometimes his mom seemed like a completely different person than the one he remembered. But maybe he was remembering her wrong. Maybe she had never known his first grade teacher's name from last year. Or who his best friends were. Or that Nevaeh Logan was always trying to kiss him at recess. And that her name was "heaven" spelled backwards.

Maybe he had to just keep lying to himself, as well.

"Why thank you, sweetheart."

She never used to call me sweetheart.

"But how about if I open this at home? Santa stopped by this morning and said I can leave here today. That's the present he gave me."

Mason's eyes widened and his jaw dropped, in almost perfect sync with his father. *Wait til Cammy finds out.* Their mother was coming home! And he didn't even care about the whole Santa lie. *She probably doesn't remember that I don't believe in him anymore anyway.*

SERENA SNUGGLED up against Oliver in their bed. The boys were finally in bed, too—their candy cane sugar high finally dissipated enough to let sleep take over. She was exhausted. Between the excitement of leaving the hospital and the excitement of it being Christmas, she was spent. Coming home on Christmas probably wasn't the best idea, but she had begged the doctor for days and promised to be extra careful.

Oliver pulled her into him and she pressed her nose to his warm shoulder and took a long, deep inhale of the scent of his skin. She remembered what his skin smelled like. And she definitely remembered the first night she'd spent with him. After the night of the firemens' carnival, she had returned to her "normal" life in Washington, DC. When she hadn't heard from him after two days, she took matters into her own hands and rung up the St. Caroline Fire Department. Luckily, he was on duty.

She went back to St. Caroline the very next weekend. Oliver

took her to a lovely restaurant for lunch, then they went for a drive in the countryside in his pickup truck. It turned out to be a long drive, to accommodate the hours of talking they ended up doing. It felt like she had known Oliver Wolfe forever. When he reached over and held her hand as he drove, she knew she was going to sleep with him that night.

By late afternoon, they were in her room at the Chesapeake Inn. To say they devoured each other would not be understating the matter.

"Penny for your thoughts, love." Ollie's voice yanked her back into the present.

"I was thinking about our first time."

"Mmm." He pulled her even closer. "Sex, room service, then more sex, then room service dessert … I had to marry you after that because everyone in town knew I'd spent the night holed up at the Inn. Even my mother knew."

She stopped her own giggles by pressing her lips into the crook of his neck, then began working her way up to his jaw. This too, she remembered. Ollie's body and all the things it was to her.

Comfort. Refuge. Exhilaration.

She slowly slid her hand down his bare chest to the point of his hipbone, where it encountered the flannel of his pajama pants.

"We used to sleep in the nude," she murmured.

"Mmmm, then we had kids. Who have the alarming habit of strolling into our room unannounced in the middle of the night."

She felt his hip press up into her palm. "Did you speak to the doctor about when we could resume marital relations?" She ran her thumb along the edge of the waistband.

"I forgot."

"The Oliver Wolfe I remember would never have forgotten marital relations."

His chest bounced with a silent chuckle. "Okay, so I didn't forget. But I'm a man. I can't ask another man when I'm allowed to make love to my wife."

"Guess we'll have to play it by ear." Her hand moved a few inches over and down.

Oliver groaned. "That's not my ear."

She stretched her body toward his head, ignoring the sharp pain in her right leg. She kissed the curve of his ear, then took the lobe gently between her teeth.

"Remember that first night? How I made you come when I bit your ear?" she whispered.

"Baby, I remember everything about that night."

"Do you remember how you made me babble incoherently?"

"I do remember exactly how I pulled that off." He turned his face toward hers. Just before capturing her lips in a kiss, he added, "You were quite the vixen."

The kiss was by turns hard and soft, desperate and loving. She had always been able to lose herself in Ollie this way. No matter what else happened, she had Oliver Wolfe at the center. Loving him was enough.

She was exhausted tonight but she wanted to be his vixen again. Her greatest fear was that he would "stray," as her father had many times. Too many times for her mother to even keep track of. She had vowed never to put herself into her mother's position—trapped inside a man's life without even the benefit of his love and affection to compensate.

She told Oliver that she would understand if he had been with someone else while she was in the hospital. She hadn't meant that. Not at all. She'd been fishing for a confession or a clue. In reality, she'd be devastated to learn that Oliver was unfaithful.

He gently broke the kiss and cupped her face in his wide hands. She met his eyes with her own and their gazes sparred, each trying to draw out the other's immediate intentions. She knew what he wanted, this first night home together. She also knew he was too good a guy to press for it.

She was exhausted from the day and the boys and Oliver's family coming over. Sleep would feel so good right now. Instead, she whispered in his ear.

"Make love to me, Oliver."

CHAPTER 12

"*M*iss Ashley!" Cam drew out the final syllable of Ashley's name into a long squeal. The front door was barely closed when he launched himself at her.

Serena watched as the other woman picked up Cam in one smooth movement and hugged him to her chest. Even in a winter coat, Ashley Wardman looked too thin and frail to pick up a five-year-old boy, especially one who was a little tall for his age to begin with.

Mason, on the other hand, approached Ashley more cautiously. "I'm sorry for your loss," he said. Clearly, someone had rehearsed that line with him—that someone being Oliver, she assumed. Or maybe Matt. He seemed to have spent considerable time with the boys over the past several months. Or Becca Trevor? She, too, was now a fixture in their lives.

"Thank you, Mason." Ashley set Cam back down on the floor. Just as quickly as he'd arrived, Cam scampered off to the living room and the boys' sea of Legos. Mason gave his mother and her guest one last look before turning to follow his brother.

"He's an old soul, that Mason." Ashley unbuttoned her coat and hung it up in the coat closet, before following Serena into the kitchen. It was the afternoon of New Year's Eve and she'd come to visit.

"He is," Serena agreed. "Seven going on fifty sometimes. Coffee or tea?"

"Whatever you're having."

"I was thinking about tea." She pulled open the pantry door. "We have quite the collection and I'm guessing it's not Ollie who's the tea drinker." She gave Ashley a rueful glance before plucking out a box of orange pekoe. Joking about her memory loss helped put other people at ease around her, she'd found.

"I can confirm that it's you." Ashley pulled out one of the kitchen chairs and sat down, while Serena put a kettle of water on to boil.

"I'm sorry about Ben, too." She unwrapped two tea bags and dropped them into stoneware mugs. They were nice mugs. *At least my old self had good taste.* "I know I said that over the phone. You went out of town for Christmas?"

Ashley nodded. "I went home to Minnesota for a few days. I needed to get out of town."

"I can imagine."

Serena wracked her brain for something to say next. Everyone said that she and Ashley Wardman were close. Best friends, even. Since the morning she remembered Ben, she had pieced together a few other bits about the Wardmans. She remembered Ashley being a photographer. The upstairs hallway was lined with portraits Ashley had done of the boys over the years. She also had a sense that the house Ashley had lived in with Ben was very small. And filled with lots of books. Every once in awhile, another memory would flash through her mind— quickly, as though someone turned on the light and then immediately switched it back off.

But looking at her right now, it was hard to pull up anything else. Ashley was on the shorter side, like Serena. Her hair was medium brown and cut into a blunt shoulder-length bob.

Diamond studs twinkled from her earlobes. Her makeup was tastefully done—a little eyeliner and mascara, a swipe of blush.

"This is awkward. I'm sorry." The kettle began to whistle and Serena busied herself with pouring water over the tea, carrying the mugs to the kitchen table.

"No apology needed." The conversation fell silent again, until Ashley spoke again. "If you need any help—you know, with the boys or around the house or you need a ride somewhere, just ask."

Oh, I couldn't. You've got enough going on—"

"I have absolutely nothing going on. This is the slow time of year for weddings at the Inn. It's not good for me to have so much time on my hands. I need to keep busy."

Serena watched as Ashley swallowed the lump in her throat.

"Thank you, then. The boys do seem very comfortable with you."

"I adore Mason and Cam. I'll babysit any time. You and Oliver probably need some quality time alone together."

Serena nodded. They did need some time alone. Now that Oliver was back full time at the fire department, some days they passed like ships in the night. And when he was home, it seemed like he didn't know how to act around her.

Ashley looked around the kitchen as she sipped her tea. "Oliver's done a lot of work on the house."

Serena followed the other woman's gaze. Ashley knew her entire life better than she did. Her children. Her house. Hell, probably even her husband.

"Did the house need a lot of work?" she asked quietly.

Ashley laughed, and Serena felt the sound catch on something in her own chest. If only she could reach in and grab onto it, hold it long enough for it to reveal its secrets. Ashley Wardman's laugh … it had to be familiar to her. As familiar as Serena's house was to Ashley.

"No, your house has always been lovely."

A thought occurred to Serena, and she was momentarily surprised that it hadn't occurred to her earlier. In addition to her house and family, Ashley knew *her* better than she knew herself.

Or maybe not. After all, who was she if she couldn't remember her old life?

"I'd be surprised if you liked this color, though," Ashley added, gesturing at one of the red kitchen walls.

Serena began to laugh. "I don't, actually. What color was it before?"

"It was a very pale grey. The whole downstairs was painted in the same shade."

Serena tried to envision the white kitchen cabinets and black granite countertops against a backdrop of light grey. "I think that was probably more 'me.' I think I like a house that's decorated in a soothing way." Yes, she really did believe that. "I like neutrals."

Ashley smiled. "You do like neutrals."

"This is so weird. I'm sorry. I feel like I have to begin every sentence with 'I think' because I don't really *know* what I would have liked."

"You'll get your memory back, Serena. I know you will." She stood and rinsed out her mug in the sink, then carefully set it in the dishwasher. "You know, one of the things that we had in common was that both of us moved to St. Caroline for a man. You, because Oliver lived here, and me, because Ben took a teaching job here. You befriended me right away, even though you were busy with a new baby."

"I feel like I'm having to befriend everyone all over again. It's just … unsettling, having everyone else know things about me that I no longer know about myself. And when I do remember something, it's so random and never what I need to know at the moment."

Ashley pulled her chair right next to Serena's and sat down again. "I know you don't remember our friendship, but after Ben you were the person I was closest to. Now he's gone and I really need a friend to get me through this."

Serena reached out and touched Ashley's hand, then wrapped hers around it.

"And knowing Oliver," Ashley continued, "you're going to need one, too."

~

"WHO HAS SEWN BEFORE?" Becca Trevor looked out over the motley group of women assembled in the upstairs classroom at Quilt Therapy. "Anything. Even if it's just something small."

Next to Serena, Ashley cautiously raised her hand. "I've made some throw pillows for around the house."

"Okay, good. Anyone else?"

Serena watched as several other women called out their sewing histories. A table runner. A tote bag. An apron. Her own hands stayed right where they were, firmly planted on the long white table. She had no sewing history whatsoever. Her mother was never the artsy-craftsy type. Not even in that rich, Martha Stewart   why-yes-I-have-the-time-to-make-my-own-drapes way.

Her parents' house in New York was professionally decorated. She much preferred the house she lived in now. It wasn't fancy, but it was comfortable and neat—and it reflected the people who lived there. Well, except for the newly red kitchen. Her mother would probably cringe were she to ever set foot in it, which Serena doubted would happen only when hell froze over. And maybe not even then.

She and Oliver weren't rich. They could have been, if her parents hadn't revoked her trust fund. Ollie had always said he didn't care about that. She wondered, though, if that was really true. *He's marrying you for your money.* Those were her father's words when she announced her engagement to a handsome, responsible, kindhearted small town firefighter. *You can have your trust fund when you come to your senses and marry someone more appropriate.*

She had yet to come to her senses.

"Well, this class requires no sewing experience," Becca continued.

Serena refocused her attention on the present. Michelle Trevor had talked both Serena and Ashley into taking a quilting class with Becca. So here they were. Serena looked doubtfully at the small stack of fabric before her on the table. The class was so beginner level, the students didn't even have to pick out the fabric. She'd gotten a mix of blues and greens, while Ashley's luck of the draw had netted her reds and purples.

"We're going to be making a string quilt in a wall hanging size. It has only four blocks, so if you mess one up it'll be easy to just make another."

Becca looked and sounded like a different person here than when Serena saw her at Oliver's dad's house. She looked older today in her skinny blue jeans and oversized black turtleneck. Authoritative, too. She was more in her element here, Serena thought, than at the Wolfe house, surrounded by all that testosterone. The absence of Angie Wolfe was palpable when the entire family got together.

That was why she had agreed to take this quilting class—in honor of her late mother-in-law.

"This is what your finished quilts will look like."

Becca held up a square that looked to be roughly three feet by three feet. From this distance in the back row of the classroom, it looked impossibly complicated despite Becca's assertion that the project was for beginners.

Within minutes, both Serena and Ashley were standing at the long cutting table that ran the length of the room's side wall. They busied themselves with cutting long strips, slicing through the fabric with the store-provided rotary cutters. She had to admit, there was a certain sort of zen peacefulness to it, a rhythm to the slicing and stacking. It was a relief to focus her mind on something relatively mindless, instead of her struggles to remember who she was. Now that the holidays were over and the boys were back in school, the house was quiet and still for six hours a day.

Too quiet. Too still.

Her empty mind was always too ready to fill the silence with worry.

Becca was walking down the line of women, peering over hunched shoulders at their handiwork. "How's it going?" she asked as she reached Serena and Ashley.

"Still have all my digits." Ashley wiggled her fingers.

"Digits are good." Becca laughed, then turned back to the class. "Okay, when you have all your strips cut, head back to the sewing tables. Spread out your strips and line them up next to each other. Think about the order you might want them in."

Serena carried a handful of dangling strips back to her seat, where she proceeded to shuffle them around, trying to decide on the most pleasing combination. She glanced over at Ashley, who had expertly combined hers into what looked like a perfect arrangement.

"You're good at this," Serena said.

"I was an art history and photography major. I learned a few things about color and compositional balance."

"Pretty sure mine isn't going to have that."

"Here." Ashley leaned over and moved a few of Serena's strips around. "What do you think?"

All of a sudden, Serena was hit with a blast of déjà vu so intense that it took her breath away. She closed her eyes to try and hold on to it. Memories snuck up on her, but they could sneak away just as quickly.

"Are you okay?" Ashley asked.

She opened her eyes. "Yeah. I get these flashes of ... something. Like something is trying to break through in my brain. But then it's gone as quick as it comes."

"What triggers it?"

"I don't know." She shrugged her shoulders. "It seems to just happen randomly."

~

"Mom? I forgot to tell you something."

Cam was sitting in the bathtub, rubbing shampoo through his dark, wet hair. Serena watched him from her perch on the toilet seat.

"Oh yeah? What did you forget?"

Cam forgetting something was not a surprise. He and his older brother were like night and day. Where Mason was buttoned down, Cam was like a rubber ball bouncing off every available surface. Mason sized up his surroundings, even if that was just the dining room table. Cam was more apt to notice what was in a room about five minutes after he entered it.

"The teacher gave me a note for you. It's in my backpack."

"Oh. And what's the note about?"

Oliver had said he was worried that Cam might not be adjusting to school as easily as Mason did. She wondered whether that was really the case, or whether that was Oliver making assumptions based solely on the differences between the boys—and on the fact that Mason shared a temperament and outlook with his dad.

Cam is definitely more like me. Even though he looked more like Oliver—tall and loose-limbed with dark hair that was on the straighter side. Mason, on the other hand, favored Serena in appearance. Shorter, more compact, curly black hair he would take scissors to if it got longer than he liked.

"I don't know. It's in an envelope." He gave his head one final rub. "I'm ready to rinse now."

A note in an envelope. That sounded rather ominous, she thought, as she knelt next to the tub and began to rinse the shampoo from Cam's hair. "Did you get in trouble today?"

"No." The note of indignation in his voice was unmistakable.

"Okay. I'll read the note when you're out of the tub." She ran her fingers through his dripping hair. "I think you're all rinsed."

While Cam toweled off and put on his flannel pajamas, Serena called downstairs to Mason, who was picking up Legos. "Anyone interested in a bedtime story?" There was a beat of silence before she heard his footsteps heading toward the stairs.

"Are we waiting for dad?" Mason's head appeared over the risers.

She peered into the boys' bedroom, at the clock on the wall. "He's supposed to be home any minute now but it's getting late."

As if on cue, the fire station's siren began its slow, high-pitched whine.

"Yeah. He won't be home now," Mason said dejectedly as he trudged into the bedroom. Serena followed and climbed up onto the bed with him.

Was this normal? Oliver was hardly ever home, at least not when the boys were awake. *Or me.* Ashley was right. She and Oliver did need some alone time. But she needed time with the boys, too—that was her number one priority. And all four of them needed time together as a family.

And when he *was* home, he could barely contain his frustration sometimes. Not with her, but with the whole situation. He'd been expecting that when she woke up, she'd have to catch up on four months of life. Instead, she was scrambling to catch up on seven years.

"Cam? You almost ready?"

"Almost!" A minute later, Cam walked through the doorway, his wet hair severely parted and combed flat against his head like some 1930s gangster. She felt a little flutter in her heart. Day after day, it was obvious how hard the boys were trying to be helpful to her.

After a few minutes of discussion, they settled on a book by a local author, Douglas Preston. He had written it as a fundraiser for the Chesapeake Inn's summer camp. According to Oliver, she didn't know him. Until last year, Douglas Preston had lived in town only during the summer when camp was in session. The name sounded vaguely familiar, though.

The story concerned a group of best friends, all of whom happened to be blue crabs living in the Chesapeake Bay. It was a cute story and one that the boys seemed to know by heart.

"You read it better than dad does," Cam said when she turned the final page.

"It's not exactly dad's favorite story," Mason pointed out.

Serena set the book on the nightstand. "I can see how that might be." It was probably too whimsical for his taste. "Has Mr. Preston come to your school to read the book in person?"

"No," the boys answered in unison.

"Well. That seems like a missed opportunity."

The boys collapsed into a fit of giggling and snorting.

"What's so funny?"

"Dad says that all the time," Cam replied.

"Well, that was a missed opportunity," Mason mimicked his father speaking.

Serena tried to suppress her own laughter, but failed miserably. She knew she should reprimand Mason but his imitation of Oliver was spot on. She let it go, in favor of a pleasant end to the day and in her own growing recognition that Oliver could be hard to live with sometimes. He didn't adapt well to changing situations—which was an odd quality in a firefighter.

Instead, she pulled the boys close and they all snuggled for a few minutes, the feel of their warm, solid bodies in her arms a balm to the confusion and disorientation that governed her days. After a few minutes, Cam began snoring softly. She managed to slide out of the bed and heft him up onto her hip. Cam wasn't heavy so much as he was all arms and legs.

She grimaced as her own leg crackled with pain. She lumbered toward Cam's bed, each step slow and deliberate. Then she felt Mason's small hand on her back. At his age and size, there was nothing he could do if she were to stumble or fall beneath the weight of his little brother. But the gesture touched her. These boys were good kids.

My boys are good kids.

When she made it to Cam's bed, she lowered him gingerly onto the mattress. Together, she and Mason managed to get the covers pulled up without waking him. She walked Mason back to his bed and gave him a tight hug before tucking him in.

"I love you so much, Mason. You know that, right?"

"I love you too, Mom." He lifted his face to plant a kiss on her cheek.

They were easy kids to love. As she closed the bedroom door behind her, her mother-in-law's voice drifted through her mind. *Oliver might be a hard man to love.* Angela had said that to her once, early in Serena's relationship with him. At the time, she'd been too head over heels in love with Ollie to give his mother's words even a second thought. She had loved him enough to accommodate his quirks.

Downstairs, she retrieved the teacher's note from Cam's backpack. It was a "Welcome home" card. *Dear Mrs. Wolfe, We are all so glad to hear that you are back home. I am delighted to have Mason's younger brother in my classroom this year. Cam is an energetic and well-mannered student, and a complete joy to have in class. I know it is probably too early for you to even consider this, but when you feel up to it—I would love to have you as a parent volunteer again. You were one of the best reading aides I've ever had. Best—Chelsea O'Connor.*

Serena tried to conjure up an image of Chelsea O'Connor. When she couldn't, she closed the card and stuck it on the refrigerator with a magnet. Upstairs, she put on her pajamas and climbed into bed. There was no telling when Oliver would be home. She smoothed out the wedding quilt Angie had made for her and Oliver. It was a Double Wedding Ring pattern, according to Michelle Trevor. It looked much harder to make than the project she was working on in Becca's class. Serena couldn't even imagine how one would sew all those curved pieces together.

She had promised Michelle that she would use the quilt. When she came home from the hospital, though, she found it already on their bed. Oliver had begun using it at some point. She didn't ask why, for fear he might change his mind. When they first got married, they had agreed that it was a little weird to sleep beneath—make love beneath—something his mother had created. Now that Angie was gone, it felt comforting to Serena to sleep beneath the quilt. She wished they had used it while she was alive.

CHAPTER 13

"We're free." Oliver exhaled, put the SUV in drive, and backed out of his dad's driveway. The boys were spending the evening—and most importantly, the night—with Paps, Uncle Jack, and Aunt Becca. "What do you want to do?" He turned to look at Serena in the passenger seat. Their eyes locked for a moment and he swallowed the lump in his throat. "You are so beautiful."

Once upon a time, those words would have caused Serena to throw herself into his arms. Today, he wasn't even sure what he was seeing in her eyes. Doubt? Skepticism? Or maybe he was reading too much into things. Maybe he had let his expectations get out of control all those months she was in the hospital.

"Thank you." She laid her hand on top of his, gave it a gentle squeeze.

"So where to?" he rephrased the question. He knew where he wanted to go—straight back home where he could lose himself in her beauty, immediately.

"This might sound weird, but I'd like to go to the cemetery." She pulled her hand back into her lap as he used both hands to make a sharp turn onto the cross street. "To see your mom's and Ben's …"

That absolutely sounded weird to Oliver. Well, not so much that she wanted to visit their grave sites, but that she wanted to do it on their date. They finally had time alone together and she wanted to spend it at the cemetery?

"I don't want to stay long," she rushed to clarify. "I just want to see them."

"Sure. We can do that, babe. Whatever you want." He redirected the car toward the edge of town, where the St. Caroline Country Club and then the St. Caroline Cemetery were. "Do you mind if we stop and get flowers on the way?" he added. "We've been trying to keep them on mom's stone."

They drove to the supermarket in silence, even as Oliver wracked his brain for things to talk about. What did they used to talk about when they went out together? The boys? Probably, he guessed. It was on the tip of his tongue to ask her but she wouldn't remember either, obviously.

He'd gone so long without having her to talk to, he felt out of practice all of a sudden.

Ask her about her day.

If I do that, we'll end up talking about the boys. Then he caught himself and stole a glance over at Serena. Was he talking to himself out loud? He'd fallen into that habit when she was in the hospital, to the point where the boys sometimes poked fun at it.

Then tell her about your day.

"How are things at the station?" Serena asked, as if pulling the words straight from his brain. "Anyone new start since last summer?"

"There's a new guy, but dad and I aren't sure he's going to work out long term."

"How come?"

"Not a good team player is, I guess, the most diplomatic way of putting it."

"Oh. So why hasn't your dad let him go yet?"

"We're too short-staffed and the state is breathing down our necks as it is."

"The state? Why's that?"

Oliver signaled to make a left turn into the supermarket's parking lot. "It's the weekend people. Every time you turn around, there's another new mansion going up. And every time there's a call to one of their homes, the owner complains to the governor's office afterward."

"Complain about what? Response time?"

"Response time. Water damage to their artworks. We didn't save the stables after we got the horses out. Maybe if they didn't contest their property tax bills every year, we'd have the budget to staff up."

He pulled the SUV into a spot near the store's entrance. "I'll just run in and grab some," he said.

"Get some for Ben?"

"Sure."

Inside, he picked out a large bouquet for his mother's grave and a much smaller one for Ben Wardman. Personally, he didn't see the necessity of getting flowers for him but he didn't want to argue over it either. What he wanted was to get this part over with as quickly as possible.

Fifteen minutes later, he was pulling the car through the scrolled iron gates of the cemetery. The setting sun was low in the sky but still bright around the edges, at odds with the cold temperature of the day and their present surroundings. But Serena wanted to be here, and he would do what she wanted.

"Mom's is closest," he said. "Okay if we go there first?"

"Of course."

The cemetery looked nicer in the summer, he thought, as he steered the car along the narrow path. Today the grass was winter-yellow. The trees were bare branches, with nothing shading them from the ice blue sky. They passed a freshly-dug grave, the dirt dark and wet looking. He averted his eyes even as he wondered whose it might be. He was unaware of any recent passings in town, but occasionally a weekend resident would buy a plot in the cemetery. Personally, he didn't get the logic of having yourself buried in a town where you had no family. Who would come visit your grave?

As his mother's headstone came into sight, he gently braked the car to a stop. There was another bouquet of flowers already there and a matching arrangement on her twin brother's stone, next to hers.

"I guess dad was here earlier," he said, opening the SUV's door and then hurrying to the passenger side to help Serena out. He took one of the bouquets from her arms. The frozen yellow grass crunched beneath his good dress boots. He wasn't dressed for a trip to the cemetery. He was dressed for a date with his wife. Khaki pants, the turtleneck sweater she had given him for Christmas two years ago, the one she said matched the deep blue of his eyes. She hadn't remarked on his choice of clothing today—she wouldn't remember that she gave him this sweater.

You were never that crazy about the sweater before.

It's itchy around the neck.

"Ollie?" Serena hurried to catch up to his long strides. "Did you say something?"

"No. I mean, I'm glad I wore this sweater today. It's cold out." He pressed his lips together, hard. He really needed to break this habit of talking to himself out loud.

"Ashley said we can walk to Ben's grave from here," she said after he nestled the flowers against his mother's stone. "But we can drive, if you want to."

"No, I'm fine. It's not that cold out." He laid his arms across her shoulders and pulled her against his ribs. Even encased in her puffy winter coat, she felt small and fragile. He was supposed to be taking care of her, but how could he do that when she wanted to do things like visit the cemetery? How was that supposed to be good for her?

They stood silently for another minute and stared at the flowers, then he gave her shoulders a squeeze before dropping his arm to take her leather-gloved hand into his own bare one. Oliver was the only person he knew who actually kept gloves in the glove compartment. Unfortunately, that's where they were right now. The old Serena might have reminded him before they left the car. The new one said nothing as their shoes crunched along the path toward Ben Wardman's final resting place.

And why was St. Caroline *his* final resting place, anyway? The Wardmans weren't from around here. Didn't he have a hometown to be buried in? Or parents who'd purchased a family plot? This was another issue the town's government was struggling with—the cemetery was going to reach its capacity faster than projected if new people kept moving here.

"Ash said Ben's mom wanted to bury him in Minnesota."

Great. I was talking out loud.

"Is that where he's from?"

"Yes. One of the suburbs of Minneapolis. That's where he and Ash met, when they were in grad school."

"So why didn't they bury him there?" He scanned the headstones up ahead, trying to see Ben Wardman's name in the dusk. He hadn't gone to the funeral. He could have hired a babysitter for the boys but, with their mom in the hospital, Oliver didn't want to draw attention to the idea of death.

"Ash said he wanted to be buried here."

"Huh." He spotted a headstone that was surrounded by flowers. A lot of flowers. *That's probably it.* "Was I talking to myself out loud back there?"

"No. Why?"

"I was wondering why they buried Ben here, that's all. Then you brought it up." As they drew closer, he saw that the grave with flowers was, in fact, Ben's. *It doesn't exactly need more flowers.*

"Maybe I'm reading your mind."

"How's your leg?" He changed the subject. The last thing he needed these days was *anyone* reading his mind.

"Good. It's good today."

"The cold doesn't bother it?"

"Not so far."

She stepped ahead of him to approach the grave. He stood back and watched while she kneeled in front of the headstone, surveyed the profusion of blooms, then laid her flowers off to the side. Ashley must be coming every day. *No reason for us to be here.*

Ashley and Serena had befriended each other immediately, but he and Ben never hit it off. There was no one specific thing Oliver could point to that he had disliked about the man. Part of it was probably that he and Ben had built-in social circles that their wives didn't. Oliver was from town—he had friends that dated back to kindergarten. He had the guys at the station. Ben had socialized with other teachers.

But Ashley and Serena were both newcomers to town, and neither had full time employment with the coworker relation-ships that normally brought. But people in St. Caroline had always liked Serena. *Hadn't they?* Granted, he and Serena tended to do family-type things. *That happens when you have kids.* You hang out with other people who have young kids. You go to kids' birthday parties and Little League games. Help out with all the silly school fundraisers like selling wrapping paper and hoagies. Serena was a champ when it came to stuff like that. She could organize the hell out of anything.

But Ashley, though, was the only person she did girl-type stuff with. Shopping, lunch, that quilting class they were taking. Things that didn't involve young kids.

Friend-type things.

And his mom, now that he thought of it. Ashley Wardman and Angela Wolfe had been Serena's close girlfriends.

Serena stood suddenly. He rushed to her side to offer his arm for support. Together, they stared at the words carved into the granite for another long moment. Then they left, not talking as they climbed back into the SUV. And even though Oliver did not believe in ghosts or any of that woo-woo stuff, the same questions that had tormented him for the past month flitted in and out of his brain like apparitions.

Normal Oliver was whispering in his ear. *Why was her first memory of Ben? Why not you? Or the boys? You guys are the important men in her life.*

Hell, Oliver would even settle for a memory of one of his brothers. Well, maybe not Mattie. But her best friend's husband? *Why?*

~

THE BLUE CRAB BISTRO was crowded, and Oliver silently congratulated himself on making reservations. For two. He'd left Normal Oliver on the side of the road. He was determined to let nothing spoil this evening out with his wife.

He waved at Sean Crane behind the bar. Sean's parents owned the Blue Crab; Sean tended bar on weekends. During the week, he was a teacher at St. Caroline High and thus a colleague of Ben's. Oliver didn't hold that against him, though.

Really, he had nothing against Ben Wardman. Other than that the man had been his wife's first memory after four months in a coma. *But hey, other than that ...*

Sean waved back as Oliver and Serena followed the hostess, a young high school girl, to a table tucked away in a quiet corner. Just as he had requested. Serena wanted to eat out, but he didn't want every other person in St. Caroline coming over to say "hello." This was their alone time, and they needed it. Or he needed it, at least.

No sooner were they seated than Sean himself brought over two sparkling glass flutes of rosé champagne. He wasn't a champagne kind of guy—well, what guy was?—but he had called the restaurant that morning to ask Sean to bring some over when they arrived.

"On the house for you two lovebirds."

They clinked their glasses together.

"To us," she said.

"To us," he agreed.

Leave the cemetery back in the cemetery.

He watched as she took a sip of the champagne. *You're the luckiest guy in the world.* First, that he had ever met Serena in the first place. Second, that she—improbably enough—fell in love with him. And now third, that she was back home safe and sound. Oliver wasn't a praying man but if he were, he'd know not to ask for anything else ever again.

Not even another child. That was a topic both he and Serena had conspicuously avoided since she got out of the hospital—the fact that she was pregnant when the accident occurred ... the fact that she was carrying a girl.

He took a tiny sip of champagne and pushed the thought from his mind.

"Our honeymoon in Hawaii," Serena said. "They greeted us at the resort with this kind of champagne. Pink."

Matt had suggested trying to trigger Serena's memories by starting with something she was unlikely to forget. "Then work your way forward," Matt advised. As much as he hated taking advice on women from his brother, he was desperate to find a way back to his old life.

"They did," he agreed.

She smiled slyly at him. "You arranged this, didn't you?"

"Guilty as charged." Inwardly, he breathed a tiny sigh of relief. "I remembered how much you liked it."

"And I remember how much you hate champagne."

"For you, I'll drink it." To prove his point, he lifted the flute to his lips and swallowed half the drink in one gulp. "I'd drink anything." And he would. He'd eat bugs like people on those television shows do, slay monsters, run a thousand miles—anything to keep Serena in his life.

Battle your own doubts?

I'm working on it.

"We should go back to Hawaii someday," she said.

Her smile lit up his heart. Hell, everything about his wife lit up his heart. That curly hair his fingers were itching to get to right now. Those soft lips. The womanly body beneath that pink blouse and dark grey pants. Her slightly chubby toes that he had once spent a leisurely hour painting bright red polish on. Before the boys were born. He had tried to match the kitchen walls to that polish, as best as he could remember it. *I should do that again.* He'd made a complete mess of it—the nails, not the kitchen—but she had simply laughed it off. That was back when neither of them could do any wrong in each other's eyes.

He took another quick sip of champagne to help mask what he knew was a stupidly sappy expression on his face. "Just the two of us, or with the boys?" he asked.

She pretended to think for a moment. "They would have a blast there, wouldn't they? Though I'm not sure we could get Cam into a helicopter. Mason, no problem, but Cam?" She shook her head lovingly.

She remembered the helicopter ride from their honeymoon. A rush of heat blanketed his heart.

Things are going to be fine.

He had to just keep reminding himself of that.

Patience, Oliver.

He was about to reach across the table and take her hand in his when the waitress showed up with menus and a recitation of the evening's specials. Creole pasta, a roasted prime rib, and a double thick pork chop. Oliver let his eyes scan the menu, though he knew what he wanted already.

You always get that.

If it ain't broke, don't fix it.

"What are you getting?" she asked, not lifting her eyes from the menu.

"The New York strip." He waited for her to mention that he always ordered the New York strip, joke about what on earth a cut of beef had to do with the Big Apple. He'd looked it up once online. The name began at a restaurant in New York.

But tonight, all of that seemed to sail right over her head.

"Mmm. I'm leaning toward the mushroom stroganoff," she mused.

Mushroom stroganoff? She hated mushrooms. It was a vegetarian dish, too. Was his wife now a vegetarian? How was that going to work? He and the boys were committed carnivores.

Let her figure it out.

"That sounds good, too," he pretended to agree. What she ate for dinner wasn't important.

After the waitress returned and took their orders, he asked, "Do you remember this place?"

Serena looked around at the exposed brick walls and the weathered pine floors. The restaurant was in one of the oldest buildings in St. Caroline. Local lore maintained that George Washington had slept there. Oliver wasn't sure that was true, but neither did it seem out of the realm of possibility.

"Maybe? I'm not sure. How many times have we been here?"

"Lots." He tried to tamp down the disappointment in his chest. "It was our go-to place for birthdays and anniversaries."

He followed her gaze as she scanned the dining room. Most of the tables were for two, filled with couples.

"Oh. I'm sorry, Ollie. I'm sorry that I don't remember it. That's why you made reservations here?"

"It's okay, babe. I just thought that if we went someplace we'd been before, it might spur some memories."

"Haven't we been to most places in St. Caroline?"

"Yeah, true." He ran a finger around the rim of his water glass. "But I wanted to take you to a nice place tonight."

"Well, this is nice." She smiled at him. "And I'll definitely remember it now."

Their meals arrived and they ate quietly for a few minutes before she added, "You know, we might have to settle for just making new memories. The doctor said he can't promise how much I'll recover."

"I know. But it's worth a try, isn't it?" *We had so many good memories.* He swallowed those words with his steak.

She shrugged. "I just don't want to get your hopes up." She swirled a mushroom in the sauce on her plate. "I feel like the more I try to remember things, the harder it becomes."

He reached across the table and touched her wrist. "So let's talk about new memories, then. How is your quilting class going?"

"Good. Though Becca might have a different take on that." She laughed. "I don't think I'll ever be any good at it—certainly not as good as your mom was—but it's kind of fun. It's growing on me."

She spent a few minutes describing the string quilt she was making in class. The waitress brought dessert menus. While they considered apple crumb cake, Tahitian vanilla creme brulee, and blackberry sorbet, Serena spoke again.

"I'm going to volunteer in Cam's classroom, starting next week."

He looked up. "Oh? You are?" He set down the menu. "Are you sure you feel up to it? There's no rush to jump back into things."

"The teacher asked. She needs someone."

"How will you get to the school?" She wasn't cleared to drive yet. According to the doctor, it would be a few months.

"Ash said she'd drive me. This is the slow season for wedding photography. At least around here."

"Oh. You've already discussed this with her?" *Why not me?*

Why hadn't she consulted with him before deciding to do this? He was about to voice his complaint, but her shining face stopped him. She was excited about this.

That's a good thing, Ollie.

He bit back the complaint. "Well, Cam will love that. Mason always did."

~

RIGHT NOW, Oliver was exactly where he wanted to be. At home, flat on his back in bed, his wife's nearly naked body on top of his. Skin on skin. He had missed that almost more than anything—the feel of her bare skin on his. The warmth, the scent, the taste. With the boys at his dad's house for the night, it felt like they were on a date from long ago. They could make love until dawn if they wanted to.

He wanted to.

He also wanted her to continue doing exactly what she was doing right now, leisurely kissing and licking his neck … his jawline … his cheek. He knew exactly where her soft lips were headed, and a certain part of his anatomy stiffened in sweet anticipation.

When her lips brushed the curve of his ear, his eyes rolled back in his head.

"Mmm," she whispered. "If you get any harder, we'll need to call 911."

Her warm breath filled his ear and flowed straight down to his groin, taking more blood flow from his brain with it. "Please don't do that. Matt's on duty tonight."

She lifted her head and looked into his eyes, her lips parted in a smile that was equal parts sexy and mischievous. He reached behind her back and unhooked her bra. It was lacy and black. He wasn't sure he'd ever seen this one before.

"Is this new?" He slid the wisp of fabric down her arms as she sat back up. "I like it," he added. He liked lingerie best when it was lying on the floor next to their bed.

He let his hands slide slowly down her ribs until he reached the matching bottoms. Her hips were rocking back and forth, scrambling his thoughts. He slipped a finger beneath the elastic. "You're still a little overdressed, love."

She leaned forward, resting her hands on either side of his shoulders as he slid the sheer black fabric down her legs. She kicked them off her ankles and settled her hips back down, her eyes closing. He was content to just watch her move her body above his, against his, her arousal and pleasure washing over her face in waves.

He wondered what she was thinking right now.

He knew it was a bad place to go. A bad, dark place. A place he knew he'd regret exploring. Normal Oliver had hitchhiked home and waited for them in bed. Now he was whispering in Oliver's ear again.

It's not what she's thinking about. It's who.

Was she fantasizing about Ben Wardman?

He wasn't better looking than me. Sure, he was a runner and a soccer coach. But Oliver was a firefighter. He ran. He lifted weights.

You've put on a little weight recently.

Well, okay. He had. He and the boys had relied on takeout and fast food a little too much when Serena was in the hospital. Oliver could cook, some, but all three of them had tired of his rather limited cooking repertoire pretty quickly.

Maybe she bought the lingerie for Ben and that was why it looked new to him. Granted, her lingerie never managed to stay on for very long, so it wasn't something Oliver had ever paid a ton of attention to. He was more interested in what was beneath the sexy pieces of fabric.

Above him, her breasts rose and fell with her breathing. She slowed the movement of her hips. He knew what she was doing.

She was pulling herself back from the brink, letting her body calm down for a moment so she could savor the sensations longer.

Did Ben know she liked to do that? He'd been a smart guy, after all. A teacher, college-educated. Oliver had gone straight from high school to the fire department. Ben could probably talk about a wide range of subjects. What did Oliver know? St. Caroline. Fires and how to fight them.

He traced the tip of his finger around the soft indentation of her navel. The sound of her sudden, sharp inhale was satisfying to his ears. *I know how to please her in bed.* She didn't seem to have forgotten how she liked to be touched.

It was always a fool's dream to think we could hold onto a woman like Serena.

He felt Normal Oliver's presence hovering above the bed. *You always knew that. I told you she was out of your league.*

The pace of her rocking picked up again, and Oliver settled his hands on the points of her hip bones. He lifted her gently and then lowered her back down. There was a moment's resistance and then he was deep inside her. *Heaven.* He mentally elbowed Normal Oliver out of the way. Serena was biting her lower lip, a sign that she was close to her orgasm. He pulled her down until they were pressed together, chest to chest.

It was terrible to think ill of the dead. He knew that. But all the same, he wasn't entirely sad that Ben Wardman was gone. He had enough things on his plate these days. *Last thing I need is competition.*

Serena began making those little mewing sounds he loved so much. He pressed his hands against her back, holding her tight as her body began to convulse with wave after wave of pleasure. Before she could come down from the orgasm, he flipped her over onto her back.

Take that. He mentally shoved Normal Oliver out of the way. *Ben Wardman isn't here anymore.*

CHAPTER 14

*S*erena stopped in the open doorway of the classroom, and discreetly scanned the walls and clusters of tiny desks. She did that everywhere she went these days, looking for something she might remember, a face or some small object that might look familiar. Once in awhile, it happened—that vague sense of *I know that person.* Every time, she had to fight the impulse to call up Oliver and tell him. It got him too excited— and sometimes agitated—as he tried to puzzle out why that thing instead of another, more logical thing. Why this person and not someone else. It was a question she didn't have the answer to.

The doctor was fond of saying that the human brain was one of life's most enduring mysteries. If a medical professional didn't understand her brain, she certainly couldn't.

The classroom wasn't giving her that vague sense, though. It looked familiar, in the way that all classrooms sort of look the same. Desks and chairs, winter coats on hooks, brightly colored posters and handmade decorations on the walls, the low-grade hum of young kids concentrating. She was about to step through the doorway when the noisy hush was split by a "There's Cam's mom!"

Twenty heads spun around to look at her. Cam's smile was so wide she feared his face might crack.

"Mrs. Wolfe is here!" the teacher exclaimed, a beaming smile on her own face.

After the note Cam brought home, Serena had run into Chelsea O'Connor in the produce aisle at the supermarket. She didn't recognize Cam's teacher, though maybe she would have if the other woman had been in context—in a classroom, in other words. Dressed in sweatpants and a winter parka, she had looked like any other weekend shopper.

Today Chelsea looked like a kindergarten teacher in a brightly patterned dress over black leggings and funky short boots. Serena imagined she couldn't be too much older than she and Oliver were.

She stepped into the room, noticing another mother standing by the large white board. Serena smiled and nodded at her. The nod was returned but not the smile, and Serena wondered whether she knew the other woman. It was disconcerting to run into people and not know whether she was supposed to know them. Or what they might know about her.

"Who's ready for some word study?" Ms. O'Connor asked rhetorically.

The classroom response was a little mixed. Cam seemed unaware that a question had even been asked. His eager eyes were glued to his mother.

Serena was impressed by how quickly Chelsea O'Connor herded the kids into three groups. *Differentiated instruction.* The phrase popped into her head.

"I gave you group three," Chelsea said quietly to Serena, handing her a stack of worksheets. "You were always so good with the kids who are struggling a bit."

Serena took a deep breath as she watched the teacher sit down with the largest group, group two. *I hope so. At least I didn't forget how to read.* She took one more glance at Cam, who was evidently in the group of kids working above grade level.

She scanned the worksheet, which was photocopied on bright yellow paper and contained three columns of words. "Hat, hot, and hit," she said as she passed them out. "Those are the sorts for today." *Sorts.* It was coming back to her, and her heart skipped a beat. She knew what to do here. Pass out the safety scissors from the plastic basket. Have the kids snip and cut their worksheets into individual words.

"Can anyone read today's words for us?"

Sat. Cat. Bat. Cot. Got. Spot. Fit. Kit. Lit. Pat. Rat. Lot. Tot.

The kids quietly cut and sorted the words into columns, their tiny faces stern with concentration. Strolling around the cluster of desks, she peered over their hunched shoulders as they moved words around, considering and reconsidering their choices, quietly whispering the vowel sounds. When she glanced over at Cam's group, she found him looking at her, his words already neatly sorted.

"Cam is such a bright boy," Chelsea O'Connor had said to her in the supermarket. "Has a wicked sense of humor, too." That remark surprised Serena. Cam nearly always played second fiddle to his older brother at home—partly because he looked up to Mason, despite their daily squabbles. She couldn't remember deferring to her older brother that way. She'd always felt perfectly equal to Peter, despite their three-year age difference. Maybe because they had always gone to different schools, it felt as though they led different lives.

Come to think of it, her entire family had seemed to live separate lives. Once she and Peter were teenagers and off at their boarding schools in Connecticut, their lives diverged entirely from that of their parents.

"Mrs. Wolfe?"

She looked down at the little girl who'd just spoken her name. The girl's word sort showed some confusion between the "a" and "o" sounds. Serena was about to slide a few of the words around when the girl spoke again.

"Can Cam come over to my house again to play?"

Just like that, Serena was thrown out of her momentary triumph of confidence. She had no idea who this little girl was. But "again" would seem to indicate that she was a friend of Cam's.

"Umm, sure. If your mom is okay with that."

"I'm sure she will be." The little girl was coated in confidence. "Do I have these right?"

As Serena leaned over to help her, two pieces clicked together in her brain. That inexplicable sense of déjà vu she experienced while arranging her fabric strips in Becca's quilting class? Her brain had been remembering this—helping kids sort their words in an elementary school classroom.

"I'M JUST GOING to brush my teeth, then I'll be right back. Okay, dad?"

"Sure thing, bud." Oliver watched as his oldest son marched off to the bathroom in his pajamas. The maturity in Mason's voice these days broke his heart. *No one ever tells you that about having kids.* That being a parent will break your heart all the time. And always at a moment when you're not expecting it.

I told you that. At least a hundred times.

Okay, so his mother had probably said that to him at least a hundred times when Serena was pregnant the first time. But just because something was a cliché didn't mean it wasn't true.

"Dad? Can you help me?" Cam stood in front of his chest of drawers, wearing a pajama top and underwear, his long legs skinny and winter-pale. He held up a pair of pajama bottoms, the legs somehow twisted and tied up. Cam shook the pants, clearly frustrated.

Oliver was lying on Cam's bed, the night's chosen bedtime story on the quilt next to him. He swung his feet over the edge of the bed. "Let's see 'em." He took the twisted pajama pants from his youngest son's hands. "Looks like they weren't folded up properly before someone put them in the drawer."

Cam let out a giant exhale. "I know. I was in a hurry."

Oliver fought back a smile. Cam and Mason were like night and day, yet it was a difference that increasingly worried Oliver. Mason just seemed way too old for a seven-year-old sometimes. Even a seven-going-on-eight-year-old. He knew he hadn't been that mature at that age.

Oh hell no.

His mother always had a bit of a salty mouth. Did Serena swear around the kids? It was a question that had never occurred to him before, but lots of new questions were occurring to him these days.

No, she doesn't.

Yes, that was certainly the answer he would have given before the accident. It was like their lives were divided in two now— B.A., Before the Accident, and A.A., After the Accident.

Only because you look at it that way.

No other way to look at it, he thought.

He held the pajama bottoms up for Cam to look at it. "See how the legs are looped around each other, bud?"

"Yeah." Cam didn't sound terribly convinced that simple fabric physics was to blame here.

"So take one end in your hand and push it back toward me. You have to look at these things like they're a puzzle you have to solve."

The expression on his son's face was doubtful, but he grasped one pajama leg in his fingers and worked it back through the knot. "But it's still twisted."

"Well, we're not finished yet. Whoever tied these legs together clearly has some training in sailor's knots." He winked at Cam.

He had started teaching the boys how to tie knots as soon as they could walk, practically.

You're a good father.

Yeah, teaching your kids to tie knots ... Father of the Year!

But the comparison seemed to be working for Cam, who carefully worked loose the knotted pajama legs.

"There you go! See?" Oliver gave the pants a final shake and handed them back to his son. He watched as Cam hopped from leg to leg, putting them on. He felt that little pinch in his chest again—Mason would sit on the bed to pull on the pants. Mason displayed an alarming fascination with firefighting (or maybe just with fire), but was otherwise a calm, methodical kid. Cam, on the other hand, didn't even need walls to bounce off of. He could bounce off of thin air.

Oliver scooted back up the bed and patted the mattress next to him. "Did you brush your teeth, bud?"

Cam gave him a toothy, horse-like grin. "Yup. Mason made me go first."

Oliver wondered why that was so, but refrained from asking. Some questions you don't want the answers to. Even when you're a parent.

True that.

He opted for a more innocuous query instead. "How was school today?" Oliver knew how school had gone, from Serena's perspective. He had come home to a wife who was practically bouncing off the walls herself. Going into Cam's classroom left her more animated and excited than he'd seen her since before the accident.

"Mom came to my room!"

"I know, bud. How was that?"

"I wasn't in her group. But everyone clapped for her at the end."

Oliver wondered whether the other mother got a round of applause.

"I wish mom was my teacher," Cam added.

"Why's that?" Oliver heard the water go off in the bathroom, then the squeak of the towel ring as Mason dried his hands.

"If she was my teacher, I wouldn't have to miss her when I'm at school."

"You miss mom during the day?" Oliver resisted the urge to add, "what about dear old dad?"

Cam nodded solemnly.

"Well, bud, she's always here waiting for you when you get off the bus." Oliver wrapped his hands around his younger son's waist and pulled him closer. "You know where I always had to go after school?"

"Yeah, I know. The station. Uncle Mattie's told me, like, a million times."

"Well, Nana was a professor at the college so we couldn't stay by ourselves at home."

"I miss Nana, too," Cam said. Oliver felt his little boy shoulders sink an inch. What was taking Mason so long? He was too young to be admiring himself in the mirror the way Matt did when they were kids.

Oliver thought he heard a soft laugh. Sometimes he could hear his mother as clear as if she was standing right in the room with him. It was a little unnerving, truth be told.

I'll go check on Mason.

Like that right there. He could understand his brain serving up his mother's pet phrases or her pithy advice. But something like that? It made no sense. Serena wasn't the only one with brain problems.

"I miss Nana, too, bud."

"I don't like missing people."

"Well, at least you don't have to miss mom anymore. Right?"

"Right." Cam impatiently picked up the bedtime story book.

Oliver tried to push back at the thought pestering the edges of his brain. *I miss the old Serena.* Not that she was completely different since coming home from the hospital … but she was a little different. He couldn't quite put his finger on it. He had never been good at that sort of thing, emotional stuff.

No, you never were.

"Dad, can I ask you something?"

"Sure, bud. What is it?" Oliver was glad to have Cam interrupt his ruminations. "Mason, you almost done?" he called toward the bathroom.

"Jackie says she's going to miss her mom when she dies."

Or maybe not so glad. He had no idea how Jack and Becca were going to handle this situation.

"But I thought Aunt Becca was Jackie's mom," Cam continued. "Aunt Becca's not dying, is she, dad?"

At the sound of Cam's sniffled tears, Oliver pulled his son onto his lap and hugged him tight. "No, no."

"I don't want Aunt Becca to die, too!" Cam wailed loudly.

Oliver heard footsteps pounding up the stairs. Serena. He began to rock Cam in his arms. "Aunt Becca's not dying. It's … it's complicated, buddy." Oliver was wracking his brain for how to explain his brother's situation when Serena burst into the room, out of breath from running up the stairs. Mason shot into the room right behind her.

"But Jackie says—" Cam was full on sobbing now.

Mason climbed onto the bed and squeezed his younger brother's cheeks between his hands. "I explained all this to you, Cammy."

He did? When? Oliver looked helplessly up at his wife, who— he realized—might not fully or perfectly understand the situation with Jack and Becca yet either. *When are things going back to normal? WHEN?*

"How can she have two mommies? We don't have two mommies."

Mason's small hands wiped Cam's tears from his cheeks, like

he was squeegeeing a windshield. "Shhh, Cammy. I told you. Becca is Jackie's *original* mommy."

Oliver held his breath, in anticipation of Mason's explanation. From Serena's widened eyes, he could tell she was doing the same. She came over and sat at the foot of the bed. Then Cam lost it entirely.

"Who's *our* original mommy?" he wailed.

"Mom is our original mommy." Mason's voice was as calm and measured as his little brother's was frantic and uncontrolled. He gave Oliver's knee a gentle nudge. "Dad, I got this," he said softly.

Oliver slowly pushed himself off the bed and escorted Serena from the room. They stood outside in the hallway, straining to hear what Mason was going to say to Cam, but Mason was silent.

"Come on," Oliver whispered to his wife. He cocked his head toward the stairs. Mason wasn't going to talk to Cam until their parents were out of earshot. As much as Oliver wanted to hear what Mason would say, he knew he needed to trust him. His sons had a brotherly bond that had only strengthened since the accident. He was proud of Mason, too, for the way he had taken on more than a seven-year-old should have to—and done it mostly without complaining.

They tiptoed down the stairs to the kitchen. Oliver leaned his elbows on the granite island and listened, but all was quiet upstairs. There were no more panicked shrieks from Cam. Serena stood elbow to elbow with him, her shoulder touching his bicep.

"I'm sorry," he said, leaning his head down to nudge hers.

"For what?"

"For my insane family. You have enough to contend with without having to explain the whole Jack and Becca situation to the boys."

"Sounds like Mason understands it."

Oliver shrugged. "He understands bits and pieces of it. He gets that my brother and Becca are going to be Jackie's parents from here on out, but I don't think he really understands how Jackie came to be living in Ohio in the first place."

"Well, it's a little beyond a seven-year-old's ken."

"Ken? What does that mean?" Oliver pushed himself up off his elbows. *Ken? Did Serena learn a new language while she was in the coma?*

"It means 'understanding,'" she replied.

"Oh. Where did you learn that word?"

"I don't know. College? A book? NPR?" She touched his forearm. "Are you okay, Ollie?"

"Yeah, I'm fine. I think we're all having a little trouble understanding the Jack and Becca thing."

"Seems pretty straightforward to me. But I'm not talking about that. I mean you. Are *you* okay?"

"I'm fine, babe. You're back home. We're all together again. I don't need anything more than that."

Serena opened her mouth to speak, but just then came the soft sound of feet padding down the stairs. A moment later, Mason appeared in the kitchen's doorway.

"He's out." Mason nodded to the two of them. "I explained it again."

"Thanks, bud," Oliver said.

"What did you tell him?" Serena asked.

"Just that Becca is Jackie's original mom, but Becca was too young to be a mom so Jackie was adopted by a nice lady. But now that lady is sick and Jackie is coming here to live because Becca is old enough now."

Huh. That was kind of the gist of it.

Serena walked over to Mason and hoisted him up in her arms, kissing his cheek. "You're a good brother, you know that?" Mason half nodded, half shrugged. "Thanks for taking care of Cam and daddy while I was in the hospital."

Oliver watched his wife and son. He wanted to join them, but his feet remained rooted to the tiled kitchen floor. His relationship with the boys was tighter than ever, and Serena had fallen easily back into her bond with them. But there was a distance between him and Serena sometimes.

When she set Mason down onto his feet, his son turned and gave him a thumbs-up before heading back upstairs.

Don't be jealous.

I'm not!

She and the boys need to bond.

I said I'm not jealous.

But he was. Just a tiny bit. There was a time—like, say, two months ago—when Mason would have given him a hug and a kiss before bedtime, not just a thumbs-up.

Serena turned and looked at him. "What's your schedule like next weekend?" she asked.

"I'm off. Why?"

"Let's take the boys and go away for a weekend. Not anywhere far. I think they need a fun weekend and a change of scenery."

"I think we all do," he agreed. Yeah, getting away was a good idea. Maybe they needed a break from the pressure of trying to be a normal family again. "Where do you want to go?"

"I don't know. The idea literally popped into my head just now."

He walked over to her and took her hand in his before going up the stairs to their bedroom.

At the top of the stairs, she turned to him and added, "What about the new Air and Space Museum? We used to talk about taking the boys there. Did we ever do that?"

He shook his head. "Yeah, they would love that. Matt, Jack, and I always loved the original Air and Space Museum. The old planes and space suits ... wait." He tugged on her shoulder as she was about to disappear into their bathroom. "You remember that? That we wanted to take them there?"

Her eyes widened as she looked up at him. Then a deep frown of concentration creased her forehead. "I do." She bounced up and down on her toes. "I do! Ollie, I remember that!"

He scooped her up in his arms and carried her into their bedroom, swinging her around until they were both a little dizzy. "Your memories are coming back, babe!" He kissed her hard before they both tumbled onto the bed. Things were looking up.

CHAPTER 15

*I*t was an unseasonably warm day and Serena paused
for a moment after the fireproof door of the elementary school closed with a heavy thud behind her. As a coastal
town, St. Caroline's winters were pretty temperate, unlike the
winters of her boarding school years in Connecticut. She might
not remember last year's winter but her memories of hurrying
from building to building on campus while trying not to breathe
in the frigid air were as sharp as ice.

Still, going from thirty-five degrees to sixty degrees overnight
was unusual, even for St. Caroline, and she wanted to savor the
warmth for a moment or two. She almost wished the boys were
still preschool-aged—she could pack a picnic lunch and the three
of them could spend the afternoon at Secret Beach.

She cocked her head to one side. Had she done that with the
boys? Taken them for picnic lunches and some play time at the
beach? She must have, right? Why else would it have occurred
to her?

She scanned the visitors' parking lot, looking for Oliver. She'd
been relying on Ashley for rides around town, but a couple in
Annapolis had hired her to take photos of their newborn twins

today. Serena dug her phone out of her purse as she strolled toward the visitors' parking lot and tapped in a text. *Come over for dinner tonight.* Ashley had confessed that the new year was hitting her hard—"I thought the holidays would be the worst," she'd confessed, "but it's starting to feel real now, that Ben is actually gone." Oliver's shift at the station began at four so it would be just Serena and the boys at home. *Bring your quilt blocks. I can help you catch up.*

She looked up from her phone just in time to see Oliver's black SUV pull up to the curb.

"Sorry I'm late," he said as she climbed up onto the passenger seat. He leaned over to kiss her.

"You're not late. I just got out."

"I had to stop by the station for a bit."

"Oh. I thought you didn't have to go in until later this afternoon."

"I don't, but some folks from the governor's office are in town today. You probably don't remember the fire at Mona Barrett's house last summer."

She thought for a moment, then shook her head. "But I don't remember every call you guys have ... wait. Isn't Mona Barrett the Secretary of State?"

"Yup. That she is. And the governor has been getting an earful from her and some of the other part-time residents. They're not convinced the St. Caroline fire department can save their fancy, expensive mansions in an emergency."

Serena stared out the passenger side window as Oliver vented. The subject of the wealthy summer homeowners in town had always made her uncomfortable. After all, it was no secret to anyone that she came from exactly those kind of people, the kind of people who could afford multiple homes. It wasn't the way she wanted to live, but the town was more dependent on the part-time residents' money than they liked to admit. All those nice restaurants and cute shops needed more customers than lived year-round in the surrounding neighborhoods.

From her purse came the gentle ping of a text notification. She lifted her bag from the floor of the car and dug through it for her phone.

"Who's that?" Oliver asked.

She tapped on the screen. "Ashley. I invited her for dinner tonight since you're going to be at the station. She's been feeling a little blue since the holidays."

"Oh. Okay."

Serena shifted her gaze from her phone to her husband. She heard disapproval in his voice. "Is that not okay?"

"It's fine." His voice was still tight, even for a man who was normally more buttoned up than most. "It's just that I feel like you spend a lot of time with her and not with anyone else in town."

"She's my best friend." She was beginning to wonder whether Oliver liked Ashley—or whether he even knew her. "And she has time to spend with me. Not everyone does."

Up ahead was the intersection and the turn that would take them to their house.

"I don't seem to have too many other close friends in town," she added quietly. "It was Ash and ... your mom. They're the people I was closest to, it seems. After you, of course."

Oliver braked the car to a stop at the intersection.

"Was there someone else I was good friends with? Someone I'm not remembering?"

When he didn't answer, she turned her head to the side window. But instead of Oliver making a right turn in the direction of their house, he proceeded straight through the intersection.

"Where are we going?"

"I thought we'd go car shopping. I'm assuming you don't want to make the trip to Virginia this weekend in my car."

"Why not? Plus, I haven't been cleared to drive yet."

"You always said the SUV rode like a truck. And we need to replace the minivan at some point."

"Did the insurance cover it?"

"They did. The car was a total loss. I just didn't want to replace it before … without you along to pick one out."

That wasn't what he'd been about to say. *Before I knew if you were going to wake up.*

"Well, you know me. I'm not really a car person. I don't care that much what kind of car I drive." Growing up in the city, cars weren't really a big part of her life—other than cabs. Her parents both had BMWs, but those were only used on weekends to get from the New York house to the Connecticut one.

"You know I would never be presumptuous enough to pick out a car for you without your input," Oliver said.

No, he wouldn't. That was true. She was about to give him a smile when other thoughts intruded. Thoughts of a different kind of insurance.

"What about the hospital bills? Did the insurance cover all of that?"

"Most of it."

"How much is most of it?"

Oliver turned the car down another street. "Dad paid for what the insurance didn't cover."

"What? He can't do that, Ollie."

"He used some of the life insurance from mom."

"No. We have to pay him back. How much was it?"

"You were in the hospital for four months." He paused at an intersection. "It was a lot," he added quietly.

"How much is 'a lot?'"

He didn't answer.

"Ollie, either we're in this together or we're not."

"It was a little over seventy grand."

Her breath caught in her throat. "We don't need to buy another car yet. I can't drive it yet anyway."

"We should get you started practicing."

"I can practice in the SUV."

"You never liked driving it."

She stared sightlessly as the houses and front yards thinned out the closer they got to the edge of town. He was right. She was never comfortable driving the SUV. *Maybe I'm just not a good driver.* Her parents weren't, not that her father would ever admit to that.

They drove past strip malls and car dealerships, the businesses that every town needed but that no one wanted to live next door to. Least of all people like the Secretary of State. She spotted the now-empty lot where the Trevor family's quilt shop used to stand.

Oddly enough, she remembered where Quilt Therapy used to be. She didn't mention it to Oliver, though. Truth be told, she was remembering more things than she told him about. It felt childish after awhile to bombard him every day with "guess what I remembered today?" And he attached too much significance to everything when even the doctor had cautioned that there would be no rhyme or reason to any of it.

Oliver turned the car into the car dealership. Behind the low, grey building row after row of shiny new cars glittered in the sunlight. Serena wondered whether this was where they'd bought the other car. Not that it mattered. Not all memories were equal. Some were downright unimportant.

She hopped down from the passenger seat before Ollie could get around the hood to help her. A tall, heavyset man burst from the office building and strode quickly toward them.

"Serena!" he boomed. "Oliver! My man!"

She felt Ollie's hand on the small of her back, then heard him whisper, "Charlie Thomas. I went to high school with him. Took his younger sister to the prom."

Serena fought back a snort of laughter. "I'll try to be nice."

"So what are you two looking for today? Another minivan? Our Valentine's Day specials don't start until next week but I'll speak to the manager. For one of our first responders, I'm sure he'll give you the incentives today."

"Sure, we'll look at some minivans. Maybe a sedan?" Oliver turned to her. "What do you think? A sedan?"

"Mmm. A minivan might be better, with the boys getting older and bigger."

"Well, we got plenty of minivans around this way. Follow me." Charlie turned and began walking toward the back of the lot.

"Besides," she said quietly to Oliver, "would I have survived if I'd been driving a smaller car?"

He shook his head. "Possibly not."

In Oliver-speak, that meant "definitely not."

He slung his arm across her shoulder and squeezed her into him as they followed Charlie. He stopped at a row of gleaming minivans in a rainbow of pearlized colors. She couldn't remember what color their old minivan had been. She slipped out from beneath Ollie's arm to wander in and out of the aisle of cars, letting Oliver and Charlie discuss upgrades, packages, and safety features.

Ten minutes later, they had the keys to a shiny blue minivan, the color of which reminded Serena of blue birds she had seen in Puerto Rico over spring break one year. *Another useless memory.*

There are no useless memories.

That sounded exactly like something Angie would have said.

"Can I ask something weird?" she said as Oliver fiddled with knobs on the dashboard, responsibly acquainting himself with the functions and features of the car before driving off the dealer's lot.

"Sure, babe. Ask away." He cranked up the heat, causing a blast of air to hit them right in the face. "Sorry." He dialed it back down.

"Do you ever, like, talk to yourself—not aloud, just in your head—in the way your mom used to talk?" Realizing how weird that sounded, she leaned her body toward the passenger side door, anticipating a burst of laughter from Ollie.

"Oh god, all the time." He turned toward Serena with a sympathetic smile. "Some days it's like a constant running commentary."

"You had a good mom."

"I did." He leaned over and pulled her toward the car's center console. "You're a good mom, too, Serena."

"I was?"

"You were and you *are*. Mason and Cam are two lucky boys to have you as their mother." He cupped the back of her head in his hand and kissed her. "How about we go find someplace private to park this jalopy and make out in the back?"

She smiled into his lips. "Is there someplace private in St. Caroline?"

He pretended to think for a moment. "I could always call Elliott Parker and tell him we're going to park in his back field for awhile."

He let his fingers trail through her hair as he released her head. The sensation sent a tiny shiver down her spine.

"I'm not sure Charlie would be okay with us off-roading in this vehicle."

Oliver laughed and pressed the ignition button. "Yeah, probably not. He was nice enough to let us take this out for a test drive by ourselves."

"Unlikely that the deputy fire chief is going to steal a car."

He shot her a mischievous look. "One of these days I'm going to let my wild side out. Then you'll be sorry." He winked.

"Just warn me ahead of time, okay?"

For a moment, things between them were relaxed and normal, like old times. But it was getting harder and harder to sustain those moments. It was her fault, obviously. She was the one who couldn't remember things. And increasingly that made them feel like strangers. Instead of getting closer to each other after the hospital, it felt like they were drifting further apart.

Oliver steered the minivan off the dealer's lot and immediately launched into a recitation of the car's features. Heated seats, heated steering wheel, driver assist technology, pre-collision braking.

"Even the headlights respond to the driver's steering," he added.

"Seems like there are a lot more gizmos in cars these days than I remember."

"Yeah, just imagine how many there'll be when the boys are driving."

"Ugh. I'm not ready to think of them being that old."

She knew Oliver wanted the safety features for her. Cataloging them out loud helped him feel more in control. She understood that about him, his need to have everything under control. It was a part of his personality that had been sorely challenged over the past year.

Five minutes later, Oliver turned the minivan down a narrow country road and pulled up to a small house. She recognized it as a former fishing camp. They dotted the outskirts of town, the ones that hadn't been razed for mansions and summer estates, that is.

"What's this?" she asked. "You didn't go real estate shopping while I was out, did you?" That seemed unlikely for Oliver, but what did I know these days?

"No." He put the car into park but left the engine running. "This is where Matt lives."

"What are we doing here?"

"Switching places." Oliver opened his door, then came around to open the passenger side. "I want you to drive for a bit."

A fluttery feeling skittered over her heart. "I'm not cleared to drive yet."

"You'll be fine." He took her hand and helped her out of the minivan.

"What if I have an accident? This isn't even our car."

"Better their car than ours." He grinned boyishly. "Serena, I'm not worried. We'll just drive a little on the roads out here where there's no traffic. We won't go into town."

She shot him a dubious look but hauled herself up onto the driver's seat. She sat there for a moment, assessing, trying to tap into some feeling of familiarity. Was driving like riding a bike? One of those things you never really forget how to do?

She clicked her seatbelt into place, right before Oliver did his.

"Well. We're strapped in." She released the parking brake, then executed a three point turn to get the car pointed back toward the main road. So far, so good. "Where do you want me to go?"

"Wherever you want. Just stay outside town. There won't be many cars on the road at this time of day."

She drove cautiously at first, then grew a little more confident.

"How do you feel?" he asked.

"Good." Her lips spread into a wide smile. "Muscle memory is kicking in, anyway."

Oliver had missed that smile so much. He didn't realize exactly how much until she was away for four months. No matter what happened at work, just knowing that she was home waiting for him made it all okay.

She took a few turns and looped around Elliott Parker's land. Oliver watched the familiar landscape pass by. He couldn't imagine waking up one day and not remembering any of this, the way storm clouds gathered low on the horizon in the summer. Or the faint, salty smell of fish and bay water on a breeze.

This was home for him.

He knew his brothers didn't feel the same way about St. Caroline. Hell, lots of the kids he went to high school with didn't. They all wanted to get out of Dodge before the ink was dry on their diplomas. But Oliver had never really felt that tug—to leave town, live somewhere else. Why? Everything he wanted was right here. His parents and brothers, his friends. A job he loved and was good at. Serena and the boys. His fishing boat. What else did he need?

He looked over at his wife, feeling his heart swell with love and contentment. He knew his reputation around town was that of a stable man—code for "boring." But the world needed stable, boring people. And he might not be a worldly man, but he was smart enough to know that at least some of his appeal for Serena was probably that he was so different from her father.

The distant whine of an ambulance siren snapped him from his reverie. He focused his gaze on the landscape outside the car. *Oh no.* They were headed straight toward the site of the accident.

"Are you ready to turn around and head back?" He tried to keep his voice as nonchalant as possible.

"Mmm. Do you mind if we drive just a little further? I know where we are. I used to come this way when I would meet your mom for lunch at the college."

She definitely hadn't been meeting his mom on the day of the accident. His mother was in the hospital for the final time at that point. Jack was at her bedside when the call came in.

"I always admired your mom," she continued. "Being a college professor and raising three boys at the same time."

"Yeah." They were about a quarter mile from the site. "She was lucky to find a tenure track job in the area." Less than a quarter mile. "Hey babe, I really don't think we should keep going this way. Let's pull over at this next road and turn around."

"Don't worry. I won't drive all the way to the college."

"It's not that ... it's ..." The spot was just ahead now and Oliver's heart was racing. He tried to avoid this stretch of road whenever he could. When he couldn't, he held his breath and kept his eyes trained straight ahead on the road, not looking at the tree that stood twenty feet back from the shoulder. The tree his wife's car had been practically wrapped around. "This is where the accident happened," he blurted out.

He felt the car slow beneath him.

"Oh," Serena said.

She slowly steered the car over to the side of the road.

"I don't think we should stop here," he said.

"Why not?"

"Bad memories." That hardly did it justice. "This is where the worst day of my life happened."

She put the minivan into park, set the brake, and pushed the ignition button to cut the engine. He looked at the lovely wood-grained dashboard, the leather trimmed seats—and began to wonder whether they could even buy this car now. Would he think of this moment every time he looked at it? Like that even mattered, he realized a split second later. He would never drive through this intersection without thinking about the accident, no matter what car he was in.

"Maybe I'll remember something." Serena unsnapped her seatbelt. Oliver left his buckled. "You can stay inside. Just tell me where it happened," she added.

He said nothing, just stared at that damned infernal tree.

"Or we can do that 'warmer and colder' game."

"You hit that tree up there," he replied finally, quietly. "On this side of the road."

"The big white oak?"

"That would be the one," he confirmed.

Serena got out of the car and started walking toward the tree. For the first few steps, she favored her right leg, the one that was broken in the accident. Then her gait became normal. The incongruity of the scene struck him. It was a sunny day. A downright gorgeous day for February. And he was watching his wife walk straight toward the tree that nearly killed her.

He jammed the base of his palm against the seat belt lock and flung it open. Then he shoved open the door and ran after her.

What if she did remember something? He couldn't let her face that alone. He wasn't that kind of man.

"Serena! Wait!"

She stopped and turned. The look of mild surprise on her face stung him. *She thought I was going to stay in the car.*

"Tell me what happened." She took his hand in hers.

He took a deep breath. "Your car ran off the road here." He scanned the macadam for the thick, dark tire marks from that day but they were long gone. "It hit that tree. That's all we know. You might have swerved to—"

"Shh. Don't put any ideas into my head. I want to feel what I remember."

He followed as she marched up to the tree. On the day of the accident, it had looked huge and immovable, malevolent almost, its branches heavy and thick with summer-green leaves. Today, denuded of its foliage in winter, it appeared smaller and weaker. Serena ran her hand over the wide scar on the trunk where the car had stripped away the bark. She reached back, as if to wave him forward.

"Come here."

He hesitated. His lungs felt raw from the crazy storm of emotions swirling inside him, emotions he couldn't pin down long enough to even name. But she was spreading her palms wide and flat over the bark and he could pin down one thing—he did not want to touch this tree. But a real man had to be at least as brave as his wife. So he stood behind her, his palms on her shoulders, his face easily clearing the top of her head and putting him face to face with the white oak.

"This tree almost killed you," he said. Mature white oaks were massive trees, with hard lumber.

She ran her fingers along the edge of the scarred bark. "It didn't, though. And I'm the one who ran into it."

She pulled his hands off her shoulders and placed them, palms down, on the trunk. He supposed he should feel something beneath the calloused skin of his hands—some connection to the tree or nature or mother earth. But he he felt nothing. Except ... that wasn't exactly true.

He leaned down and pressed a kiss into the top of Serena's head, then rested his chin there. "I felt so inadequate that day," he began, gathering his thoughts and words together. "With Dad and Matt restraining me, and all I could do was stand there, helpless while other people cut you out of the car."

"Why didn't your dad make you leave?"

"He wanted me to. But there was no way I could go until I knew you were okay. I thought I was about to lose everything that mattered to me." He pulled her back against his chest, breaking her kumbaya moment with the tree and wrapping his long arms around her.

All he had ever wanted was an average life. Nothing special, nothing extraordinary. He didn't need everyone to think he was smart and ambitious, like Jack did. He didn't need every day to be a party, like Matt. He wanted a wife and kids, a modest house, a yard in which to throw a football or a baseball with his boys, a summer vacation at the beach. He wanted his dad's job someday when his father saw fit to retire. It would be nice to maybe have a daughter, in addition to the boys.

He wanted his parents' life, basically. Minus the bad parts like when his mother's twin brother died on a call ... or his mother dying of cancer in her fifties.

You don't get to minus the bad parts.

"Did you remember anything?" He began to walk her backward, away from the killer tree.

She spun around so they were facing the minivan and walking forward toward it. "No. I'm sorry, Ollie."

"I just can't imagine why you were driving out this way, without the boys. You asked Charlotte Trevor to watch them."

"Has anyone asked her why I left the boys with her?"

"The police spoke to her."

"And what did she say?"

"You told her you had an appointment and that you'd be back in a couple hours."

"Maybe I was going to the OB. I was pregnant."

They stopped next to the minivan. "The doctor's office said you weren't scheduled for an appointment that day."

"Oh." She walked around to the passenger side. "You'd better drive back. Don't want to push our luck with the dealership."

"Sure."

They climbed back into the car, buckled their seatbelts, and then turned to look at each other.

"Maybe I swerved to avoid hitting a deer," Serena suggested. "Maybe the sun was too bright in my eyes. Maybe a tire blew out and I lost control of the vehicle." She sighed. "I wish I knew. But I look at Ashley and think 'if this accident is the worst thing that happens to us, we're doing pretty good.'" She reached out and stroked his smooth cheek. "Becca said you let your beard grow out while I was in the hospital." She flipped her hand over and ran the tops of her fingers over his skin. "I don't think I've ever seen you with a beard."

"I can't have one in the fire department."

"I know. But you grew it out when you were on leave."

He shrugged. "Just for a little while. The boys gave me a hard time about it, so I started shaving again."

She smiled. "You'd do anything for Mason and Cam."

"I would."

"Let's just be happy, Ollie. For them, at least. I know you want answers and I want them, too. Maybe we'll find them someday. But in the meantime, let's enjoy what we have. We have a lot."

She was right. They did have a lot. And other people had it worse than they did. Ashley Wardman, to be sure. To be a widow at her age? Oliver still had the life he wanted. Every day, he went to a job he loved. And every day, he came home to his beautiful wife and handsome boys in their comfortable home. They were going to drive back to the car dealership and buy this new mini-van, something not every family could afford. But they could.

He leaned over and kissed her. "You're right, babe. Let's go buy these new wheels for you, then grab some lunch before school lets out."

CHAPTER 16

"Boys?" Serena called into the living room, where Mason and Cam were adding to their latest Lego masterpiece. "Homework time!" She rolled her eyes at the faint sounds of grumbling.

"They get homework at this age?" Ashley carried two cups of strong, dark coffee to the dining room table.

"Yeah, it's surprising. Well, Cam doesn't get much. A worksheet once or twice a week." She pulled out a chair and collapsed into it, took a sip of coffee and giggled. "He said something really funny the other day. He said, 'Mom, why do I have to color in the worksheet, then cut up the worksheet, and then glue the worksheet back together again? Why can't I just move on to the next worksheet?'"

Ashley clapped a hand over her nose to keep from snorting hot coffee. "Out of the mouths of babes. What did you tell him?"

"I gave him a brief explanation of learning styles, that it helps reinforce the material for some kids if they have to do the additional steps."

"You sound just like Ben. Theories of Teaching 101."

"He was still making kids cut up worksheets in high school?" Serena winked at her friend.

"I think he would have, if he thought they'd actually do it."

"Mom!" Mason's voice sounded from the other room. "We're trying to do homework in here!"

"Sorry, sweetie! We'll keep our voices down."

"Indoor voices!" Cam added, in a voice that wasn't exactly "indoors."

"Your boys are so adorable," Ashley said, in a quieter "indoor" voice.

"Exhausting, but adorable."

"You do look tired tonight."

Serena took a giant sip of coffee. "Oliver wanted to buy a new car today so we can drive it to Virginia this weekend."

"Romantic weekend away?"

Serena shook her head. "No, we're taking the boys to the Air and Space Museum. Family weekend away."

"That sounds like fun. Exhausting, but fun."

"We need to get out of town for a couple days. Really, it's more for Oliver than for the boys."

"Why so?"

Serena lowered her voice further to make sure the boys couldn't hear. "He needs a distraction. He's obsessed with me getting my memory back. But honestly, there are some things I don't want to remember. Like the accident."

"Good heavens, no. That would be awful." Ashley drained the rest of her coffee. "Sometimes I wish I had no memories. It hurts too much to remember Ben."

Cam took that moment to carom into the room, a worksheet clutched in his hand.

"Done! Before Mason!" He drew out the last syllable of his brother's name into one long victory cry.

"Let me check it over," Serena said as Ashley returned to the kitchen for more coffee. "Okay, looks good. Put this in your backpack. Then why don't you go up and get your pj's on, then come down for a bedtime snack."

Cam hurtled himself into the mudroom to deposit his homework in the backpack, then raced upstairs.

"Where do they get the energy?" Ashley set the mugs of fresh coffee on the table.

"The air, I think. Oxygen seems to be a stimulant." She took a sip. "Can I ask you something?" She hesitated, then forged tentatively ahead. "You can decline to answer, if you want."

"Ask away."

Serena looked at her friend, dressed as she often was these days—in jeans and an oversized wool sweater that had to have belonged to Ben. Maybe she shouldn't ask this of her. After all, what Ash had gone through was far worse than her own life. But the question nagged at her as much as it did Oliver.

"When we were test driving the car today, I ended up driving to where the accident happened. Not on purpose."

"Oh. Wow."

"Apparently, when I dropped the boys off with Charlotte Trevor, I said I had an appointment and would be back in a couple hours."

Ashley shrugged. "I can't imagine taking those tornadoes of energy to a doctor's appointment."

"But the doctor told Ollie that I didn't have an appointment scheduled for that day." She hesitated another moment. Ashley might know where she was headed that day. But Serena was beginning to worry that she might not like the answer—when she tried to imagine an answer that made sense, she came up empty every time.

She took a deep breath. She had to ask anyway. "Do you know where I was going that day? Did I tell you anything about an appointment?"

"No. If I knew, I would have said something by now."

"Don't you think that's odd? That I wouldn't have said something to a close friend?"

Ashley shrugged. "Honestly—and please don't take offense at this—but you were always a very private person. I know everyone sees you as the more extroverted half of your marriage, but you still play things close to the vest." Ashley took a hurried sip of coffee. "Actually, you're much more open now."

"So I'm kind of a different person now?"

Ashley shrugged again and nodded. "Yes. But not in a bad way. It's not like you're totally different or anything. It's you, but *more* of you. If you know what I mean." She smiled in an attempt to soften her words. "I mean, I like it! It's a good thing."

"I feel kind of different. I think. It's hard to say when I don't remember a lot from before. But, like, I look in my closet and I think, 'Why on earth did I buy *that?*' There are things I clearly did that I can't even imagine myself doing now."

"I probably also wasn't the greatest friend last summer, with Ben being sick. It all happened so fast." Ashley wiped a finger beneath her teary eye. "I thought I'd have more time."

Mason appeared, as if out of nowhere. His dark hair was ruffled, like he'd been worrying pieces of it around his fingers. He laid a small stack of papers on the table, then touched Ashley's forearm. "I'm sorry for your loss, Ms. Ashley." He glanced over at his mom, then added, "I wanted to be coached by Coach Wardman someday."

Ashley leaned down and hugged him. "Thank you, Mason. I like to think his spirit will always be hanging around the soccer field. That was his happy place."

"Hey bud," Serena said. "Why don't you go put on your pajamas and bring your brother down for a snack? He seems to have gotten sidetracked up there."

Mason gave her a thumbs-up and she leaned back into the chair, massaging her temples.

"Maybe you just needed a break that day," Ashley ventured.

"You were pregnant. Your mother-in-law—whom you were extremely close to—was in the hospital. You have two energetic kids. Who wouldn't need a couple hours to themselves? Or maybe you were going to the hospital to see Oliver's mom?"

"If I were going to the hospital, that's the way I would go."

"See? If I had to guess, I'd say that's where you were headed. Because you wouldn't have taken the boys with you to the hospital."

"No. Never. Ollie and I discussed how to handle Angie's illness, where the boys were concerned … wait, I just remembered that! Oliver and I talked about what to tell the boys. I recall that very clearly."

"See?"

"And I might have just told Charlotte that I had an appointment so the boys wouldn't accidentally find out that I was really going to the hospital."

"Right! That has to be it."

Serena nodded, as much to herself as to Ashley. That had to be it. She was on her way to see Angie when the accident happened.

CHAPTER 17

"*L*ook at that plane!" Cam shouted. "It's going to crash!"

Serena watched through the windshield of the new minivan as an airliner flew over the highway ahead of them, its long white body heavy and at an alarmingly low altitude.

"The wheels are down!" Cam's arm shot into the space between the driver's and passenger's seats.

"Sit back, sweetie," Serena said, not taking her eyes off the lumbering plane. "Is your seatbelt still on?"

"I think we're close to the airport, boys. That plane is going to be landing in a few minutes."

"Freaky wow!" Mason finally chimed in.

"I want to see the plane land!" Cam added.

"Well, according to the museum's web site—and we all know the internet doesn't lie—there is an observation tower where you have a great view of the planes landing *and* taking off," Oliver said. He was in full dad mode behind the wheel of the new minivan, carefully piloting them to their destination—the Udvar-Hazy Center in Chantilly, Virginia. It was part of the Smithsonian's National Air and Space Museum.

"We can see them take off, too?"

"Cammy, dear, I need you to sit back in the seat. We're almost there." She shot Oliver a questioning look. They had to be close, right? A plane had practically landed on the highway.

Oliver gave her a quick nod. "Hey guys, before we do get there, let's review some ground rules. Okay? This is going to be a big place, with a lot of people. So no running off by yourself. Understood?"

Serena twisted around in her seat to look at the boys. "And indoor voices only, please."

"In space no one can hear you scream," Mason said.

"Yeah well, we're not going to be in outer space. We're going to a museum here on planet earth," Oliver replied, rolling his eyes.

"Uncle Mattie said there's a space shuttle at the museum."

"Your Uncle Mattie is occasionally right."

The boys rode out the rest of the drive in agitated silence. Oliver pulled the car into the parking lot, cut the ignition, and checked his watch. "We made pretty good time, even hitting rush hour traffic around Annapolis. Why don't we check out the observation tower first, have lunch, and then do the rest of the museum?" He looked over at Serena for her agreement.

She nodded. "Sounds like a plan." Then quieter, "Give everyone a chance to calm down a bit."

After thirty minutes of watching planes take off and land, they hit the fast food restaurant. Serena munched on french fries and tuned out the boys' excited chatter. She couldn't think when she had last flown in a plane. She and Oliver flew to Hawaii for their honeymoon but that was over seven years ago now. That was Oliver's second time on a plane. His first was to a fire training academy in Texas. It was possible they hadn't flown since, what with the boys and all. It was possible Oliver had only ever flown twice.

How many times had she been on a plane? She was certain

her first time was before she could walk. Her family had taken multiple vacations every year—summer, spring break, winter break. When she and her brother were teenagers, they'd gotten shipped off to internships with family friends or her father's business colleagues. Those had been of more use to her brother than to her. She ended up getting married a year out of college and becoming a stay-at-home mother.

Her parents were of the opinion that they had wasted a lot of money on her education.

She held tightly onto Cam's hand when at last they made their way to the main part of the museum, a cavernous hangar filled with every imaginable kind of flying vehicle. The boys' eyes grew as wide as flying saucers, and no wonder. There were aircraft on the floor. Aircraft hanging, suspended, from the soaring white ceiling. Aircraft everywhere. She heard Oliver take a long, deep inhale.

"Okay, guys. Let's start over here—" He consulted the paper map in his hands. "—with pre-1920 aviation. We'll try and go chronologically." He looked down at the boys' eager, upturned faces. "That means oldest to newest."

Serena hung back, reading the exhibit descriptions, as the boys circled each aircraft, gawking at the wings overhead and listening as their dad pointed out interesting features. He wisely glossed over the backstory to the Enola Gay. The boys were too young for that—and Cam, especially, was too sensitive. Cam couldn't even bear to go fishing with his granddad; he didn't want to hurt the fish.

After they oohed and aahed over the sleek, dark curves of the Blackbird reconnaissance plane, they deviated from chronological order. Mason had spotted the space shuttle in the back wing of the museum. Serena's leg was starting to ache, so she waved Ollie and the boys on and found a bench to rest on. Oliver shot her a worried look.

"Go on," she mouthed back. She tapped her thigh.

The boys were going to be exhausted tonight, she thought as she watched them join the crowd of people surrounding the shuttle. Going away for the weekend was a good idea. It was total sensory overload for Mason and Cam, but in a good way. As far as she knew, this was their first time in a museum. That was the downside of growing up in a small town. Serena had probably visited the Met in New York when she was still in a stroller. Not that she remembered it. Just like the boys probably wouldn't remember this day. For a few years they would and then the day would fade in their memories, pushed back by the onslaught of days ahead.

She watched as Oliver lifted up Mason so he could get a better view over the heads of the crowd. Then he did the same for Cam. It didn't matter that they wouldn't remember this day twenty years from now. Right now—today—they were having the best day of their lives. She sat with that thought for a minute, as Oliver and the boys disappeared around the back of the shuttle. Kids live in the present. Mason and Cam could bicker and squabble over who knocked over their latest Lego creation or who should get the last juice box in the one flavor that suddenly either of them will drink—and the next day act like it never happened. Each morning, their lives started all over again, fresh, a blank slate, nothing but potential as far as the eye could see.

She envied them that. Not having to worry about what happened a year ago. Or mistakes that were made and couldn't be undone. Some offhand remark that someone else took the wrong way. Or realizing that what you thought you would want forever isn't even what you want today. She closed her eyes for a moment, shutting out the noise and busyness of the museum. When she reopened them, Oliver and the boys were headed her way.

"The boys want to check out the Concorde in the other hangar," Oliver said. "Then we thought maybe we should see one of the movies in the IMAX theater. The space one starts in about thirty minutes."

"Sounds like a plan." She accepted Oliver's outstretched hand and allowed him to help her stand up.

"How's your leg, mom?" Mason asked.

She smoothed an errant lock of dark hair on his head. "It's better, thank you. It just needed a rest."

The Concorde dominated the other side of the museum's main hangar. The plane was long and sleek, its white body tapering to sharp points at each end. Large blue letters spelled out "AIR FRANCE" just behind the cockpit. Standing below it, the plane looked impossibly large—much larger than Serena remembered it.

Mason ran back from the information display, Cam on his heels.

"Mom! Mom! It's a supersonic plane!"

"I know that." She smiled over at Oliver.

"It makes a sonic boom when it flies," Mason added.

"Did I ever tell you that I flew on the Concorde?"

The boys fell silent, their expressions skeptical as if they were waiting for the punchline to a joke. It was Oliver who spoke first.

"You did?"

She nodded. "Twice, actually. When I was a kid. We flew it from New York to Paris."

"You flew in *this* plane?" Mason pointed back at the Concorde.

"Well, maybe not that exact plane. But one of the Concordes. They had more than one."

"Wow." Oliver shook his head. "You never mentioned that."

She shrugged. "Guess it never came up in conversation."

Which it hadn't—because Serena wasn't in the habit of mentioning her childhood or her family to people in St. Caroline. Obviously, Oliver knew some of the details. But her parents had cut her off when it became clear that she was determined to marry him. She hadn't been back to New York since. Oliver had never been to her parents' homes—the Park Avenue mansion or the Connecticut weekend home. Nor even to her neighborhood.

Plenty of wealthy people owned mansions and estates in and around St. Caroline. The locals, even Oliver, believed they understood that world. But what passed for great wealth in St. Caroline … well, New York City was of an entirely different order. Serena was embarrassed to say she had grown up like that. The excess, the waste, the hubris.

Everyone in St. Caroline thought of her as "a girl from the city," and their imaginations imputed a certain lifestyle to her past. But their imaginations fell well short of the reality, and she preferred to keep it that way. When she moved to the Eastern Shore, she had reinvented herself as what she considered to be a "normal" person. A person who liked a slower, less glitzy life, who clipped coupons for the supermarket and didn't need a trendy new restaurant opening up every six minutes.

"Are there museums in New York?" Cam asked.

She reached down and hoisted him up onto her hip. "There sure are. Quite a few."

"With dinosaurs?" Mason expanded the scope of his brother's question. "Nevaeh at school said she went to a museum where they had dinosaurs and fossils."

She looked over at Oliver and lifted her eyebrows in question. Another road trip on the horizon?

"I'm pretty sure the natural history museum on the Mall has dinosaurs and fossils. And other cool stuff," Oliver said.

Good point, she thought. Washington, DC was much closer than New York. Still, a part of her wanted to show "her city" to the boys.

Oliver glanced at the watch on his wrist. "If we're going to make the space movie, we should head over there."

She let the weight of Cam's body slide from her arms as Mason fell into step beside his father. As soon as Cam's sneakers hit the polished concrete floor, he ran to catch up.

Serena took one last look back at the Concorde. She and her brother, Peter, had been privileged to get to fly on it. Privileged to go to Paris as kids. She was ten years old the first time she went; she remembered the Seine, the ornate buildings, the croissants that were better than any she'd ever tasted in the States. Mason and Cam wouldn't be jetting off to Paris as children. She and Oliver certainly couldn't afford that.

She turned away from the plane and hurried to catch up to the boys.

OLIVER SAT down on the pool's edge next to Serena. Mason and Cam were already in the water. Both boys had fallen asleep halfway through the space movie and now, after dinner at the hotel, were catching a second wind of energy.

"You're not getting in?" she asked, kicking her right leg lazily through the water.

"Maybe later." He ran a finger along the bare skin of her thigh. "I'm bushed, you know? Mom and dad used to take the three of us to the zoo in Washington every summer." He shook his head, laughing softly. "They must have been out of their minds. Three boys?" He laughed again, this time a little louder. "I do remember they had their hearts set on Jack being a girl. Didn't happen."

"You remember your mom being pregnant with Jack?"

"I do. Not with Mattie, but I was five when Jack was born. Between starting school and another baby in the house, it was a lot of change. That's what I remember. All the change in our lives."

"You don't do well with change."

"I know."

She laid her hand on his to stop his finger tickling her thigh.

"I think I might know where I was going the day I had the accident," she said.

"You do? You remember?"

"Well, I don't remember, really. But there's only one scenario that makes any sense. I was probably going to the hospital to see your mom. And I left the boys with Charlotte because we agreed that we didn't want them to see her there."

He mulled over this idea for a moment. "But why wouldn't you have told me you were going?"

She shrugged. "Maybe it was a spur of the moment thing. Maybe she called me? You can't always be reached when you're at the station. Doesn't that make sense to you?"

It did make sense, in a way. Serena had always been the daughter his mother never had. *The daughter Jack was supposed to be.* He bit back a tiny smile. So yes, the idea of Serena going to visit her in the hospital did make sense. In fact, the idea had already occurred to him.

But.

Jack was at the hospital visiting mom when the accident happened. Why would Serena be headed there at the same time?

You're letting your imagination run away with you.

He knew that. He'd never had any reason to question his wife's fidelity to him. So probably the simplest answer was the most likely one. He looked at the boys splashing and swimming in the pool, like little energy-making machines.

"Or maybe you just needed a break from the boys," he said.

CHAPTER 18

"*H*ey guys. Happy Valentine's Day."

Oliver was helping Serena up onto a bar stool. He looked up to see Becca standing behind the bar, her reddish-brown hair pulled back in a ponytail.

"Thought you weren't working here anymore." He and Serena were at Skipjack's to have a quick drink before heading over to the Inn's fancier restaurant, Evangeline's, for dinner.

"Just for tonight. Mike needed someone to fill in. Jack's at the station, so it's not like I have a date for Valentine's Day."

"Welcome to life with a firefighter," Serena said as Becca laid two square cocktail napkins in front of them.

"What can I get you?"

"White wine?" Serena asked. "What do you recommend?"

Oliver smiled inwardly. At least *that* hadn't changed about his wife. When they first started dating, he was surprised that she wasn't more knowledgeable about wine and drinks. Given her background, he expected her to be worldly and cosmopolitan in everything. Then he learned about her father's drinking and it made more sense.

"Mike has a new sauvignon blanc from New Zealand, if you'd like to try that. I thought it was excellent."

"Sure. I'll give it a go."

"I'll have whatever IPA you have on draft tonight." Oliver let his fingers graze his wife's hair, let one of her dark curls swirl softly around his thumb.

It was Valentine's Day. He was out with his wife for a nice dinner and then an evening of hotel sex—he even booked the same room she stayed in the night they met. He was certain she would remember *that* little detail. So yeah, it was going to be a good night. They'd made it this far, despite everything that had happened since Valentine's Day last year. *Things are going to be okay.*

Becca returned with their drinks. "Where are the kiddos tonight?"

"They're at home. Ashley is babysitting," Serena answered.

"By babysitting, we mean spending hours and hours playing with Legos," he joked.

Serena looked over at him with a smile. "We'd better make the most of tonight. She may not do this for us ever again."

"You know you can always ask me and Jack to babysit," Becca offered before leaving to tend to another couple at the other end of the bar.

"It's busy tonight," Serena remarked.

Oliver scanned the restaurant. Every table sported an arrangement of red roses. Serena's roses were already up in the room, along with a box of chocolates he ordered special from a tiny artisan chocolatier in Pennsylvania. The Inn's owner, Sterling Matthew, had put the flowers and candy in the room himself. Oliver had responded to enough false fire alarms at the Inn over the years—the man owed him.

"Even this early," she added.

It was only five o'clock, but most of the tables were full. When he and Serena discussed timing, they decided to make an early dinner reservation—just in case the boys ended up being too much for Ashley. Starting the evening early guaranteed them at least a few hours together, even if the date had to be cut short.

A few minutes later, they watched as Becca reached into her apron pocket and pulled out her phone. She glanced at the caller ID, then held it up to her ear. Within seconds, her face blanched white. She leaned on the bar's glossy wood, just listening. When she set down the phone, she turned to Oliver and Serena, her face stricken.

"There's been a shooting in Boston. Cassidy's in the hospital."

"What's she doing in Boston?" Oliver asked, trying to process what Becca had just said. Cassidy Trevor shot?

"She's there for a business conference." Becca's voice broke and she pressed her fist against her mouth. "She was supposed to come home tomorrow."

Sterling Matthew appeared out of nowhere, slipping behind the bar.

"You. Go," he said to Becca. "I'll take over here."

While Becca ripped off her apron and hurried from the bar, Oliver pulled out his phone to call his brother, Jack.

"I need you to come in," were the first words out of his brother's mouth. "Cassidy's been shot and Mattie's heading up to Boston."

"Why's he going?"

"He and Cassidy have been seeing each other."

"They have? Since when?"

"I don't know. Couple months, I think. Hey, I've gotta go. I need you to come in and cover for Matt."

"All right." He turned to Serena.

"It's okay," she said before the words were even out of his mouth.

"I'll make it up to you. I promise." He leaned in and kissed her.

❧

THE FIRST THING Serena noticed when she opened the front door to the house was the spicy scent of pizza. Ashley had the boys' number. Pizza was their current number one favorite meal. The more pepperoni, the better.

The second thing she noticed as she picked her way across the Lego-strewn floor of the living room was an expensive-looking camera sitting in the middle of the sea of plastic. She shifted the roses and box of candy to one arm so she could pick up the camera. She carefully set it on the coffee table that was semi-permanently pushed aside to make room for feats of Lego engineering.

The boys' heads snapped up the instant she entered the dining room.

"Mom! Mom! We're having pepperoni pizza!" Cam exclaimed.

"Mom! Mom! Miss Ashley is helping us take pictures of our Legos!" Mason belatedly realized he was speaking with his mouth full, and hurriedly gulped down what he was chewing.

She shot Ashley a look of sympathy. Ashley might not want kids after an evening with the pure adrenaline that was Mason and Cam.

"Where's dad?" Mason asked, in a calmer voice.

"He had to go into the station."

Ashley's face fell in sympathy. "Oh. Sorry," she mouthed.

Serena shrugged.

"That's life with a firefighter. Keep that in mind, boys. If you ever marry a firefighter, half your dates will end this way."

Mason rolled his eyes. "Girls aren't firefighters."

"Yes, they are! Amy at the station—hello?"

Serena bit back a laugh at the indignant tone in Cam's voice. Mason's days of having an unquestioning, adoring younger brother were numbered.

"Okay, one," Mason allowed.

"Hey guys, I need to speak with Ashley for a moment. Save me a slice, okay?"

Ashley followed her to the kitchen. "Those flowers are gorgeous."

Serena held out the roses for her friend to sniff, then laid them on the counter. She set the box of candy next to them.

"So Oliver got called in? I didn't hear any sirens or anything."

"He had to relieve Matt. There's been a shooting in Boston. At the hotel where Cassidy Trevor was staying."

"Oh god. Don't tell me …"

Serena nodded. "Cassidy was injured. Matt is headed up there. Apparently, the two of them are dating."

"They are? Well, I'm not surprised, I guess. They co-chaired the winter festival. They struck me as being pretty good friends."

"More than friends now." Serena opened a cupboard and retrieved two bags of microwave popcorn. "Want to stay and watch a movie with us?" The relief on Ashley's face pierced her heart. Her friend had been dreading going home to an empty house on Valentine's Day. "I've got expensive candy," she threw in for good measure.

"Far be it from me to turn down chocolate."

AN HOUR LATER, the carpeted floor of the basement TV room was littered with an empty pizza box, two nearly empty bowls of popcorn, and a half dozen deflated juice boxes. Serena and Ashley were stretched out on opposite ends of the corduroy sectional, her Valentine's Day candy open on the sofa between them. On the floor, Mason and Cam were sprawled on pillows. An animated movie about space aliens played on the television.

Cam will be lucky if he stays awake to the end.

Serena was hit with a sudden memory of this exact same scene, only with Angie on the sofa instead of Ashley. The boys had adored their grandmother. And their grandmother had adored them.

They are pretty damn adorable.

Angie's death had left a gaping hole in Mason and Cam's lives, a hole no one else would ever be able to fill. *Even if they learned to swear from her.*

Oh, they were picking up some of it from Mattie, too.

Serena suspected that. Mason and Cam adored their uncle, as well. She offered up a silent prayer for Cassidy. The Wolfe family just could not catch a break these days. She hoped Oliver could set aside his obvious dismay at the idea of Matt and Cassidy dating, and offer his brother some comfort and sympathy. He was the one person who knew exactly what Matt was going through right now.

Her phone vibrated on the sofa next to her. She picked it up and swiped away the lockscreen. It was a text from Oliver.

Bored. Wish I was with you.

She texted him back. *Wish that too. Any word from Boston?*

Matt managed to get a flight out of Baltimore. Cassidy just went into surgery.

How serious is it?

Dunno. A minute passed before his next message. *How are the boys?*

She pointed her phone at Mason and Cam and snapped a quick photo. The boys were too engrossed in the movie to even notice. She texted it to Oliver, then added, *I love you.*

I love you too, babe.

CHAPTER 19

The next morning Serena put the boys on the school bus, waved goodbye to Oliver as he headed to the gym, and then did what she did most mornings—wander aimlessly through the house. On the days she volunteered at the elementary school, she woke up feeling a sense of purpose and direction. On the days she didn't, she ... did laundry and vacuumed and wrote out grocery lists and made dentist's appointments for the boys and discovered socks and underwear beneath beds and searched the internet for new ways to serve vegetables that the boys would tolerate and ... collapse into a chair in the den, wondering what the point of it all was.

Growing up, she had looked down on her mother for hiring out the mundane, rote details of running a household in favor of serving on nonprofit boards and raising money for playgrounds and arts programs. She was starting to rethink that attitude. Sure, sometimes folding and putting away laundry gave her the warm, rosy feeling that she was taking care of the people she loved the most. Other times ... *wasn't I just doing this fifteen minutes ago?*

It wasn't just that she couldn't remember the recent years of her life. She was having trouble imagining *this* as her life.

She leaned forward in the den's office chair and flipped open her laptop on the desk. She was still working her way through the thousands of emails that had accumulated while she was in the hospital. It was a Sisyphean task—as soon as she deleted a hundred, another fifty appeared. *Clearly I was a big online shopper.* Of course, one didn't have much choice, living in St. Caroline. There wasn't even a Walmart nearby. Most people drove to Annapolis or to the outlets on route 50 for any serious shopping. She wondered where Oliver had taken Mason and Cam for back-to-school shopping last year.

She deleted emails until her knuckles began to ache and stiffen. Then she dragged a cardboard box from beneath the desk. Apparently Oliver was just tossing junk mail and catalogs into it, rather than putting it out for recycling. She didn't bother to wonder why—he'd had enough on his plate while she was in the hospital. She flipped through it absentmindedly. There was an alarming volume of mail from Talbot College. The boys were way too young to be getting brochures from colleges. She *definitely* wasn't ready for that yet.

She spent a few more minutes sorting through the box, just to make sure there was nothing important in there. A brightly colored postcard caught her eye. From the college, of course. She flipped it over and scanned the text. It was for an open house for the teacher certification program. If you had a bachelor's degree already, you could get certification in less than two years. *Interesting.* She glanced at the date. The open house was last November. *Oh well.* She tossed the card back into the box.

After lunch, she cleaned the boys' bathroom, then hoisted onto her bed a large plastic box filled to the brim with quilting fabric. Angie had left it for her. Tears pricked at Serena's eyes. She never had the opportunity to thank Angie, or say goodbye— or tell her how much her friendship had meant to her. She felt motherless now, too.

She unsnapped the plastic latches on both ends of the box and lifted away the lid, wondering how Angie had decided which fabrics to give her. She remembered her mother-in-law's huge stash of fabric, practically enough to open a fabric store of her own. She lifted lengths of material from the box and laid them out on the bed around her. From the quilting class with Becca she was gradually learning what everything was called—fat quarters, jelly rolls, calicoes, reproduction fabrics. And the colors—cheddar, turkey red, double pink.

She wanted to make her string quilt from class larger. Becca told her that Angie had always liked batik fabrics. It turned out that Serena was drawn to those also, and she dug through the box looking for anything that looked hand-dyed, marbled, or stamped with images of leaves or flowers. She unfolded a length of turquoise fabric covered with tiny, pale palm fronds. The color and design made her think of Hawaii, and their honeymoon. She set it aside and looked for more in the box.

Oliver joked the other evening that she had been bitten by the quilting bug. She laughed along with him, until it occurred to her that he might not want to see her quilting, that it might remind him too much of Angie. He denied it, but of course Oliver would. He prided himself on being level-headed, rational, calm under pressure. A firefighter had to be all of those things, but sometimes she wondered whether he really had emotions underneath it all. He said "I love you" to her every single day, but did he mean it—or was he just saying what a good husband was supposed to say to his wife?

Ollie's desire to be a good, stable husband and father was part of his appeal, initially. And he was those things—the things her own father hadn't been quite so good at. Her father had been more interested in the appearance of an attractive family—beautiful wife, accomplished kids—than in the reality of one.

She set aside several more folded lengths of fabric. Ollie seemed different lately. Distant, more closed off than usual. She tried to talk to him about it, but he merely agreed with everything she said. *Yes, we have a great life. Yes, I love you. Yes, everything's okay.*

She could tell that everything wasn't okay, though. And worrisome thoughts were hanging around more and more frequently. In trying to marry a man who was completely different from her father, had she ended up marrying one who was just a different version? Oliver wanted a particular kind of life—quiet, small town, family-oriented to the nth degree—but did it matter who peopled that life for him?

Her father used to say that her mother was "the perfect wife" for him, even as he embarked on affairs and drank away his unhappiness. Was that what she was too? The perfect wife for the life Oliver wanted? If she had died last fall, how long would he have waited to remarry?

She sighed. When she came home from the hospital, he was fine at first. He was like the old Ollie. But lately? She was getting the distinct impression that she wasn't meeting the "perfect wife" standards.

She gathered up the batiks and set them aside, then put the other fabrics back in the box and snapped the lid into place. Was she getting the quilting bug? It was certainly a relaxing activity. Why hadn't Angie tried to get her interested in it before?

Not as pushy as Michelle Trevor?

Serena bit back a laugh as she lugged the box back over to the closet. Sometimes her thoughts were alarmingly blunt. She paused for a moment before closing the closet door. It saddened her that Mason and Cam didn't have their grandmother in their lives anymore. How much of her would they even remember? Cam—probably not much. She couldn't recall much from when she was five years old. Not even her first day of kindergarten.

She did have fond memories of her maternal grandparents and their home outside Atlanta. Her mother used to take her and Peter to visit on school breaks. While her mother lunched with childhood friends, Serena would hang out in the kitchen with her grandmother and bake. Bread, cakes from scratch, buttermilk biscuits, cookies. *She was the one who domesticated me.*

She shook her head at the thought of Mason and Cam ever being "domesticated."

They won't be feral forever.

Feral, that was an apt term for her boys. They would have a close relationship with Oliver's dad, Tim, but they had never even met her parents. What was wrong with her mother and father? She sent birth announcements both times, but all she got back was deafening silence. She had thought that the arrival of grandkids would make them get over their displeasure with her marriage. *I thought wrong, obviously.* Years ago, Peter had bugged her about forcing the issue with their parents. "You know mum just goes along with whatever dad wants, even if she doesn't agree with it."

Maybe I was too stubborn. Her parents started this, and she wanted them to fix it. She hated the thought of begging her own parents to see their grandkids. But she hated the thought of Mason and Cam not knowing their grandparents more.

They came to see you in the hospital.

True. Oliver did mention that. He had called to let them know about the accident. But he didn't let the boys meet them.

He wasn't sure you wanted that.

She hadn't.

She jumped off the bed and ran downstairs to find her phone before she thought better of the whole idea and changed her mind. She tapped in her mother's cell number and listened while it rang on the other end, her heart pounding in her chest. She shouldn't be nervous about talking to her own mother.

But she was.

Her mother's voice mail picked up. *Should I hang up? She'll see that I called. She won't call me back.*

You never know.

I'd be surprised.

There was the beep after her mother's greeting and then silence. Serena's heart was in her throat. *Words! I need words!*

"Hi mum" ... did you call her "mum?"

Right. Start simple. "Hi mum. It's me. Serena." Her mind went blank again.

You're home from the hospital now.

"I'm home from the hospital now ... just wanted to let you know ... don't know if Oliver called to tell you or not ..."

Mention the boys.

"... hope you and dad are well. I was thinking about bringing the boys to New York some time ..."

The museum!

"... um, they want to go to the natural history museum and see the dinosaurs."

Perfect!

"Call me ... if you have time."

She hung up. There was no way her mother would call her back.

You never know.

CHAPTER 20

Oliver and Matt stood on the sidewalk outside St. Caroline High School, watching a crowd of students wait for the building to be cleared. The fire alarm had gone off just as the final lunch period was ending. Some of the students were still drinking from bottles of water and small cartons of milk. Others rubbed their arms up and down in an effort to stay warm in the February chill.

Oliver glanced over at his brother, who was uncharacteristically quiet today.

"How's Cassidy?" he asked.

Matt shrugged. "She's home. That's all I know."

"You haven't been over to see her? I thought you two were dating."

"We're not."

"Jack said—"

"It was more of a friends with benefits situation. But it's over now, okay?"

Oliver studied his brother's profile. He could see the tightness in Matt's square jaw and the tension in his shoulders, even beneath the heavy turnout gear. "Got it."

Oliver was under the impression that the Trevors weren't overly enthused about Matt's interest in Cassidy. He could understand that. Matt's reputation wasn't exactly sterling where women were concerned.

Still, he felt bad for his younger brother. Hopping on a plane and flying up to Boston to see a woman in a hospital wasn't normal behavior for Matt. Maybe his love 'em and leave 'em days were coming to an end. It was just too bad that he had picked a woman he couldn't have.

Across the way, two other firefighters pushed open the heavy steel doors to the school. They spoke briefly to the principal and vice principal. A minute later, the crowd of kids surged toward the open doors.

"How's Serena?" Matt asked.

"She's fine."

"How are the boys?"

"Good. They're good."

It was only Oliver that wasn't "fine" or "good." Serena had called her mother a few days ago. He wasn't sure what to make of that. Did she not remember just how estranged she'd been from her parents?

His attention drifted from the students to the slice of soccer field he could see behind the far corner of the school. "You knew Ben Wardman," he said.

"Yeah, just through soccer and all."

"Serena really took the news of his death hard."

"A lot of people did. He was a pretty popular teacher."

"Yeah. But I don't recall her really knowing him all that well. She's friends with Ashley, but it's not like we ever went out together as couples."

"Why not?"

"I don't know. We just never did."

"Huh. Well, they were friends. I used to see them at Two Beans sometimes, having coffee together."

"Serena and Ben?"

"Yeah. Isn't that who we're talking about?"

Oliver squinted hard at the soccer field, processing what Matt just told him. He used to see Serena and Ben having coffee together.

～

SERENA HAD JUST GOTTEN out of Ashley's car at the elementary school when her phone rang. She expected it to be Ollie. He had taken to calling her at odd times during the day, just to check in. For a split second, she considered ignoring it—she was due in Cam's classroom—but then dug the phone out of her purse. Her breath caught at the sight of the area code. New York.

It couldn't be. Not after all these years. Not after three days of hopeful waiting.

She tapped the screen to answer and held the phone up to her ear.

"Serena?"

Her legs nearly buckled beneath her.

"Mum?"

There was a long silence, as though her mother wasn't sure what to say next. Serena wasn't sure, either. Then they both spoke at once.

"Did you get my message?"

"I got your message."

She heard her mother's raspy laugh on the other end.

"Serena, love, I was so happy to hear your voice."

She wondered whether that was really true, but she hadn't called her mother to confront her. She had called for Mason and Cam. She needed to keep that front and center in her mind.

"I'm out of the hospital now."

"We came to see you!"

"I know. Oliver told me." Serena was imagining a giant cloud

151

of awkwardness stretching from St. Caroline to the Upper East Side. Her natural inclination was to apologize for not calling her mother the day after she was released from the hospital. On the other hand, the only time her parents had been to see her was when she was unconscious and in a coma.

"You said you were thinking about bringing Mason and Cam to New York for a visit," her mother said.

Serena was surprised that her mother remembered her grandsons' names. "Yes. It would probably have to be after school lets out in June."

"Well, anytime is fine. We can put them up in Peter's old room."

"You and Daddy haven't moved?"

Her mother's laugh was sharp, a sound not filled with much amusement.

"No, I'd love to downsize but your father likes his space."

Just two floors of her parents' house covered more square footage than the home she shared with Oliver.

"Although he's been eyeing those new skyscrapers that keep popping up like weeds here in the city," her mother went on. "But—"

"You don't like heights," Serena finished the sentence for her. She had inherited her mother's aversion to heights, herself.

"Exactly! I cannot live on the seventieth floor of anything. Up in the clouds—literally!"

Serena imagined Mason's and Cam's reaction to seeing all those tall buildings.

"Your father and I are coming to Washington next month, however. An old colleague of his from way back is retiring and his wife is throwing a retirement party. I'm sure we could swing over your way for a few days. It's not that far, right?"

Serena's heart raced, whether with excitement or dread, she couldn't tell. "It's a two hour drive, about."

"Is there a decent hotel around there?"

Oh my. Her mother was serious about this.

"There's the Chesapeake Inn. It's very nice." A little dated, maybe, but then again she couldn't picture her parents in some trendy modern place. Her father had always been a Ritz-Carlton kind of guy.

"Perfect, I'll book your father and me a suite. Isn't Cam's birthday next month?"

Serena's heart stopped for a moment. Cam's birthday? Was it? Cam hadn't said a word about it.

He'll be six. March twenty-fourth.

Right. Her heart began to beat at a normal pace again. It was a good thing she remembered that. It was like her brain talked to her sometimes.

"Yes, we'll do a party," she said. "Cam will love that."

"So will I, sweetheart. I'll call you when the date gets closer, okay?"

"Sure … mum."

Jeez, my mother remembers Cam's birthday but I don't? And why hadn't Oliver said anything to her? Did he just assume she remembered? Or was he testing her? Her mother had hung up, but Serena's phone instantly vibrated with a text. It was Chelsea, Cam's teacher.

Are you coming today?

Serena turned and hurried toward the door. Talking to her mother had made her late. She replied to Chelsea's text. *Just outside. Sorry.* She pressed the button on the school's security intercom. As she waited to be buzzed inside, she wondered how on earth she was going to tell Oliver that her parents were coming to visit.

wo days later, Serena received a strange envelope in the mail. At first, she thought it must be from her mother—the envelope was a heavy, woven cotton paper. Pale grey. Expensive-looking. Who else did she know who would use fine stationery? She set her purse down on the small half-moon-shaped foyer table, hung her winter coat on one of the iron hooks on the wall, and flipped through the rest of the mail as she walked to the kitchen.

She'd been out driving with Ashley, and her nerves were still on edge. Not because of anything Ashley did, but just from the stress of driving. Truth be told, not knowing *why* she had the accident bothered her as much as it did Oliver. The more she thought about it, the faster her imagination began to run. *What if I had a seizure? A mini-stroke? Something that could happen again?*

She dropped the mail onto the kitchen island and climbed up onto one of the stools. She picked up the grey envelope and looked at the back. There was a small return address printed on the flap. Annapolis. So not from her mother. Probably junk mail. She rubbed the paper between her finger and thumb. *Expensive junk mail.* She slipped her thumb beneath the edge of the flap and tore it open. The sheet of paper inside matched the envelope. She unfolded it.

It was written in longhand, a neat but quirky mix of printing and cursive. According to Mason's teacher, the schools didn't bother teaching cursive anymore.

That's a real shame.

Her thoughts exactly.

The letter was short. For junk mail, it was very well done. Very convincing. Her eyes dropped down to the signature, expecting to see the name of some washed-up celebrity or minor CEO. Instead, her breath caught in her throat.

With love, Ben.

Then she took a deep breath. For a split second there, she'd thought the letter was signed by Ben Wardman. But that couldn't be. Ben had died. It was probably someone like Ben Affleck or Ben Stiller or Ben Folds or … well, those were the only famous "Bens" she could remember. Someone endorsing some product or other.

It was short and she had a few minutes before Oliver was due back from his workout at the gym, so she began to read it.

Dearest Serena …

Well, the personalization was good.

If you're reading this, then my prayers were answered and you recovered from the accident.

Really … good?

I am sorry that we did not get the chance to properly say "goodbye" to each other. We all leave this life with things undone. I have run out of time on my own.

She leaned against the kitchen island to steady her suddenly wobbly legs.

I'm writing to ask you a favor.

She sunk to the kitchen floor, her legs too weak to stand.

Mine and Ashley's wedding anniversary is March 4th. Obviously, this will be a difficult day for her. It would have been our sixth anniversary. I don't want her spending the day sitting at home and grieving. So could you do something with her that day? Distract her, keep her mind off of it. Don't tell her I asked you to, please.

March 4th was two weeks away.

I know this is an odd request, but it would ease my mind to know that you will be there for her.

With love, Ben

It really was a letter from Ben Wardman.

P.S. Don't wait for the time to be right, Serena.

She sat there, stunned, until the front door opened and Oliver walked in.

"Babe!" He ran over to her. "Are you okay? Did you fall?"

She shook her head. The letter had slipped from her fingers some minutes ago and was lying on the floor next to her knee. Oliver knelt down and picked it up.

"What's this?" He read it through. "Where did this come from?"

"It came in the mail."

"Is this some kind of joke? Because it's not funny."

He stood and plucked the envelope from the island. He scanned the return address, then disappeared into the den. Serena heard the soft chime of his laptop booting up. A minute later, he returned to the kitchen.

"The address is for an attorney in Annapolis."

"Guess it's real, then."

"He wrote this before he died and had an attorney mail it now? I'm sorry, but that's more than a little creepy."

"I think it's rather sweet. He was planning ahead and thinking about helping Ashley cope."

The expression on Oliver's face was one of skepticism. "Well, you don't have to do this if you don't want to."

"Why wouldn't I want to?" She pushed herself up onto her feet, then stood. "Ash is my friend. And if Ben went to all this

156

trouble when he was sick, it seems like the least I can do is carry out his wishes."

~

OLIVER STRETCHED out his long body on the cot. He was in the station's break room. Overnight shift. He squirmed on the thin mattress for a minute, listening to the labored groan of the worn springs and trying to find a comfortable spot.

"We need to replace these things," he said to Matt, who was lying on the next cot over.

"Maybe there'll be a little money left over after we build the new station."

"Doubtful."

"Yup."

They lay there in silence for awhile, Oliver studying water stains on the ceiling that he'd known by heart since he was a kid.

"So Serena got a letter from Ben Wardman today," he said, at long last.

"Come again?"

"Serena got a letter from Ben. He wrote it before he died and his attorney mailed it out."

"That's ... weird?"

"I'll say. His and Ashley's wedding anniversary is March 4th, apparently. He wants Serena to spend the day with her. Keep her from dwelling on it."

"Huh. Well, he's a good husband—even in death."

Yeah, raising the bar for husbands everywhere. Oliver kept that thought to himself. He had practically memorized the entire letter. Granted, it was short. And to the point. But then there was that P.S. A postscript.

P.S. Don't wait for the time to be right, Serena.

What did that mean? Wait for the time to be right for what? Why would another man be saying that to his wife?

"How friendly did they look when you saw them in Two Beans?"

"Ahh, I don't remember, man. I didn't really think anything of it at the time."

"I think they were having an affair." There, he'd said it—the thing that had been percolating in his mind for weeks now. *Serena and Ben had an affair.* He heard Matt's cot squeak as his brother rolled onto his side to look at him, but Oliver kept his own eyes trained on the water-stained ceiling.

"Really? Because Ben never seemed the type. He adored Ashley."

"You never know about people, though."

Matt made no reply to that.

Oliver knew he should probably shut up. But he was on a roll now and who better to talk this over with than Matt? Matt had more experience with women than Oliver and Jack combined.

"Have you ever slept with a married woman?" Oliver asked.

"Not that I'm aware of," his brother replied, in a tone that suggested he might be getting bored with this conversation.

But Oliver persisted. It was one of his worst qualities—according to his mother and, well, pretty much everyone—his talent for getting stuck on a path and being unable to redirect.

"You think I should confront her?" He rolled his head to one side and looked across at Matt.

"I'm not really the best person to ask for relationship advice. Lord knows, I've made a hash of things lately. What's your evidence for this?"

"You saw the two of them together. He was the first person she remembered when she woke up. And now she gets this letter?"

"Seems a little flimsy to me."

"And where was she going on the day of the accident? Without the kids? Why would she need to drop off Mason and

Cam with a babysitter in the middle of the day?" He stared up at the water stains again.

"I guess it depends on what consequences you're willing to tolerate. You know, the guy is dead. Even if they did have an affair, it's over now."

"If it happened once, it can happen again."

"I don't think—"

Matt's response was interrupted by the station's alert system. Oliver shot a quick glance across the room at the light stack flashing on the wall, then pulled out his phone to check the app the department used to communicate the location of emergency calls coming in. In seconds, he and Matt were off the cots and sprinting downstairs, the conversation they were having immediately forgotten.

CHAPTER 22

*S*erena stood on the porch steps, hugging her arms to stay warm, watching the school bus drive off. She lifted a hand to stifle a yawn. It was seven-thirty in the morning, and she'd had a fitful night of sleep. There was a serious fire overnight, two houses on the other side of town. Two families displaced.

She always worried when Oliver had the overnight shift. Not that the overnight shift was any more dangerous than a daytime one, but she had things to distract her during the day. At night, it was too easy to simply lie awake and worry.

She was turning back toward the front door when Oliver's black SUV pulled into the driveway. She waved at him as the garage door lifted, but there was no wave back. He must be exhausted after the night he had. She'd go in and kiss him "hello," then let him go straight to bed.

In the kitchen, though, Oliver poured two mugs of coffee. He slid one across the island as she approached. She tried to ignore the alarm bells going off in her head.

"That's not decaf," she pointed out.

"That's fine."

The alarm was ramping up to a five-alarm siren now. Why would he be drinking regular caffeinated coffee before going to bed?

"You're not tired? That was a big fire last night." She could see that he was tired. There were dark circles beneath his eyes, the lines around his mouth more pronounced.

"It was. Someone put out hot ashes from a fireplace and caught their garage on fire." He pulled out one of the bar stools and sat down. "Have a seat."

She did as he asked. "What's the matter?"

"You had an affair with Ben Wardman."

The alarm bells fell silent, so silent that she wondered whether she was back in the coma. *Maybe I never woke up?* But no, Oliver was still sitting there, his blazing eyes boring into her, evidently waiting for a response.

"What?" she managed.

"You heard me. Don't make me say it again. It was hard enough the first time."

"No, I didn't. Why would you even say such a thing?" She pushed away the coffee mug. Just the smell of it was turning her stomach.

"Matt said he used to see you and Ben having coffee last year."

"I don't remember that."

"You didn't remember that you had kids, either. Yet they exist."

Serena struggled for air. What was going on here?

Breathe. Breathe.

"Pretty large leap from having coffee to having an affair," she said quietly, warily.

"And you got a letter from him yesterday."

"Asking me to do something for his *widow*. If we'd had an affair, would he ask *me* to do that?"

"And he was the first person you remembered when you woke up."

She threw her hands up in exasperation. "Can't you hear how ridiculous this sounds?" She waited for him to agree. Instead, he said nothing. "Maybe you should go take a nap," she suggested. This had to be the stress and exhaustion of his overnight shift talking.

"I think I will."

She watched his back as he walked out of the kitchen and headed for the stairs, waiting—hoping—that he would turn around and say something. Anything. But she knew he wouldn't. Oliver was the strong, silent type. It was one of the things she loved about him. *One of the many things.* Their trip with the boys to the Air and Space Museum felt like years ago already. Oliver was relaxed and happy that weekend. And now? Now he was accusing her of having an affair.

I'm pretty sure I would remember that.

She listened to the water turn on and off upstairs in their bathroom, then his footsteps moving across the floor to the bed. She wanted to march right up there and talk this out. But she sensed it would be futile at the moment. Her husband wasn't good at talking things out under the best of circumstances, and this certainly wasn't that.

It might be better to just go about her day and see what he was like later. They had six hours before the boys got home from school. She dumped out her cold coffee and poured a fresh cup, splashed it with milk. She leaned against the island as she drank. March 4th was only a week and a half away. She would do what Ben had asked her to do—not for his sake, but for Ashley's. She could ask her out to lunch or dinner, but that might be too obvious. Knowing that Serena was trying to distract her would only call attention to what she needed to be distracted from.

It had to be something involving other people, not just the two of them.

Tea at Evangeline's is always lovely.

Tea. *Wow. I haven't been to tea since I was sixteen.* Her mother had enrolled her in an etiquette course, one that Serena remembered as being interminably long and dull. Manners, the art of small talk, when to use which fork. Evangeline's probably did a nice tea, though, if it wasn't too late to make a reservation.

She took another quick slug of coffee, then poured the rest into the sink and put the mug into the dishwasher. She glanced at the clock on the microwave. It was five past eight. Lucy Wyndham's yoga studio, where Ashley used to take classes, was open early. As Sterling Matthew's fiancé, Lucy could probably pull some strings for her at Evangeline's, if needed.

Serena grabbed her coat and purse—and the keys to the minivan—and headed for the garage. She crossed her fingers that Oliver was too zonked out to hear the garage door lifting.

SHE EASED the minivan into a spot right in front of Studio L Yoga. Fortunately, parking was easy on Main Street in the winter. In the peak summer season? Forget about it. But today, Serena didn't even have to attempt parallel parking. She let out a little sigh of relief as she turned off the engine and got out of the car. The doctor hadn't cleared her for driving yet, but technically she still had her license.

Yeah, Oliver was going to be furious when he discovered she was gone, but she drove by herself. She would never drive with the boys in the car until the doctor said it was okay, but Ashley had taken her out driving a lot lately. Being dependent on Ashley and Oliver whenever she needed to leave the house was getting old.

It also made her realize how dependent on Oliver she must have been before the accident.

How did she let that happen? Become financially dependent on a man? It was the one thing she had sworn never to do—get trapped inside a man's life like her mother had. Even a good man like Oliver Wolfe. Things could happen to good men, too—especially when they were firefighters. And what then? Life insurance wouldn't last forever. And the older you got, the harder it was to find a job. Her mother had learned that lesson the hard way.

Serena opened the door to the yoga studio and took a deep inhale. It always smelled so good inside. Lavender and something … citrusy. She couldn't put her finger on it. It was relaxing and invigorating at the same time. No wonder Ashley loved to come here. She peeked discreetly through the window separating the front office area from the actual studio, where Lucy was finishing up a class. Serena scanned the studio, looking for Ashley. She didn't see her.

A moment later, the studio door opened and twenty sweaty women poured out, along with a faint trickle of New Age-y music.

"Hey girl." Lucy made her way through the students donning shoes and fleece jackets. "You're finally coming back to class? We've missed you."

Serena froze. "Uh …"

Lucy's face fell. "Oh sorry. I forgot that … and jeez, that doesn't make it any better, does it?"

"It's okay. So I used to come to class here?"

Lucy nodded, her cheeks bright pink with embarrassment. "With Ashley. I am so sorry, Serena."

"Don't worry about it. I wonder why Ashley hasn't said anything to me about class."

"Probably because she hasn't been here much lately. So drag her in here, okay?"

Serena moved closer to the front desk to allow people to get to the front door. Each time another person left, a blast of chilly air dispersed some of the studio's lavender scent.

"I'll try," she promised Lucy. "The reason I stopped in today, though, is because her wedding anniversary is coming up. March 4th."

"Ohhh." Lucy nodded her head slowly.

"And I want to do something for her that day. To keep her mind off of it, you know?"

She wasn't going to tell Lucy—or anyone—about the letter from Ben. The fewer people who knew about it, the less likely Ash would be to find out. And Oliver was right about one thing—getting a letter from a dead man was more than a little creepy. Ben's heart was in the right place, certainly, but she wondered if maybe he should have sent the letters out before he died. Granted, she herself had been in the hospital—with uncertain prospects for recovery—but Oliver would have saved the mail for her. Hell, he'd saved an entire box of junk mail.

"I was thinking perhaps tea at Evangeline's?" she continued. "But it might be too late to set that up."

Lucy smiled broadly. "Oh, I love that idea. And getting into Evangeline's won't be a problem at all. March is the deadest month at the Inn. No special holiday weekends and the weather isn't quite nice enough yet." She reached beneath the counter and pulled out her phone. "I'll text Sterling now."

"Umm …" Serena watched as Lucy thumb-typed. "I'm not sure who all to invite, though. Ash seems to mostly be holing up at home these days, and for the life of me I can't remember who her other friends might be."

Lucy looked up from her phone, a soft look in her eyes. "You and Ashley were always thick as thieves, so you're the most important person to invite."

"But I don't want it to be just me and her. That would be too obvious that I'm trying to distract her from the anniversary. I mean, you're invited of course. If you want to come."

"I would love to come. You could ask Michelle Trevor and her daughters. They would certainly come if they're free that day. And if you want, I can invite a few people so it doesn't look like the event is being held just for Ashley. There are people in town who would like to help her get through this, if she'd let them."

"I know. She won't even let me help much. She's not able to picture a life without Ben yet."

"Well, try and get her back in here. I worry about her, too. And as for you, we've started a mom and me class on Saturdays. Bring those adorable boys of yours."

Serena couldn't stifle a grimace. "I'm not sure how adorable they'd be in a yoga class." She tried to picture Mason and Cam being still enough to do yoga."

"You might be surprised."

The studio's front door opened, admitting another blast of cold air and several students for the next class. Serena needed to be on her way if she didn't want to get roped into a yoga class right that minute.

"I would be surprised," she said to Lucy. "But I'll keep it in mind."

Lucy's phone vibrated and she glanced down. "Sterling says Evangeline's is wide open that day. Just give him a call."

It was a ten-minute walk from the yoga studio to Quilt Therapy on Azalea Street, so Serena slipped on her gloves and left her car parked where it was. She would stop by the shop and speak to whichever Trevor was working this morning, except … she looked up at the sky as she walked. The sun was still struggling to break through the early morning clouds. Quilt Therapy didn't open for another hour.

The aroma of coffee beckoned, and Serena quickened her pace until she reached Two Beans coffee shop. She could kill some time here with coffee and a muffin. She slipped inside and joined the long line of customers. Was it always this busy? She craned her neck to look toward the back of the shop. Nearly every small bistro table along the back wall was occupied. Her eyes lifted toward the spider plants hanging in baskets from the ceiling. How did they keep those alive all winter long? Her house plants always seemed to die once the temperature dropped outside—like they knew it was winter.

Two Beans was a nice space, but she wasn't sure it was around when she first moved to town. Or been around in this incarnation. The shop felt familiar to Serena, but was that because she remembered it—vaguely—or simply because it was a coffee shop, a familiar sort of place? She had practically lived in coffee shops during college. There was a sameness to a lot of them—small wooden tables, a sofa or two to make it look cozy, inoffensive music playing in the background. Maybe that was the point. No matter which one you were in, you were bound to feel comfortable there.

The line snaked toward the long marble-topped counter and Serena moved forward a few spots. She studied the black chalkboard menu. Latte, cappuccino, flat white, espresso, mocha, drip coffee in both light and dark roast, chai tea, hot chocolate ... all standard fare. The only thing that stuck out to her as different was the Vietnamese coffee. She had no idea what that was, which meant either it was a new addition to the menu or Serena wasn't really remembering this place, after all.

When finally it was her turn at the counter, she was faced with a woman about her own age, her dark hair in a thick braid off to one side. The name "Mai" was embroidered on the brown and white striped apron she wore. The barista was clearly of Vietnamese descent, so that explained the coffee.

"Hi Serena," Mai said, smiling brightly. "The usual?"

Her greeting caught Serena off guard. She had a "usual" here? Apparently so. If only she knew what it was.

Say yes.

Why not? How unusual could her usual be?

"Sure," she answered, "and a slice of the coffee cake, please."

When she left the register a moment later, she was carrying a small wooden tray with the coffee cake and a glass cup of Vietnamese coffee. *I'm more unusual than I thought.*

She found an open table and set down her tray, then shed her winter jacket, draping it over the back of the chair. She took a small bite of the coffee cake, chasing it with a sip of the coffee. *Whoa.* That was some sweet coffee. She hadn't paid much attention when Mai was making it, but that was clearly not plain milk in her glass. She took another tentative sip. She wasn't sure she liked it. In fact, her teeth were beginning to ache a bit from the sweetness.

The front door to the shop opened and closed, and Serena felt the energy in the large room alter just ever so slightly. Then a voice from the back of the shop called out, "He-yyy Matt-tay." She looked up to see Matt Wolfe striding toward her. She gave her brother-in-law a neutral smile.

"You're bright-eyed and bushy-tailed this morning," she said when he leaned over and rested his elbows on her table.

"Yeah, I'm younger than your husband." He snorted. "From the expression on your face a moment earlier, you don't seem to be enjoying that drink."

She shrugged.

"What can I get you instead?" He stood up.

"That's okay, You don't have to get me anything, Matt."

"I insist."

"A drip, then, please. Black."

A few moments later, Matt was back with her coffee. He waved off her money. "My treat." Then he carried his own coffee to the back of the shop and sat by himself at a table there. Not that Serena minded. She wasn't feeling overly charitable toward Matt these days. She had half a mind to walk back there herself and demand to know why he was filling her husband's ear with wild tales.

She looked around Two Beans and tried to picture where she and Ben might have had coffee, if Matt's story were true. At the table where an older couple was sitting? On one of the sofas? Or in the back, away from prying eyes? But nothing triggered a recollection.

I didn't remember taking yoga classes. Or what my usual order here was. She tried to shut down the thought that was barreling toward her like a runaway train, but it was no use. Maybe she *did* have an affair with Ben? It was hard to imagine, but ... *maybe I was a different person back then.* She sipped her coffee and let the doubts swirl in her mind.

No. It was impossible. She loved Ollie. She gave up her trust fund, her fledgling career, her family in order to move to St. Caroline and marry him. And she regretted none of that. Where did Matt get off telling Oliver she'd had coffee with Ben? When would that have happened anyway? Ben was a teacher. It's not like he could sneak out of the classroom in the middle of the day to go have coffee!

She waited to hear that voice in her head ... waited to hear it agree with her. Waited to hear it say, "You absolutely did not have an affair with your best friend's husband." But the voice was silent.

CHAPTER 23

Serena peered through the large front window of Quilt Therapy. The shop always had some sort of charity quilt stretched out on a big quilting frame near the front. She could be wrong, but it seemed like some customers came just to work on the quilt and then left without buying anything.

Today, only Cassidy Trevor was seated there, one hand beneath the layers of fabric, the other working a tiny needle on top. That was a good sign, she thought, as she quietly opened the shop's door. It meant Cassidy was recovering from her injuries. But what wasn't a good sign was the way Cassidy looked up and eyed her warily.

Did Ollie... Serena wanted to believe that her husband hadn't blabbed about the letter or his suspicions to other people, much less his brothers. From the expression on Cassidy's face though, her faith in Oliver might be misplaced.

"Hi there, Cassidy!" She wasn't going to act guilty. "How are you doing?" She also wouldn't let on what she knew about Cassidy and Matt's relationship. According to Oliver, they weren't supposed to be dating, but secretly were. The Trevor family was prioritizing Jack and Becca's relationship, which made sense on the one hand. There was a child involved.

On the other hand, she felt for Cassidy. She had walked a mile in those pinching, blister-inducing shoes. She knew what it was like to have your family disapprove of a relationship, to try and tell you whom you could and couldn't love. Granted, it might be for the best in Cassidy's case. Matt was no Oliver. Unless his personality had done a one-eighty at some point and Serena just couldn't remember it, her brother-in-law wasn't exactly the type to settle down.

"I'm fine," Cassidy replied.

"Is your mom here?"

Cassidy nodded. "Mom!" she called out. "Serena Wolfe's here!" Her eyes never left Serena's face. "Sorry, I'd go get her but I'm supposed to stay off my leg."

Serena nodded. "I understand." A pair of crutches leaned against the wall.

Michelle appeared from the back hallway. "Hi there. What can I do for you? Don't tell me you've used up all of Angie's stash already."

Was it her imagination or was Michelle's demeanor also cool? But she smiled. *Not everything is about me,* she reminded herself. Michelle certainly had her own sources of stress—a business to run, two daughters in love, an unexpected grandchild.

"No, not yet." Serena looked around the empty shop. "I wanted to invite you and—" She looked over at the quilting frame. "—Cassidy and Becca and Natalie to a tea that Lucy and I are hosting for Ashley Wardman."

Lucy probably wouldn't mind if Serena gave her co-hosting status. An invitation from Lucy carried a little more weight around town.

"Oh, that's a lovely idea," Michelle exclaimed. "When are you thinking?"

"March 4th." She lowered her voice, even though no one else

was in the shop yet. "It's her wedding anniversary. We don't want her to be alone and dwelling on it that day."

Michelle pressed her hands together. "Excellent idea. Ashley doesn't seem to be doing well. She looked better over the holidays."

"She had a lot of support over Christmas. But she feels like everyone has moved on now."

"Oh dear. That's not good. Well, I should get moving on the support group."

"What support group?" Cassidy re-entered the conversation.

"I want to start a combination grief support-quilting group for women in town."

"Here at the shop?" Cassidy asked.

Michelle nodded. "Here and maybe also host a group at the nursing home. We don't do enough with them, and I think we should."

"I volunteer there all the time." Cassidy stopped quilting for a moment. "Those are good ideas, Mom, but you need to keep me in the loop. Okay?"

Serena was beginning to think she should quietly make her exit. Clearly, she was in the middle of an ongoing point of contention between Michelle and her daughter.

"We'll talk about it later." Michelle turned to Serena. "So where are you and Lucy thinking about having this tea? At the Inn?"

"At Evangeline's."

"Oh that *will* be nice," Michelle said. "I don't think I've been to tea there since Angie's bridal shower." She gave a little laugh. "And that's been awhile! Count me in. Cassidy?" Michelle turned toward her eldest daughter.

Cassidy nodded and shrugged at the same time. "Sure."

The younger woman wasn't radiating enthusiasm, exactly, but —mission accomplished in Serena's mind. She had a venue and guests. Still, as she left the shop, Cassidy's cool reception had her feeling a little unsettled. Not that she and Cassidy were ever friends—*at least I don't think we were*—but for a woman whose sister was marrying Serena's brother-in-law, her vibe had been rather unfriendly.

Don't take it personally. She's in love with Mattie. Not exactly the easiest person to love.

There was that voice again. She would try not to take Cassidy's coolness personally. But things were getting very personal lately. Or, as Mason had taken to saying, "Things are gettin' *real.*"

∽

WHEN SHE GOT HOME, she found Oliver awake and cleaning up the kitchen.

"Thank you," she said, nodding toward the sponge in his hand while holding up the paper bag in her own. "I stopped by the Burger Barn." She set the bag on the kitchen island and began pulling out food. "I got you a double cheeseburger. And fries for the boys when they get home."

She was trying to act normal, hoping that Oliver had thought things through a little more clearly while she was gone. "I decided to try their veggie burger."

"Why? Are you becoming a vegetarian now?"

She set down the veggie burger. Based on his tone of voice, things were not back to normal.

"It sounded good, that's all." *Oh hell. In for a dime, in for a dollar.* I ran into Matt at Two Beans. Did you tell him about the letter?"

Oliver didn't say a word as he unwrapped his cheeseburger, pulled out the lone leaf of lettuce, and gingerly set it aside. *What? I've forgotten that he doesn't like lettuce on his cheeseburger?* She slapped her hand hard on the island's granite top. "Did you?"

She would take his silence as a "yes."

"Dammit, Ollie! Can't we keep some things between just us? I

JULIA GABRIEL

suffered a *head injury*. It's not my *fault* that I can't remember things."

"I know that." His voice didn't sound that convinced. "You're not cleared to drive yet."

"I know. But I was fine. I have a doctor's appointment next week. I'll ask him then if it's okay. And don't worry—I won't drive with the boys in the car until I'm officially cleared."

"Please don't."

Hot tears stung her eyes. Their marriage was unraveling. That's what was happening here, wasn't it? She could feel it in the pit of her stomach. She didn't bother unwrapping the veggie burger. Her appetite was completely gone now.

"You're accusing me of something I can't remember. And I can't believe you don't see how not fair that is to me. What evidence do you have that I cheated on you, Oliver Wolfe? Your brother said he saw me having coffee? Unless we were having sex on the table, that's not really proof." The words were barreling out of her mouth now. "And I received a letter mailed to me by his attorney, asking me to do something for his widow. I'm Ashley's *best friend.* Who else would he ask? She doesn't have *family* in St. Caroline."

She forced her lips closed before she could say something she'd regret later. Instead, she took a long deep breath to stem the tears that were threatening to spill over any second.

"Here's the thing," Oliver said. "*I* don't remember you socializing that much with Ben. Sure, you hung out with Ashley a lot, but—" He made a back and forth gesture with his hand. "—the four of us never went out together."

"Ollie, it's hard to socialize with you! You have weird work hours. You're at the station for seventy-two hours straight, then you have three days off. You spend a lot of time at the gym. I mean, I know that's in the nature of your job and ..."

And Ben was always so busy with soccer. It all came back to her in a rush. He coached the high school team in the fall, ran the spring youth soccer league, and spent two weeks every summer running clinics at a soccer academy outside Annapolis. *Ashley and I always talked about getting the guys together.* But their schedules never synced. *Great. Fighting with Oliver is causing me to remember things.*

Just then, they heard the low grumble of the school bus outside.

"The boys are here," he said. Which meant this discussion had to be shelved for another time.

Serena rushed to the front door. The bus driver wasn't allowed to let kindergartners off the bus unless there was an adult there to meet them. She burst out onto the porch just in time to see Cam's dark head bobbing down the aisle, Mason waiting for him at the bottom of the bus steps. She waved to the bus driver and smiled.

"Hey guys," she said as her sons raced up the stairs to the porch. "I got you fries!"

The boys were home. Whether Oliver liked it or not, their marriage had to go back to normal until bedtime.

"WE NEED TO SIGN OUT, SON."

Oliver turned away from the elementary school's wide bank of doors. His father was standing in the doorway of the office. "Right. I forgot."

He and his father had spent the morning at the school, conducting refresher CPR training for the custodial and administrative staff. He followed his dad into the brightly lit office. A sign-in log book lay on the counter. His father wrote his name, glanced up at the clock on the wall, and then scribbled the time.

"Oh look," he said, pointing to a line in the log book.

Oliver leaned in to read the name. Serena Wolfe.

"She volunteers in the boys' classrooms." His father held out the ballpoint pen. Oliver took it and hastily signed his name.

"I bet she's good at that," his father added as they pushed open the fireproof front doors.

Outside, the sun was shining in defiance of Oliver's current mood. "I guess so."

As they walked to the red fire department car, he scanned the visitor parking area. Sure enough, there was the new minivan. She had driven herself to the school. He wished she'd told him she was volunteering today. He and his dad could have swung by the house and picked her up.

You were kind of a dick to her yesterday.

She was asserting her independence, that was it. Serena was never the shy, retiring type to begin with. Not a strict follower of rules. That was one of the things that had attracted him to her. She was the type of woman who would strip down and go skinny-dipping the night she met someone. The type of woman who would pick up and move to a small town because she fell in love with a man who lived there.

Still doesn't excuse your behavior yesterday.

He was channeling his mother again.

"It's nice that Serena helps out at the school." His father chuckled. "Your mother never could have done that."

"Why not?"

"Would have been only a matter of time before some salty language slipped out." Tim chucked him lightly in the arm. "She tried her best around you boys when you were young, but …" Tim shook his head. "Listening to Mattie sometimes, I'm not sure how successful she was."

Always figured you'd pick it up somewhere. But I didn't raise you to be those words.

Yup. Oliver could hear her saying exactly that.

CHAPTER 24

$\mathcal{E}$vangeline's looked just as Serena remembered it. Where Skipjack's was casual and nautical-themed—white-washed wood and crisp navy and white uniforms on the staff—Evangeline's was elegance all the way. Dark wood floors, a high coffered ceiling, and walls that were the color of champagne. With softly lit glass chandeliers, the room practically glowed. Instead of a bar, bartenders rolled small glass-topped carts from table to table with an assortment of wines and spirits.

This was where Oliver had proposed to her. *He must have spent half his paycheck here.* There was the table where they sat, next to a tall velvet-draped window. He had gotten down on one knee, the whole nine yards. Oliver Wolfe was a by-the-book kind of guy.

"Penny for your thoughts." Lucy appeared out of nowhere.

Serena smiled. "Oh, just remembering. This is where Oliver proposed."

"Oh how sweet!"

"Then I got pregnant on our honeymoon. That ended our fine dining days for awhile."

"That's what babysitters are for."

And trust funds. She had spent the past week poring over their bank statements and the college funds—small still—for the boys. She and Oliver were careful with money, that was clear. But why on earth were they trying to live on one income? Sure, they had started a family right away but plenty of mothers worked. Oliver's mother had.

Oh, she knew that Oliver preferred that the boys come home after school instead of going to an after-school program. But Mason and Cam might enjoy that, actually.

She pushed aside that question and focused on Lucy's smiling face.

"Are we all set up?" she asked, glancing around the still empty restaurant.

"We are. Let me show you." Lucy turned and started walking toward the back of the restaurant. Serena followed. "We reconfigured the private dining room."

"Oh wow."

In the private dining room, the walls were a deeper shade of amber and the drapes were thrown open to frame the view across the Inn's back lawn and out over the sparkling water of the inlet. Right in front of the windows sat a grouping of upholstered sofas and low, round tables topped with pink and gold china. A buffet held platters of tea sandwiches—cucumber, strawberry-chicken salad, smoked salmon—ricotta and tomato tartlets, white chocolate-covered strawberries, heart-shaped macarons, and cream scones with blackberry whipped cream.

Light classical music played softly in the background. Chopin, Nocturne Number. 2, Opus 9. Next would be a Bach prelude, followed by something from Mozart. She thought for a moment. A flute and harp concerto?

She stopped and closed her eyes. How would she know the order of the music? Or that the scones were topped with *blackberry* whipped cream? She wasn't close enough to the table to tell. It could just as easily be raspberry or blueberry. But she knew it was blackberry—because that's what Evangeline's always served with high tea.

Only ... I've never been here for tea ...

"Are you okay?" Lucy lightly touched her arm.

She opened her eyes. "I used to work here." She shook her head in wonderment. "I was a waitress here at Evangeline's."

"You were?" There was confused concern in Lucy's eyes. "I don't recall—"

"It was years ago. Before my boys were born."

"Ahh. Before my time."

Serena nodded. "Wow. I can't believe I remembered that. It was the music." She paused. "See? It went from Chopin to Bach. And the whipped cream on the scones is blackberry."

"Hmm. How long ago was this?"

"Seven years ago? Roughly?"

Lucy gave a tiny frown. "Maybe I should talk to Sterling about a menu refresh. And the music, too."

"Oh no! It's fine the way it is. If it ain't broke, don't fix it. Right?"

"There they are!"

She and Lucy turned to see Michelle, Becca, Cassidy on her crutches, and Natalie headed their way. Also three women from yoga, the Inn's wedding planner, and the wedding planner's assistant. Despite March temperatures outside that were still more winter than spring, everyone had donned lighter attire—flowery dresses, pastel scarves, nude hosiery.

"We'll make spring arrive by sheer force of will," joked Michelle, twirling to show off her skirt.

Ashley was the last to arrive, and Serena could tell immediately that her friend knew exactly what day it was. Suddenly the idea of distracting Ashley from her wedding anniversary seemed ridiculous. What made Ben ever think Ashley might be fooled into forgetting? Some things required a head injury to forget.

She hurried over to Ashley, part of her wanting to beg forgiveness for going along with Ben's idea.

"I'm underdressed, aren't I?" were Ashley's first words.

"No, you look great. Lovely."

Ashley wore a loose tunic printed in a brown and black abstract pattern over black leggings, short brown leather boots on her feet. Of all the guests, she was the only one dressed for the actual weather outside.

"This is cute." Ashley tweaked Serena's sleeve.

Serena glanced down at her floral-printed dress. "It seems a little big. I half thought it might be one of my maternity dresses. You know, second trimester." She gave a little laugh.

Ashley's pause was just a beat too long.

"Oh, dear. It is, isn't it?"

Ashley shook her head. "You're still a bit thinner than you were. That's all."

But Serena had the sinking feeling that Ash was sparing her feelings. *Just as you're trying to spare hers.* "Well, I'm going to fatten myself up here today. Come. I saved you a seat next to me."

Waitresses in tailored black pantsuits were pouring Earl Grey tea into the delicate pink and gold china cups while Lucy encouraged everyone toward the buffet table. Serena filled a small plate with tiny egg salad sandwiches and scones.

"Thanks for inviting me," Ashley whispered as she sat on the sofa next to her.

Talk quickly turned to the subject of Becca's upcoming wedding. Serena tried to catch Michelle's eye. A wedding maybe wasn't the best topic for Ashley today. But Ashley threw herself wholeheartedly into the discussion—Becca and Jack had hired her to do the photography.

"Do you want pictures at the bachelorette party?" Ashley was asking.

"Depends on whether it's at a male stripper show," Natalie

laughed, then seemed to remember who else was present. "Sorry, mom."

Michelle waved her off. "I'm not going to the bachelorette party, so …" She waved her hand again, not bothering to even finish the thought.

"I want it to be someplace Jackie can come to."

The room fell dead silent at Becca's request.

"Why not here?" Cassidy suggested. She looked around. "This is really nice."

Serena listened passively as plans and ideas for the party swirled around her, her ears only perking up when someone mentioned Jack's bachelor party. She knew vaguely that Oliver was planning to go, but she was surprised to learn now that the party was the weekend her parents were coming. Ollie had rather conveniently skipped over that detail. Not that she had sorted out how, exactly, she was going to manage the relationship between her parents and her husband … but she still had three weeks to figure it out.

"Serena? You're invited to the bachelorette party too." Cassidy was looking straight at her.

"Oh. My parents are coming to town that weekend, to see the boys."

"Oh?" Michelle perked up. "That's wonderful!"

"Definitely more important than my bachelorette party," Becca agreed.

The waitresses discreetly began to clear away the empty platters from the buffet. Another waitress was topping off tea cups for what was evidently the last time. Serena rose from the sofa and went over to speak quietly to Lucy about the bill. They turned away from the other guests.

"Don't worry about it," Lucy whispered. "Sterling wanted to donate the afternoon. Ashley does so much work for the Inn."

"Oh Lucy, I can't let him do that. This was my idea."

"He insists. Truly."

Ten minutes later, everyone was making their goodbyes to each other and walking to separate cars. Ashley fell into step beside Serena.

"It's great you've been cleared to drive," she said.

"Yeah. Oliver still worries though."

"You were fine every time I took you out." They arrived at the minivan. "Thank you for today." Ashley wrapped her arms around Serena in a loose hug. "I know this was your idea. I appreciate it. I would have just sat at home and been miserable."

When Ashley dropped her arms and stepped back, Serena saw that her friend's eyes were misted with tears.

"Actually, it was Ben's idea."

Ash frowned, confused.

"He arranged for his attorney to send me a letter asking me to do something for you today."

Ashley's tears spilled over in earnest. Serena dug tissues from her purse and pressed them into her friend's hand.

"I'm never going to find another man like him. Everyone says 'oh you're so young, you'll meet someone else.' But I won't. Ben was one of a kind."

~

"WHERE'S MOM AGAIN?" Cam asked, looking up from the space rover he was crafting from Legos.

For about the hundredth time, Oliver replied, "she's at the tea for Miss Ashley."

"Oh. Is Miss Ashley coming home with her?"

Oliver hadn't realized how popular Ashley Wardman was with his sons. Had Serena and Ben done things together with Mason and Cam? When he was out of town for training, say? The boys didn't talk about Ben the way they did Ashley. But still. They might have been told not to.

Don't you dare ask them.

"Dad?" Mason sat on the other side of the wide pool of Legos. He held up a small brown piece. "Can you find me another one like this, only red?"

Oliver was the Lego Whisperer, able to magically root through the multicolored jumble of plastic on the living room rug and spot even the oddest, most unusual bricks. *If we divorce, she'll get the kids.* The thought rang clear as a bell as he sifted through plastic bricks. That's what would happen. She would take them to New York. He'd only see them on weekends, if that. Given his schedule, visitation would be a nightmare. Or what if she put them in boarding school? Then he'd *never* see them.

That's why her parents were coming at the end of the month. He was certain of it. They were going to talk her into leaving him and taking the boys up north. Why else would they decide to come visit, after all these years of ignoring their daughter and grandsons?

He shouldn't have agreed to go to Jack's bachelor party that weekend. What if he came home and they were gone? He looked at his sons, their heads bent intently to their individual creations, and felt faint. *I can't lose them.*

You're letting your imagination run away with you.

He sifted through the pile of plastic, looking for the piece Mason needed. *And yet you always said I was your least imaginative child.* Jeez, he was talking to his mother again. He needed her advice, her wise counsel—that's why he was constantly imagining these conversations with her.

There it was! He snatched up the tiny red brick before he lost it again in the sea of plastic. "Here you go, bud." He held it out to Mason.

"Thanks, dad."

Cam looked up from his space rover. "You're better at this than mom."

"She tries, Cammy," Mason admonished his younger brother.

"I know. I'm just saying."

As Oliver watched his sons play, his heart swelled with love. These were his boys. Yeah, he'd run into any burning building to save a complete stranger but he'd jump out of a plane or wrestle a wild animal to save his boys.

"I love you guys, you know that?"

His sons' heads snapped up, the expressions on their small faces a mixture of surprise, pity for their old man, and *is this a joke?*

"Yeah, we know," Mason answered for both of them, then bent his head again to his Legos.

Oliver resisted the urge to laugh. Had he and his brothers been that embarrassed by their dad when they were kids? *Don't answer that.* He preempted the imaginary conversation with his mom. This afternoon with the boys felt familiar, comforting. All those months when Serena was in the hospital, it had been just the three of them. Was it wrong that he missed those times, just a little? Not that he wished his wife was still in a coma! But there had been that "three of them against the world" vibe in those months, a quest for survival against the forces of misfortune and the vagaries of the universe.

You also missed Serena and wished she were around to help. You wondered how she wrangled the boys all day long without losing her mind and falling asleep on the sofa every night, too exhausted to even make it up the stairs to the bedroom.

That was true. *I didn't say it made any sense.* Feelings never did, in Oliver's experience.

"Who wants popcorn?" he asked suddenly.

Mason looked up. "Now?"

"Sure now. Why not?"

Cam spun the thick rubber wheels of his space rover with his finger. "Mom says we're snacking too much between meals."

"Well, mom's not here right now." He gave his sons a conspiratorial grin. "I won't tell if you don't."

CHAPTER 25

The kids in Cam's classroom were noisily cleaning up. Serena had come in to help with math, filling in for another parent volunteer who was sick. *Math? Me?* But it had gone well. It was kindergarten math, after all.

She looked across the barely-controlled chaos to Cam on the other side of the room. His dark hair bobbed head and shoulders above the other kids, easily the tallest child in the class. He favored Oliver in looks but maybe he was going to be really tall like his uncle Jack—six foot five. That gene must have come from Angie's family somewhere because Tim Wolfe was short and stocky like Matt. Maybe there was a giant uncle or great-great grandfather on one of the branches of the family tree.

Chelsea sidled up to her. "Quite a few of the kids had break-throughs this week."

"They really did." It was gratifying to see a child finally "get it," to have the pieces all of a sudden snap into place.

"Well, I couldn't do it without you. The PTA is holding a luncheon for volunteers next Friday. Just let Kym in the front office know if you're coming."

Serena thought for a moment. Was next week already—? "I

can't. My parents will be in town. But speaking of volunteers, I'd be happy to volunteer in your classroom next year. Even though I won't have any kids in your class."

"Oh, I won't be back in the fall." Chelsea patted her stomach. "I'm pregnant."

Serena's eyes widened. "Congratulations. This is your first?"

Chelsea nodded happily. "But I'll be sure to leave a note for the new teacher with your contact info and a glowing recommendation."

In the front office, Serena signed out of the visitor's log and turned in her badge. At the door, she stopped. On the wall was a large bulletin board covered with flyers and notices. Normally, she waltzed right past it. But today, something caught her eye—a large poster from Talbot College advertising its evening and weekend programs in education.

Teachers: Get your master's and advance faster in your career.

Career-switchers: Get credit for your professional experience and get your teaching certification in as little as 18 months!

Open House: May 9. Financial aid available.

She thought about the poster on the drive home. Teaching certification in a year and a half. She'd never considered being a teacher. But she liked helping out in Cam's classroom. No, she more than *liked* it. She loved it. She looked forward to it every week. It was the one area of her life where she still felt competent.

She pulled onto her street, pressed the garage door opener, and pulled the minivan inside. The other bay was empty. No surprise there. Oliver was spending more time at the station lately. The fire department was planning to build a second station on the other side of town. As deputy chief, Oliver was heavily involved in that.

But it was hard not to wonder whether he was spending more time at the station as a way to avoid her. They fought after Ashley's tea. She'd been upset that he hadn't told her about the bachelor party happening the week her parents would be here. Not that she would ever keep him from going to his brother's party, but the lack of communication bothered her.

Was it always like that? Had their marriage always been full of these little misunderstandings, miscommunications, emotional mishaps?

She turned off the ignition and went into the house, hanging her jacket on a coat hook just inside the door. She leaned against the wall for a moment, surveying the kitchen—the shiny stainless steel refrigerator, the sunny window above the sink, the wicker basket of paper napkins sitting on the island. A kitchen was the heart of a home. Or that's what some people said, anyway. Or maybe it was something she had read in a magazine. She couldn't remember, nor did it matter anyway. If this kitchen had ever felt like the heart of these four walls and a roof, she was having trouble remembering it now. She wasn't sure the house even had a heart anymore.

She pushed away from the wall and went into the den. She booted up her laptop, opened a browser window, and typed in the web address for Talbot College. There was a link for the Education Open House right on the home page. She clicked and filled in the short RSVP form. She had no idea how she would pay for it, but it couldn't hurt to go and check it out. Nothing ventured, nothing gained, right? If her marriage was on the rocks —and it was starting to look that way—she needed to prepare for the worst case scenario.

She had always vowed not to make the same mistakes her mother made. There was no way she was going to spend years waiting for her husband to change and watching opportunities pass her by. Chelsea wouldn't be the last teacher to leave the St. Caroline school system. If she got her certification, she'd be ready when the next opening came up.

She launched her email app and began deleting the day's messages. Viagra for cheap. A sale on boys' jeans. A clearance sale on winter clothing. More spam. Cialis for cheap. Then a confirmation email from Talbot College popped up. She clicked on it and added the open house to her calendar. She leaned back in the desk chair and stared blankly at the flickering screen.

I didn't have an affair.

She waited for that other voice to chime in and agree with her. It was like good cop-bad cop in her head. The doctor had said not to worry about it.

The voice was silent today. Now that she thought of it, it had been silent for awhile. A week, at least. Maybe it didn't agree with her anymore.

I did not cheat on Oliver. Maybe the voice was still listening. *I loved Ollie!* She pulled herself up short. *I love Ollie.* Present tense. She still loved him, even though he was driving her nuts with this affair nonsense.

Even though she wasn't sure he still loved her.

She leaned forward and began scrolling quickly through her email, all the way back to last summer. She was looking for Ben's name. If they'd had an affair, he might have emailed her. She scrolled through July, June, May, April, March … nothing. Just the usual emails from the elementary school, the fire department, local businesses—the Inn, the Purple Pickle Deli, Talbot College —reminders from the boys' dentist and Dr. Trevor, their pediatrician.

She closed the laptop. Not that the lack of email from Ben would convince Oliver at this point. He seemed to have his mind all made up. *I cheated on him and that was that.*

Her phone pinged with a text. *Are you free for lunch?* It was from Ashley.

Now? She still had several hours before school let out.

Sure. I'm at the Inn. Meet at Skipjack's?

When Serena walked into Skipjack's, she found Ashley sitting with Becca Trevor at a table by the window. Becca gave her a wide smile and a little wave when she spotted her. She looked so damn ... happy. Serena could remember feeling that way right before her wedding. When you believed that "for better or for worse" really only meant "for better." And you're certain that yours won't be one of the many marriages that dissolve in divorce. That only happens to other people.

Until it happens to you.

"I invited Becca to eat with us," Ashley said as Serena pulled out the third chair and sat down. "We were scouting photo shoot locations outside."

"Seems like plenty of good places for pictures around here."

"We're trying to recreate the wedding photo Jack's parents took when they got married here. But the treeline looks a little different now." Becca held out her phone. On the screen was a photo of a young Angie and Tim Wolfe.

Serena stared at her mother-in-law for a long moment. "Wow. They look so young." She shook her head as Becca pulled back the phone. "Ollie and I got married at the Episcopal Church."

"Well, April weather can be iffy. Jack and I may regret having an outdoor wedding if it rains."

The waitress brought over lunch menus, sparking a flash of memory in Serena. She flipped the menu over to the drinks. "The boys love those silly drinks they have here in the summer."

Becca laughed. "Oh the Crabby Lady and Monster's Claw. They're not on the menu until May."

"Were you at the school this morning?" Ashley asked.

Serena nodded as she wavered between the hamburger and the chicken salad sandwich. She was sort of craving fries, but the chicken salad would come with a pickle. "I registered for an open house over at the college," she said, absently. "They have a teacher certification program for career switchers. Not that I have a career to switch from, but ..." She looked up at the waitress. "I'll have the chicken salad."

"Me too," Ashley said, then turned her gaze back to Serena. "I am so glad you're going through with that."

Serena frowned. "What do you mean, 'going through with it?'"

"You were considering going back to school last year."

"I was?"

"Yeah, you and Ben used to talk about it. Well, I think he was more trying to talk you into it. You don't remember the day you went into the high school to shadow a few teachers?"

Serena's eyes widened. She'd been considering *high school* teaching? "Really? This was something I wanted to do before? Why didn't I do it?"

"You were worried about the cost."

"Huh." Serena tried to wrap her brain around this news. So this wasn't a brand new idea of hers. "Well, I still don't know how I'm going to pay for it. But I'm going to the open house. Baby steps."

"That's great, Serena. Really. You'll make an awesome teacher. Ben always thought so."

"He did?" And was that good or bad? How close *was* she to him? Close enough for him to have opinions on her life? "Ollie is convinced I was having an affair with Ben." *Oh damn.* The words were out before she could think twice about the wisdom of saying them, especially in front of Oliver's soon-to-be sister-in-law. She held her breath, waiting for a reaction.

But Ashley's reaction was loud laughter. "Oh that's nonsense." She rolled her eyes. "One, you would never do that to me. And two, Ben would never have done that to me." Ashley shook her head. "Our marriage was solid. Plus, Ben was sick most of last year. He was in no shape for that kind of thing."

That was true. She wondered why Oliver hadn't taken that into account.

"Why does Oliver think that?" Becca asked.

"He said Matt saw me and Ben having coffee. And then there was—" She glanced at Ashley's still unconcerned face. "—that letter."

"Hardly the action of a man having an affair." Ashley leaned back in her chair to allow the waitress to set a plate in front of her.

"What letter?" Becca asked.

"Ben arranged for the attorney to send Serena a letter last month, asking her to do something with me on our anniversary."

"The tea," Serena clarified.

"Oh that is so sweet." Becca looked from Ashley to Serena. "Do you want me to have Jack talk to Oliver?"

"No, that's okay. He'll get upset if he thinks everyone is talking about it."

"Honestly, Serena, you're the last person I would suspect of having an affair," Ashley said. "I think I would have known if my best friend and my husband were sneaking around behind my back."

Serena bit into her sandwich. She liked to think she would know about something like that, too. But maybe not. After all, she was beginning to feel like she was married to a stranger.

On the way home, she picked up flowers from the supermarket and swung by the cemetery. She had an hour before the school bus would arrive at the house. Oliver and his brothers had agreed to keep flowers on Angie's grave, with Ollie getting a pass while she was in the hospital. But she doubted he'd gone back to the cemetery since the one time they went together. Ollie was not the type to stir up emotions—particularly his own—if he didn't have to.

The grass was greening, she noticed as she walked the path to Angie's gravesite. Soon the trees would bud. The air outside was still nippy, but day by day the advent of spring was softening it. Easter was next weekend. Cam's sixth birthday party was this weekend in the fire station's community room.

And her parents were arriving this weekend, too. New beginnings around every corner, it felt like.

She just hoped she and Ollie weren't ending. Could the universe be that cruel? Her parents finally come to see her—and her family—right as her marriage was crumbling. She stopped in front of Angie's stone.

Yes, the universe could be that cruel.

She slipped the bouquet of flowers from its cellophane funnel and shoved the plastic into her jacket's pocket. Then she laid the flowers on the grass below Angie's carved name. Angela Jane Wolfe.

"Could I have come to you for advice on my marriage?" she said out loud. Belatedly she looked around. There was no one else within earshot. "Or would you have been on Oliver's side no matter what?"

She leaned down to straighten a stem, arrange the flowers just so.

"Oh who am I kidding? I'll probably always side with Mason and Cam. That's a mother's job, right?"

You always did the heavy lifting, emotionally.

She did! Right from the very beginning, too. If she hadn't slipped Oliver her room number at the carnival, he wouldn't have sought her out, bought her a cotton candy, invited her to ride the Ferris wheel with him. He would have let her slip right out of his life.

He was at the hospital nearly every day.

That's what her father-in-law said. To hear the boys talk, their dad was at the hospital 24-7. Obviously, that wasn't the case since he'd had his hands full with the boys.

The reality of that hit her. *I was in the hospital. He had the boys. His mother had just died.* Had he properly grieved her death? Or did he do the "Oliver" thing and bottle it up, put his head down, and plow through the days and months after? She guessed the latter. Shutting everything out was the only way he knew how to cope.

CHAPTER 26

*O*liver slipped into the fire station's community room with a stack of pizza boxes in his arms. He kicked shut the door behind him, to keep the noise from the rest of the station. He wasn't sure which was louder—a party of six-year-olds or a siren. He stood for a moment, watching small bodies carom around the room, and wondering whether he could safely get the pizzas over to the table without one of the kids taking him out at the knees.

Today was Cam's birthday party—and a welcome distraction from his in-laws' impending visit. *Could be worse. They could've arrived today.* He tried to imagine what Serena's rich, snooty parents would think of a birthday party held in a fire station. In St. Caroline, no one even blinked at the idea. People rented out the station's community room for all sorts of events—birthdays, class reunions, wedding receptions, holiday parties. It was cheaper than the Chesapeake Inn.

Which reminded him—he still needed to thank Sterling Matthew for not charging Serena for Ashley Wardman's tea. *We aren't made of money.*

He began to thread his way through the human pinballs

bouncing around the room, over to the long tables where Serena had set up juice boxes, plates, and napkins. A birthday cake was in the station's kitchen, set aside for later. He watched her as she stood in front of the table, talking to Becca and keeping an eye on the kids.

And now she wants to go back to school? Where would they get the money for that? Back before he proposed to her, it had occurred to him that her affluent upbringing might cause problems in the future. He would never be able to support her in the manner to which she was accustomed. Normal Oliver had pointed that out over and over. But when he was face-to-face with her, Normal Oliver got locked in the basement and the new Oliver he desperately wanted to be—for her sake—agreed to all sorts of crazy things.

Like marrying a Park Avenue Princess.

How was that ever going to work out in the long run?

He breathed a sigh of relief when he reached the tables and was able to set down the stack of pizzas. Becca gave him a crooked smile.

"Couple moments there when catastrophe was narrowly averted."

He forced a tiny smile. "Yeah, imagine what this place will be like *after* they have cake and ice cream." He turned to face the chaos. "Hey guys!" he shouted. "Pizza is here!"

The mob of kids stopped in their tracks—for a split second— then surged toward the tables en masse. "In an orderly line!" he added.

Then something close to a miracle transpired. He watched as Serena made her way through the surging sea of kids, splitting them off into two lines pointed at opposite ends of the tables. Becca and Matt handed out plates and pizza. Now that decibel levels in the room had tapered off, Oliver realized there was music playing.

She'll make a great teacher.

Yeah, Serena definitely appeared to have more authority with the kids than he did. They still didn't have the money to send her back to school, though.

"Ollie?"

He turned toward his wife's voice.

"Do you want to pass out juice boxes at the tables?"

"Sure. Will do."

Two long tables were set end to end to form one long table, covered with a birthday-themed paper tablecloth. Silly pointy hats were matched up with each folding chair. He walked up and down the table, leaning over small sweaty heads to drop a juice box in front of each kid. Cam sat like a king at the head of the table.

When he finished, he returned to where Serena stood with Becca. Matt was roaming the room, taking pictures on his camera. His brother was a good uncle. He'd make a good father someday, too, despite what most people thought of Mattie.

"Did you have your parties here?"

He was surprised to hear Serena talk, much less talk to *him*.

You've been avoiding her.

There's a lot going on at the station.

There's always a lot going on.

We're trying to build a new station across town.

Good grief, he was talking to his mother again in his head. It seemed like the more stressed he felt, the more he imagined these conversations.

"Fine. Don't answer." Serena's voice was soft, her words meant only for him to hear.

Oliver *could* remember celebrating his own birthday in this very room, albeit on a more restrained scale.

"I did. But generally just with my brothers and a few close friends from school."

"It's sort of expected these days that you invite the entire class."

"I didn't mean that as a criticism." He picked up a juice box and stabbed the tiny straw into the side. He took a sip. "Let's not fight here."

"I'm not fighting. But you've been cranky all morning."

"And you know why that is." He drained the juice box and tossed it neatly into the trash.

"Can you try and keep an open mind about their visit?"

"Will they keep an open mind about me?"

She sighed. "I thought you said you didn't want to fight." She shook open a trash bag and headed for the table, collecting spent juice boxes, empty paper plates, and pizza crusts. Just as she dropped the last plate into the bag, Sparky the Fire Dog burst into the room.

Pandemonium ensued as the kids rushed the giant dalmatian —aka his brother, Jack.

"Who wants to take a picture with me and a fire engine?" Jack called out over the din. "I can only take you in groups of three, though. Chief's orders."

Immediately the kids sorted themselves into two groups of ten. Jack glanced over at Oliver, as if to say, "can you help me out here?" Before Oliver could do anything—not that he had a plan formulated that quick—Serena had re-sorted the kids into smaller groups and resolved a few differences of opinion, one involving his own son.

Okay, so she would probably make a *great* teacher. And she did enjoy helping out in the boys' classrooms. But they still couldn't afford to send her back to school.

The universe will provide.

I'm not even dignifying that with an answer. His mother would never spout hokum like that, anyway. He set to cleaning up the empty pizza boxes while Jack shepherded kids down to the main bay. Matt followed, as the official photographer.

Oliver carried trash down to the dumpster out back, trying to regain his equilibrium. He didn't want to fight with Serena at

Cammy's party—or anywhere, for that matter. But it seemed like any little thing could set them both on edge lately. He knew it was partly because he was stressed over her parents' visit. They were due to arrive tomorrow, Sunday. But why wouldn't he be stressed? These were the people who cut off their daughter because she had married *him*. A lowly firefighter. Taken away her trust fund. As though that was the only reason he had married her.

Hell, I didn't even know she had a trust fund until they took it away. None of that had played any role in his decision to fall in love with her.

They were nice to you in the hospital.

They were civil. Not the same thing. Nor had they offered to help pay their daughter's medical bills. He shook his head as he yanked open the heavy fire door and went back inside. Why did Serena want to see them anyway? She wanted Mason and Cam to know their grandparents—but grandparents like that? His mother would have been appalled by them.

I'm appalled by a lot of things these days.

Instead of going back upstairs right away, Oliver continued on into the bay where Sparky the Fire Dog was hoisting up kids and Matt was snapping pictures on his phone. Ashley Wardman would have done a better job, probably. But she was the last person he wanted at his son's birthday. Well, third last—after his in-laws, Georgia and Peter Irving III.

He stood next to Matt. "How many more?"

"Two more. Smile!" Matt called out. "Then cake and ice cream. You ready for tomorrow?"

"Nope." He looked at Jack in the Dalmatian costume. His brother was smart, marrying into the Trevor family. They were good people.

"Maybe they'll surprise you."

"That's what I'm worried about."

Matt elbowed him in the ribs. It wasn't just that he expected

Serena's parents to be less than civil to him. It was that he suspected they were coming with other motives.

Cam was the last kid to have a turn with Sparky.

"Hey dad!" Sparky said. "Get over here and get in the picture."

At six-foot-five, Sparky was a big dalmatian. Oliver took up position next to him, and he and his brother shared the job of holding up Cam. As he smiled broadly for Matt's camera, he had the sense that one day he would look at this picture and remember it as the beginning of the end.

CHAPTER 27

"They're here!" Mason and Cam were kneeling on the living room sofa and peering out the front window, each boy holding back a drape.

Oliver saw Serena take a deep breath. He understood why his sons were excited to meet their "new grandparents," even as he was irked by the fact of their enthusiasm. Their idea of "grandparents" had been shaped by *his* parents. But why Serena wanted to see them—much less spend all day cooking for them—was a reason he could not fathom.

"You ready?" he asked.

She nodded.

She was dressed with care today. Black pants, blue button-down shirt, lighter blue cardigan. She had blow-dried her curly hair to straighten it—as much as it could be straightened—and then pulled it back with a barrette. He imagined this was how she had looked before ... *before me.*

He had dearly wanted to dress the way he normally dressed—jeans and a St. Caroline Fire Department tee shirt or sweatshirt. At the last minute, he thought better of the idea and swapped out the sweatshirt for a button-down shirt. He kept the jeans, though. He was who he was. *A better man than they give me credit for.*

Mason yanked open the front door before Georgia and Peter Irving III even reached the porch. Oliver joined the boys at the front door, gently pulling them back.

"Let's calm down a bit, guys. Okay?"

He had tried to manage their expectations, but the idea of grandparents as terrible human beings was beyond their understanding. He knew one thing, though. He was going to be furious if the Irvings treated Mason and Cam with the same disdain they held for him.

Could be worse. At least they were staying at the Chesapeake Inn. He had called Mike, the Inn's head bartender, to let him know that Serena's parents were coming.

"They're rich. They're snooty. They hate me."

"Got it." Mike understood the request immediately. "No worries, Oliver. Sterling understands those people. He'll take care of them."

"Thanks, man."

Now Oliver watched warily as the Irvings climbed the steps up to the front porch. Peter Irving was leaning heavily on his wife's arm. Both looked older than he remembered. In his peripheral vision, he identified their rental car as a Jaguar. Who knew you could even rent one of those?

Serena rushed out onto the porch to help her parents. There were no warm embraces or kissed cheeks. From where he stood, Oliver couldn't even tell if any words of greeting were exchanged. When they got inside, Serena mouthed, "You could have helped."

Yeah, he supposed he should have. But would her father want his son-in-law helping him? How was he even supposed to behave this week? As though the past eight years of silence hadn't happened? When you got right down to it, the Irvings were complete strangers to him.

He went over to take their coats and hang them in the coat closet. He handled the garments carefully, like they might be breakable. Or contagious. When he turned around, the Irvings were seated on the sofa, with Mason next to his grandmother and Cam next to his grandfather.

Suck it up, buttercup.

He went over to shake his father-in-law's hand, which was clammier and knobbier than Oliver expected. "Good to see you," Oliver said, glancing over at Georgia and extending his tight smile to her as well. "How was traffic?"

Peter Irving grunted and dropped Oliver's hand. "Not too bad, considering."

"Can I get the two of you something to drink?"

"Water for both of us, please," Georgia answered.

Oliver gratefully disappeared into the kitchen. Behind him he heard Serena's voice. She was speaking to her parents about the Inn and their suite. He took his time getting down glasses, adding ice from the icemaker, pouring the filtered water. He wished he could teleport himself to a week from now, Easter Sunday, the day they were leaving. Already, Cam's birthday party felt ages ago, instead of merely yesterday.

He took the glasses of water back to the living room, where he was surprised to find Georgia and Peter chatting animatedly with the boys—asking about school, sports, favorite subjects, what they wanted to be when they grew up.

"I'm going to be the fire chief in St. Caroline," Mason said proudly.

Bzzz. Wrong answer. Being a firefighter was not going to cut it with the Irvings.

But Georgia nodded. "Well, that's a job you can't outsource."

Oliver caught Serena's eye. Her expression was as guarded as his was. This visit was a grand experiment with huge potential for disaster. And then how would they explain to the boys why their grandparents never came to visit again? *Well, they live in*

New York and it's really far away. Mason and Cam had always bought that explanation before, but obviously that wouldn't cut it anymore. Their grandparents had somehow managed to make the long trek to Maryland this time.

"I'm going to be a professional baseball player," Cam declared.

Oliver saw Serena fighting back a grin. Cam was occupationally fickle, though the one field he seemed to have little interest in was firefighting. Peter Irving was taking Cam at his word, though, and sharing his opinions on the upcoming baseball season—which Peter seemed quite knowledgeable about.

"So I just have a few things to finish up in the kitchen and then dinner will be ready," Serena announced.

Oliver followed. The expressed purpose of this visit was for the boys to get to know their grandparents, so he would leave them to that. There was really nothing he could do to impress them anyway. Other than go back in time and be born as someone else altogether.

"So far, so good." Serena held up two crossed fingers. "I'm beginning to wonder why I invited them for the whole week, though."

"You can't plead amnesia on that one, babe." He tucked a stray lock of her dark hair behind her ear. He was hit with a sudden longing to touch her, kiss her, carry her up to bed. Remind her why she had married him in the first place. *Because I treat you like a queen. Because we're good together. Because you made me feel like I was good enough. Because the sheets smoke when we make love.*

But all of those thoughts were followed by the voice of normal Oliver. *She cheated on you. And now her long lost parents are here, after eight years? What's up with that? Leopards don't change their spots.*

At seven o'clock, Serena finally let herself relax as Oliver took the boys upstairs for their showers. They'd made it through dinner, coffee, and dessert without incident. From either her parents or her husband. Mason and Cam had poured on the charm and her parents seemed entranced by them. Oliver and her father discussed local fishing at dinner. She let her mother fill her in on what some of her old childhood friends and their parents were doing. Doctors, lawyers, finance, kids at Miss Porter's School or Hotchkiss, summers in the Hamptons or Barcelona or Montenegro or Monaco.

That could have been her life. She tried to imagine Mason at boarding school. Or Cam sitting still long enough for a flight to Europe. She couldn't picture either. Nor did she really want to. Life in St. Caroline wasn't perfect, but it was what she had chosen.

She retrieved her parents' coats from the coat closet, thankful that her mother had left her fur coats in New York. St. Caroline wasn't a fur coat kind of place. Her mother slipped her arms into her wool coat, then helped Serena's father into his.

"Do you need any help getting down to the car?" she offered.

"No, I can make it," her father grumbled.

Something wasn't right here, something that was more than just aging. Her parents weren't *that* old. She would have to ask her mother privately, later. She hugged her parents, which felt strange and unfamiliar after all these years. Then again, maybe it had always felt strange and unfamiliar with them. She stood in the doorway as they made their way back to the rental car parked in the driveway. True to his word, her father had an easier time of it going down the stairs. But then she was surprised to see him open the passenger side door and practically collapse into the car. Her mother looked up from the driver's side and gave Serena a wave. Serena waved back.

Well, it was definitely a weird evening, but it could have gone much worse.

She loaded the dishwasher, listening to the sounds of water

gurgling through the pipes from the boys' showers and teeth brushing. Ten minutes later, she heard Oliver's footsteps coming down the stairs.

"Wow. They went down fast," she said.

"They're wiped out."

"My parents were, too."

"Your dad doesn't look good." Oliver tore off a paper towel, ran it beneath the spigot, and started wiping off the countertop.

"I noticed that. Of course, they're eight years older than when I saw them last." She touched his forearm. "Thanks for being nice to them."

"It was hard sometimes." He shrugged. "Actually, what was hard was watching the boys be so excited to see them."

"I know." She let her fingertips slide down to his wrist. They hadn't been physically intimate in awhile, and she missed it. Missed touching him. No, more than just "missed" it. She was desperate for them to make love. Tonight would be ideal.

The stress of her parents' visit was over. The boys were in bed on time and so tired that neither of them would wake until morning. She let her palm cover the back of his hand, hoping he would flip his wrist around and interlace his fingers with hers.

He didn't. Instead, he slid his hand from beneath hers and finished wiping down the countertop. "I don't care how they treat me," he said. "But I can't forgive them for how they've treated you. Even if they've gotten over the horror of you marrying me, it doesn't justify their behavior in the past."

"I know it doesn't." She dropped a dishwasher tab into the holder and snapped it shut, "And I don't know if I can forgive and forget, either. But I want the boys to have a relationship with them, if possible." She pressed the "start" button on the dish-washer and closed the door with a firm click.

"They seemed to get on with Mason and Cam, so you might get your wish there." He crumpled up the wet paper towel and tossed it into the trash. "I've got an early day tomorrow. I'm going to turn in."

"I'll come with you." She wasn't tired yet—more wired, really —but she wanted to go to bed with him. They had to at least *try*. She wasn't willing to just let this part of their marriage wither and die.

She followed Oliver upstairs and changed into her pajamas—a thin cotton tank and shorts—while he brushed his teeth. By the time she finished brushing her own teeth, he was in bed with the lights out. She could tell from the cadence of his breathing that he wasn't asleep. He was lying on his side, facing away from her. She scooted her body up to his, and draped her arm over him. If he turned her down, she knew she'd likely cry herself to sleep. As far as she remembered, their sex life was always good. Ollie was a patient and generous lover, and willing to try new things when prodded.

But this was a different Ollie lying in bed right now. This was a man who didn't believe her, who suspected her of cheating on him, who was completely unreadable to her now. She considered drawing her arm back to her side of the bed, and letting it go. His rejection would slice her heart right in half.

On the other hand, she had to know. If this part of their marriage was lost, too, then there was probably no hope of salvaging it.

She pressed a kiss into his broad shoulder and flattened her palm against his chest. "Make love to me," she whispered.

She held her breath. Would he or not? It had been over a week since he'd said anything about Ben. *Maybe he's let that go.* Her heart pounded in her chest so hard she could feel the pulse behind her ears. Would he or wouldn't he? *This is Oliver we're talking about.* Just because he didn't say anything didn't mean he wasn't obsessing over it 24-7.

He rolled toward her and slid his arms around her back. She let her breath out slowly. He kissed her and, saying nothing, made love to her. He was tender and gentle, but she could tell that his heart wasn't in it. Afterward, he rolled onto his side and went to sleep, without so much as a goodnight kiss. She rolled toward the other side of the mattress and stared at the narrow sliver of light shining beneath the door. They always left the hall light on in case the boys needed to use the bathroom in the middle of the night.

She didn't know what to do about this situation. Honestly truly had no clue. Oliver had his mind made up and nothing she said made any difference. And that was beginning to worry her— because Ollie was levelheaded and rational and generally … right. He was someone who was right about things. Almost all the time, in fact.

And while everything inside her was screaming that he wasn't right about this—she did not have an affair with Ben Wardman! —it was also hard to argue with Ollie's history of being right about things.

She closed her eyes as the tears slid down her cheeks and onto the cotton sheet. She cried—for the love she was losing and for the possibility that maybe she really had cheated on Oliver Wolfe.

CHAPTER 28

Serena's mother came back the next morning, after the boys were off to school and Oliver off to the station.

"Where's dad?" Serena asked as she hung her mother's coat in the closet.

"He stayed back at the Inn to use the gym. He needs to do his exercises. Doctor's orders."

Her mother looked around, as if she didn't know where to sit.

"Come into the kitchen with me, mum. I made a pot of coffee. And blueberry muffins are in the oven." Oliver left without filling up his customary travel mug. Part of her regretted the night before. Another part didn't. It was better to know than not to know. If Ollie had bailed on their marriage, then she needed to start thinking about what was next.

In the kitchen, Serena pulled out one of the barstools at the island. Her mother hoisted herself up. She was wearing navy slacks and a St. John knit jacket in a subtle camel and ivory check pattern. As Serena poured a cup of coffee for her mother, she tried to think whether she'd ever seen her mother in jeans. She set the cup on the island, retrieved a half pint container of cream from the fridge and set that on the table, too. She supposed she should dig out the fancy cream pitcher that got used only on Thanksgiving, but she had no idea where it was.

She climbed up onto the barstool next to her mother. "Mum, can I ask you something? When Peter and I were at school, did you just wear jeans and sweatpants around the house?" She glanced down at the black yoga pants she was wearing, beneath a long tunic sweater.

"No. Most days, I had board meetings or luncheons to go to."

"Huh."

"Why do you ask?"

Serena shrugged. "I don't know. I just can't remember whether I've ever seen you in casual clothes." She took a sip of coffee. "I forgot to mention that I have some memory loss from the accident. Well, quite a bit of memory loss, actually."

"You do?"

Serena nodded. "Several years worth. It's been a rough transition back home."

"Your father had some short-term amnesia after his heart attack last summer. But it cleared up. It was the strangest thing, though. As soon as someone left his hospital room, he had no memory of them being there. Even though it was ten seconds earlier."

"Dad had a heart attack? Why didn't you let me know?"

"I mentioned it to your husband when he called about your accident."

"His name is Oliver."

"I told Oliver, then."

"He had a lot on his plate while I was in the hospital."

"Well, your father has recovered."

"He had trouble getting up the steps to the porch yesterday."

"We were sitting in the car for a couple hours. His joints stiffen up. We're getting older, you know."

Which makes their behavior all the worse. Eight years lost. But

Serena didn't voice that. Instead, she cut right to the chase. "Why did you cut us off?"

Her mother's face was impossible to read. She had to have known Serena would ask this question sooner or later. Minutes passed like hours before her mother finally began to answer.

"We wanted the best for you," she started. "We thought it was a youthful rebellion. You were extremely young, dear."

"So why visit now?"

"Your father's health scare last year left him with a keener sense of his own mortality. And I told him I wanted to come see you and the boys."

Serena studied her mother's face, trying to gauge the sincerity behind her hazel eyes. Her mother looked familiar and yet … not. She wondered how often she had thought about her parents before the accident. A lot? Or had she given up on them entirely?

"The boys are excited to have new grandparents. So please stay in their lives." She felt the way Oliver did last night. If they exited her life again, it wouldn't bother her. But Mason and Cam wouldn't understand.

"I will. We will."

The oven timer went off. Serena hurried over to grab a pair of hot pad mitts before pulling the muffin tin from the oven. She set it on a trivet to cool for a few minutes.

"What are you doing now that the boys are in school?"

"Well, I volunteer at their school one or two days a week." Serena took down two small plates from a cupboard. "And I've been taking a quilting class."

"Quilting? Now there's something I never had any knack for. Or any sort of arts and crafts."

"It's fun. The women who run the quilting shop are of the opinion that anyone can learn to quilt. I might prove them wrong yet." She laughed as she gingerly lifted muffins from the hot tin and placed them on the plates. She carried the plates to the island. "I'm also thinking of going back to school to get my teacher certification. There's a program at the local college."

"Oh? Well, I told your father that political science degree wasn't practical."

Serena bit into a muffin, the blueberries hot and sweet inside. She chased it with a sip of coffee. "I'm not sure I'll be able to afford it though." Her initial excitement at the idea had since collided with cold, hard reality.

Her mother picked at a muffin, once in awhile daintily lifting a piece to her lips. Serena finished one muffin and started in on another, less out of hunger than nervous energy.

"I'll get your father to release your trust fund."

For a moment, Serena thought she must be dreaming. Did her mother just say …?

"Why would he do that? After all this time?"

"He's been doing a lot of thinking since the heart attack. You know, men like your father—"

Her mother left that train of thought unfinished, but Serena knew what she intended to say. *Men like your father think they'll live forever.*

"When we got back to the Inn last night, he said you looked happy," her mother added.

"I am happy, mum." *Maybe not for much longer.* But that was why she had to go back to school. Her mother was right about the practicality of her political science degree, especially in St. Caroline. "I have a good life here." *If only I can hang onto it.*

"HEY GUYS! Can someone open the door for me?"

Oliver stood outside Matt's front door, a stack of hot pizza boxes in his arms. He was beginning to feel like a pizza delivery guy. Last weekend, Cam's birthday party. This weekend, Jack's bachelor party. Such as it was.

Oliver, Matt, and several other guests were on call tonight so it was just poker and pizza for Jack. *No wild boozing for us.* Not that Oliver could remember the last time he had wildly boozed. Before he met Serena, at any rate.

He was about to knock on the door with his foot when it swung open, revealing Matt in his usual attire—SCFD tee shirt and grey cargo pants. At least, Oliver had dressed up some. Well, a button-down shirt anyway. He had changed into one every day this week when he got home from work. The ice between him and Serena's parents was melting a bit, but no point in pushing his luck. So he ironed his nice shirts and wore them.

"What did you get?" Matt held the door open wider so Oliver could fit through without jostling the pizzas.

"A little of everything. Pepperoni, sausage, extra garlic, mushrooms, peppers—"

"Okay, I get it." Matt lifted the top three boxes from Oliver's arms and carried them to his small kitchen. "We have two coolers." He pointed toward the corner. "That one has beer for the guys who can drink tonight. The other is water and soda. For those of us who can't."

Oliver set the remaining three pizza boxes on Matt's counter. He felt a hard clap on his shoulder. His brother, Jack.

"Think that's enough pizza? The groom-to-be lifted a lid to inhale the cheese-scented steam.

"We can always go out for more."

"So how's it going? Surviving In-laws Week?" Jack let the lid drop.

"Hah," Matt replied for Oliver. "You've spent more time at the station than at home, seems like."

That was almost true. Oliver had squeezed as much time out of his shifts as he could and still maintain a plausible explanation. He shrugged. "It's going, anyway. They leave Sunday."

"On Easter?"

"Yup." He walked over to the coolers and retrieved a bottle of root beer. "Although they are apparently giving Serena her trust fund back." He uncapped the bottle and took a long draw. "We'll see if that actually happens."

"Wait—seriously?" Matt's eyes widened.

"Serena has a trust fund?" Jack's eyes were even wider.

"They took it away from her when she married Ollie here."

Oliver let Matt explain it all to his brother. Easier than explaining yourself how your in-laws disliked you so much that they disowned their only daughter.

"Sorry, man," Jack said. "I had no idea."

Oliver waved away his brother's concern. "She's planning to use some of it to go back to school." He looked pointedly at the stack of pizza boxes. "Do we have to wait until everyone's here?"

"Give them a minute. They're on the way." Matt set out a roll of paper towels to be used as napkins. "Serena's going back to school, too? You're aren't moving, are you?"

"Who else is going back to school?" He glanced at Jack, who had dropped out of law school—a decision Oliver personally thought his brother would come to regret. But whatever.

"Cassidy is. University of Texas at Austin," Matt answered.

"Oh, right." He recalled hearing something about that. Tough luck for his brother. Mr. Love 'em and Leave 'em finally falls in love and ... gets left. "Serena's just going to Talbot College. Well, if she gets in, that is. She still has to apply and all that."

"I doubt that will be an issue." Matt leaned over the stack of pizza boxes and took a deep inhale. "Maybe we won't wait."

No sooner had the words left his mouth than there came a sharp rap at the front door. The door opened and the rest of the guests streamed in, a mix of guys from the fire and police departments and some guys who were probably more Matt's friends than Jack's, Oliver guessed.

"I see you got the poker table all set up," Sean Crane said.

Hmm. It hadn't occurred to Oliver that Matt might invite Sean. But it made sense. Sean had replaced Ben Wardman as soccer coach at the high school. Matt had taken over Sean's assistant role. Sean might know a few things of interest to Oliver.

When the guys took up seats at Matt's dining table, Oliver made sure he got one right next to Sean—who was drinking a beer, he noted. Maybe it would loosen up his tongue.

Not that he could just come out and ask the man: say, did my wife sleep with your old colleague? But he'd figure something out.

Matt dragged the coffee table over and set three of the pizza boxes atop it, while Jack dealt cards. It took awhile but after a few rounds, the guys paused for bathroom breaks and to re-up on the refreshments. It was in Matt's kitchen that Oliver found himself alone with Sean.

And he didn't even have to make the first move.

"How's Serena doing?" Sean asked.

"Good. She's doing good. Thinking about going back to school." Now that he was face to face with the man, Oliver had no idea how to broach the subject of Ben.

"Oh yeah? What for?" Sean lifted the lid of a pizza box. "Oh good. Sausage."

"Teaching certification at Talbot College."

"Hey, that's great. I mean, obviously I'm biased here." Sean put two slices of sausage pizza on a plate. "You know, now that I think of it, I believe she shadowed a few teachers at the high school last year."

Now *this* was news to Oliver, and not at all what he'd been expecting. "Which teacher?"

Sean bit off the point of one slice, a thoughtful expression on his face. "I don't know," he said after a moment. "It was awhile ago. Last winter or spring? Some time around there."

"You guys ready out there?" Matt called over.

"Yeah, we're coming." Oliver followed Sean back to the poker table. He really didn't need to ask which teacher Serena had shadowed. Of course, it was Ben. At some point, a series of coin-cidences becomes a pattern.

He slumped into his chair and picked up the cards Jack had dealt. He was hard-pressed to picture Serena as a high school teacher, though. Elementary school, sure. Maybe even middle school. But there was no way she had ever seriously considered teaching high school kids. They'd eat her alive. "Shadowing" had clearly been just another excuse to spend time with Ben Wardman.

$\mathcal{S}$erena felt the other side of the mattress depress. She opened one eye to squint at the alarm clock on the nightstand. Five o'clock. She wondered why Oliver had bothered driving home from the party. Surely he could have crashed at Matt's place?

Not that she minded. She rolled over and snuggled up against his back. The faint scent of smoke on his skin and in his hair explained it all. She could always smell a fire on him, even though he showered at the station afterward.

"Hey," she said quietly.

"Mutual aid call," he mumbled.

So much for Jack's bachelor party. "Did you get any poker in?"

"A little. I need to sleep for an hour or two before church."

She felt his shoulders sag as he fell asleep, and rolled onto her back. She was wide awake now. *Well, at least I don't have to worry about my husband and his brothers out at some strip club, getting lap dances and tucking money into g-strings.*

After ten minutes of staring at the ceiling, Serena rolled out of bed and put on her robe. She might as well get a head start on

Easter morning and fill the boys' baskets with their chocolate bunnies and jelly beans.

~

EIGHT HOURS LATER, the boys were trading candy in their bedroom while Serena and Oliver stood outside on the porch, saying goodbye to her parents. *Finally.* They had gone to church, followed by Serena's ham dinner. But now ... finally!

Oliver shook Peter Irving III's hand, then kissed Georgia Irving on her dry, powdered cheek. He watched them slowly walk to the rental car. *A Jaguar! Good grief!* He was so tired he could barely muster the energy to be annoyed—or even to be relieved at their departure. Last night's call had been a fire at a chicken processing plant. The building had sprinklers, but not all of them were operational, apparently. As usual, the cost of prevention was less than the cost of a fire.

That sounds rather ... unpleasant.

Yeah, it was. Oliver hoped never to go on a call like that again. He hated calls where animals were involved, even chickens that were destined for the fryer anyway. People were generally easier to get out of a burning building.

The Jaguar pulled away from the curb, with his mother-in-law at the wheel. Simultaneously he and Serena let out long exhales.

"Well, it was a good visit," she said, "but I'm glad they're gone."

Me, too. Not that Oliver was going to say that, even though Serena just had.

"You didn't tell me you shadowed Ben at the high school last year."

But you'll say that?

Serena looked at him long and hard before replying. "I don't know who I shadowed. I don't remember shadowing anybody, as a matter of fact. Ashley told me I did, and I believe her. Who told you it was Ben?"

"No one. I'm just putting the pieces together."

"Well, when you get done with that, let me know. I'd be interested in learning how the story ends." With that, she turned on her heel and went inside.

CHAPTER 30

"Mom, am I going to get any shots today?" Cam's voice was laced with concern, bordering on terror.

Serena glanced up at the rearview mirror, where she could see her youngest son's worried face.

"I don't know, sweetheart. We'll have to find out when we get there."

She trained her attention back on the street ahead. The doctor had officially cleared her for driving last week, and not a minute too soon. In another month and a half, the boys would be out of school for the summer and clamoring to go to Secret Beach. And Ashley's time was getting scarce as the Inn's wedding season geared up. Jack and Becca's wedding next week was the season opener.

"I got a shot last year," Mason chimed in from the back seat of the minivan. "It hurt like a mother."

"Mason Wolfe! Where did you hear that word?"

"I dunno," he mumbled.

He did not get that one from me.

"Dad says it," Cam allowed, grudgingly.

Even without seeing it, Serena could sense the death stare Mason was giving his little brother right now. "Well, it is not appropriate language. I hope you're not saying that at school."

"The older kids say it at recess," Cam helpfully added.

"Well, you two are not going to use that kind of language. Understood? The kind of language dad uses at the station is not appropriate for other places."

"Chill, mom," she heard Mason mutter under his breath.

At the stoplight, she glanced at the rearview mirror again—just in time to see Cam mouth to his older brother, "you're going to get us in trouble."

She let it go. She *did* need to chill. The last thing she wanted was for the boys to pick up on her stress levels—or the tension between their parents. Hiding it was getting harder and harder. So far, they'd been able to keep the loud arguments to times when the boys were at school. But it was hard to bite her tongue the rest of the time, when it felt like Oliver could barely stand to be around her.

She pulled the minivan into the parking lot behind Dr. Trevor's pediatrics practice. Mason was not happy about having to tag along to his brother's annual well child visit, but Oliver was at the station. Besides, as she had pointed out, Cam always had to tag along on Mason's appointments.

Inside, Mason set himself up at the wooden train set in the waiting room, suddenly not so aggravated at having to be there. But not so magnanimous as to let his little brother follow the nurse into the back without a parting, "fingers crossed you don't have to get a shot!"

Cam whimpered softly. Serena filled her lungs with a deep breath of calm. She couldn't imagine how Angie had managed with three boys.

An infant mewled in one of the other exam rooms. *I was pregnant last year at this time.*

You might have had a third boy.

A girl would have been nice.

"Hey there, Cam." The nurse stopped at the scale. "Step on up here and let's get your height and weight."

Cam stepped up, the nurse typed in some numbers on her tablet, and turned to Serena. "Ninetieth percentile." Cam stepped off the scale. "You're going to be a tall one," the nurse said.

Cam dutifully followed the nurse into the outer space-themed exam room and hopped up onto the exam table, the white paper crinkling beneath him. The nurse took his blood pressure and pulse, while Serena watched from a chair against the wall. The nurse input those numbers into the tablet too, then said, "the doctor will be with you in a minute."

"I forgot to ask her whether I'm getting a shot," Cam said when she was gone.

"They don't hurt that much, do they?"

Right then, a piercing wail sounded from another exam room.

"They might?" he said. "I don't remember."

"Well, if they hurt a lot you'd probably remember. Don't you think?"

Cam's expression said he wasn't convinced. "Do you remember the last time you had a shot?"

Serena thought for a moment. She could lie and say, "yes." After all, she vaguely remembered a few childhood vaccinations. But anything more recent? Um, nope.

"Mason says you can't remember stuff."

"He does? Who told him that?"

Cam pressed his lips together, protecting his sources.

"I hurt my head in the car accident, Cammy. So yes … it's like there are some blank spots in my brain."

Who told him? She contemplated the short list of suspects. Mattie. Jack. Oliver. Her ire began to rise at the thought that it might have been Oliver.

"I get that in word study sometimes." Cam said, nodding. "Like I *know* the word but I just can't say it."

"That happens to everybody, sweetie. It's normal."

"So what other things can't you remember?"

Speaking of blank spots. What could she tell him that was innocent enough? She quickly wracked her brain while Cam watched her, guilelessly expecting an answer.

The door swung open.

"Hello there, Wolves." Dr. Trevor in his white coat and stethoscope strode into the room, a much bigger presence than the nurse had been. Like the nurse, he too carried a tablet. "Who do we have here? Cam?"

Saved by the bell.

"Am I getting a shot today?" Cam cut to the chase.

Dr. Trevor scanned his tablet. "Nope. Looks like you're good."

Serena saw the tension release from her son's shoulders. Quietly, she watched as the doctor went through Cam's exam, finally pronouncing him "fit as a fiddle."

"But you still need to eat more veggies, okay?" Dr. Trevor added. Then he turned to face Serena, "My wife says she hasn't seen you in the shop lately."

She shrugged. "My parents were in town the week of Easter."

He smiled. "You know, you don't have to be as crazy about quilting as the women in my family are."

"No, no. I enjoyed the class I took with Becca. It's just—" *It's just that my marriage is falling apart and I don't know what to do about it.* Ollie was dead set on the idea that she'd had an affair with Ben Wardman. She couldn't remember doing so. But she also couldn't really remember *not* doing it, either.

She went back and forth on this every day. No, more like every hour. It was hard to imagine *wanting* to cheat on Ollie. She *loved* Ollie. She had given up a lot because of that love—a chance at a lucrative career, a life of financial ease, kids who would start their lives with the same advantages she and her brother had enjoyed.

Love isn't enough. Those were her parents' words when she told them she was marrying a small town firefighter. It wasn't love that had sustained her parents' marriage, that was for sure. It was her mother's willingness to suck it up, to ignore her husband's bad behavior in exchange for a secure, comfortable lifestyle.

Serena was trying to suck it up and wait Ollie out on this, wait until he came to his senses. But so far, there was no sign of his senses on the horizon—and that worried her. Oliver Wolfe was a sensible man. As sensible as they came. Maybe she was more like her mother than she wanted to admit—insensible.

Dr. Trevor held up his hands, warding off the rest of her sentence. "It's okay. Quilting's not for everyone. How's Oliver these days?"

Dr. Trevor's words jolted her back to the present.

"He's good," she answered.

"He's grumpy," Cam chimed in.

"Cam!" She gave her son a sharp look.

"Well, he is."

"Sorry," she apologized to Dr. Trevor.

"Cam, why don't you go check on your brother in the waiting room? I need to talk to your mom for a minute."

Cam bolted from the room, as if Dr. Trevor might change his mind on the shot if he hung around long enough. When he was gone, Dr. Trevor said, "Oliver was my patient when he was younger, like all three of the Wolfe boys. Of the three of them, Oliver was always wound tight the most." He grinned. "I'm sure that's not news to you."

"Not really, no."

"There's a psychologist who's become a customer of Michelle's shop, and who is helping Becca and Jack prepare for Jackie's move to St. Caroline. And helping Jackie, too. There are a lot of things to unpack in that situation. But she's around quite a bit, so if Oliver wants to speak to her, we can arrange it."

Serena considered the idea. Oliver would probably benefit from a session or two with a therapist. He probably also would never consent to the idea.

"I'll let him know."

"Grief is an unpredictable thing," Dr. Trevor went on. "What looks like grief in one person can be 'totally holding it together' in another. I don't think Michelle has yet to fully grieve her sister's death and that was over twenty years ago. When Penny died, we rushed out to Ohio to get Becca out of foster care. We had two toddlers at home already and went on to have two more after Becca. Then when the girls got a little older, Michelle opened the quilt shop ..." He took a deep breath. "It's going to slam into her one day like a hurricane."

"I suspect Oliver didn't really have time to grieve for Angie last year, what with taking care of the boys and all." In fact, knowing Ollie as she did, she was one hundred percent certain he hadn't. Her husband prided himself on order and control.

"Well, you can't really force someone into it. But seriously, let us know if he'd like to meet with the psychologist."

"I'll keep it in mind."

OLIVER WATCHED as St. Caroline's town planner drove off in his grey pickup. Now he was alone with one Mr. Finn Brody, a partner in a Washington, DC construction firm. Mr. Brody was also an architect, and so far the favorite for designing and building the new fire station. Oliver had lobbied hard to be the person managing this project on the fire department's end, even though his only relevant qualification was that he was a fire-fighter. On the other hand, no one else in the department—save his father—was any better qualified.

Oliver had his reasons for putting this project on his plate. He wanted to be able to drive past the site with the boys and point out what daddy was doing. He wanted the boys to drive past the new station with their own children someday and point out that their grandfather was responsible for building that station.

He wanted a reason to spend more time at work.

And he wanted to show up Ben Wardman.

You're trying to show up a dead man?

So maybe Oliver didn't have a college degree. So maybe he spent a lot of time washing fire trucks. Maybe he worked with his hands.

Maybe?

Okay, no maybes about it. But he wasn't just a pretty face and a good body.

Modest maybe, too.

He had a brain, too.

You're starting to sound like the Scarecrow.

He ignored the voice in his head. Finn Brody was walking the site, taking pictures and making notes on a yellow legal pad. Every so often, he would stop and stare hard at ... something. Oliver wasn't sure what.

The site was just a flat field right now, covered in scrubby grass and goose droppings. They'd had a good meeting back at the station. The town planner explained the town's architectural guidelines. Because the new station would sit on the eastern edge of town, close to the large estates on the water and where most of the new residential construction was taking place, the town wanted it to fit in. No boxy brick building like the main fire station, built in the sixties.

"So a fire station that looks like George Washington built it." Fortunately, Finn Brody had grasped right away what the town needed.

At the moment, Brody was headed Oliver's way, tucking his pen into an interior pocket in his leather jacket. The man didn't look the way Oliver had pictured an architect looking. He was expecting someone skinny, nerdy-looking, with glasses and smooth hands. Finn Brody looked more like a construction worker—or someone who was a gym rat. Oliver was no slouch in the muscles department, but this guy made him look like a hundred-pound weakling.

Wonder what he bench presses. Not that it mattered. The guy wasn't going to be physically pouring the foundation.

"Nice piece of land you got here," Brody remarked as he stopped next to Oliver. "Town's really growing, huh?"

Oliver was getting a military vibe from Brody, too, and he wasn't sure why. Maybe it was just the really short hair. He was a good looking guy. Piercing blue eyes. His face and hands were the color of brown sugar. Mixed race, possibly.

"You've been here before?" Oliver asked.

"Yeah, once. End of last year. For a funeral, sadly."

"Oh? Whose funeral?"

"Ben Wardman. You know him?"

Seriously? Oliver was starting to feel like Ben Wardman was following him around. Not to mention, if he gave Finn Brody's company the contract to build the new fire station, now he was going to be reminded of Ben every time he saw this guy.

"Not really. My wife is good friends with his wife, though."

"Oh yeah? Ashley?"

Oliver nodded. Brody knew the name of Ben's wife. So clearly they were more than just passing acquaintances. Oliver didn't want to delve into that. *Better if I just don't know.*

"So what are the next steps?" Oliver pulled the conversation back to the immediate matter at hand. So what if the universe was taunting him with Ben Wardman? He could ignore the universe.

"Well, after we sign the contract, the first thing I'll do is create a program—a written report—that lists the rooms and spaces you need in the building with proposed sizes. Once that is all agreed upon, I will create a bubble diagram. That's a more visual map of where different functionalities will be. For example, you'll want sleeping quarters that are close to the main bay so you can get from one to the other quickly when a call comes in. Does that make sense?"

Oliver nodded. "We want a community room in this station, too, but preferably it would be further away from the main bay. With a separate entrance, even."

"Right. Exactly. That's what we'll work through with the bubble diagram. Where you want things to be, how you want people to move through the building. You can start to draw up a list of things you think aren't working as well as you'd like in the current station." He pulled a business card from his jacket's inside pocket and held it out to Oliver. "Email me with any thoughts or questions you have."

Oliver took the card and slipped it into his own pocket. "Will do." He liked Finn Brody, despite the connection to Ben. Obviously, the guy was smart. You had to go to college to be an architect. But there was something a little rough around the edges, too. He felt comfortable around that.

They turned and headed toward their SUVs, which were identical right down to color, make, and model. They'd had a laugh about it back at the station.

"What year is yours?" Oliver asked now.

"2015," Brody answered.

"Mine, too."

They had another laugh about it.

"Great minds think alike, eh?" Brody said, extending his hand for a final shake. "I'll be in touch."

CHAPTER 31

Oliver stood at the edge of the parquet dance floor set up in the Chesapeake Inn's grand ballroom. Jack and Becca were officially married now. The guests were all stuffed to the gills with asparagus bisque, crab risotto, and surf and turf. Matt, as the best man, had made his toast. The bride and groom had danced their first dance as a married couple.

Mason and Cam were on the dance floor with their new cousin and flower girl, Jackie. He had to bite his lip to keep from laughing at the sight of his sons flailing—uh, dancing—in their black pants, white shirts, and cummerbunds (blue for Mason, pink for Cam). There was a purple sock monkey in the mix, too, getting swung from Mason to Cam to Jackie and then back again. The boys were both trying a little too hard to impress their cousin with their dance moves.

They're not as repressed as their father.

Tears stung his eyes. His mother was missing this. She was missing Jack's wedding and would miss Matt's ... well, who knew if Matt would ever get married? So maybe her missing that one was a non-issue. Whatever was between Matt and Cassidy

Trevor seemed to be over now. As far as Oliver could tell, they had yet to even speak to each other today.

Evidently, Cam had dispensed with his black dress shoes at some point because he was dancing in his stocking feet. Oliver could sympathize. He looked around for Serena, and spotted her talking to Becca's youngest sister, Cam's shoes dangling from her fingers. She looked lovely in a white dress printed with yellow flowers of some sort.

Daisies.

Maybe daisies? Her wild dark hair was pulled back and subdued with a yellow ribbon. It was hard not to draw comparisons between Jack and Becca's wedding and his own to Serena.

They had gotten married in October and, while it had been warm enough for an outdoor wedding, they weren't able to afford a wedding at the Inn.

A church wedding was cheaper and Serena had hoped that it might change her parents' minds. She had hoped, right up to the very last minute. Obviously, her parents hadn't contributed financially to the wedding. His parents had, to the extent they could afford to, but Matt was in community college at the time and Jack was a freshman at Cornell.

He watched Becca happily chatting with Mike, the Inn's bartender and several other Inn employees. Not that he begrudged her and Jack this beautiful day, but the Inn had probably given them a discount since Becca worked at Skipjack's. An employee discount.

Serena used to work at the Inn.

Right ... she did. How had he forgotten that? For several months after they met, she had continued to work her job on Capitol Hill in Washington and drove to St. Caroline every weekend to see him. But then he had proposed—

We all worried that you were moving too fast.

—which was totally out of character for him. Even he had

always believed he would need to date a woman for several years before feeling comfortable enough to commit to a lifetime with her. That old adage—measure twice, cut once? He was more like measure six times, then measure twice more for good measure, and then cut.

You said you just knew she was the one.

His conversations with his mother were all coming back to him. Serena had accepted his proposal—yeah, he remembered *that* night. And the next morning and ...

I don't need to know this.

Well, that wasn't part of his conversations with his mother.

Then Serena quit her job in DC and moved into Oliver's small apartment over a now-defunct art gallery on Main Street. She took a job at the Chesapeake Inn.

As a waitress.

It all came back to him in a rush. She got pregnant on their honeymoon and had to quit because of the terrible morning sickness she had. Actually ... now that he thought of it, her morning sickness was bad last year too. She didn't go out on the boat even once last summer. Matt had used it more than Oliver had.

Waitressing. He wondered whether Serena remembered that job. Or ... *oh hell.* Did her parents know about it? No wonder they couldn't stand him. He'd taken their only daughter and turned her into a waitress. *Double hell.* After all the money they spent on boarding school and Princeton.

"Hey there." Matt suddenly appeared by his side. "Trying to pick up some new moves?" He nodded toward Mason and Cam.

"Actually, I was wondering whether it was you they picked up those moves from. They seem to have picked up quite a bit from you."

Matt held up his hands. "Hey, just trying to be a mentor to today's youth."

Ashley Wardman popped up in front of them. "Smile, guys!"

The flash went off and she leaned back to look at the shot on her camera. She frowned. "Let's try that one again. *Really* smile this time. Like you're happy to see your little brother married."

Oliver forced a smile onto his face. He was happy for Jack. Less happy to see Ashley. When she pronounced the picture "perfect" and turned to go, Oliver felt a sharp jab in his ribs.

"Dude, let it go," Matt said. "I'm sorry I ever said anything."

"Where's Cassidy?" He heard his brother's sharp inhale.

"Inside. Resting her leg."

"What's going on with you two—"

Oliver! Don't be a dick.

Matt snorted. "Yeah, bro, don't be a dick."

Oliver was confused. "Did I just say that out loud?"

Matt's head bounced with laughter. "That was mom."

"What do mean, 'that was mom?'"

"Don't you hear her voice all the time?"

"Yeah … I hear what she would say. In my head."

"We all do. Me and Jack, too."

"She did raise all three of us."

And only one left to marry off!

"See?" Matt said. "Didn't you just hear, 'and only one left to marry off?'"

Oliver was quiet. He *did* just hear that. But that was nuts. "So what are you saying? She's haunting us?"

"Yes! Jack and I told her to haunt you some more. Leave us alone for awhile."

I can multitask, you know.

Oliver's brows knit together. There was no way … he didn't believe in that kind of supernatural nonsense. After the past year, he wasn't even sure he believed in the concept of heaven and hell.

"So what did she just say?" he asked his brother.

"She said she can multitask."

On the other hand, he was certain that neither he nor Matt

were drunk at the moment. Yet they were hearing the same things. Unless he and his brother were engaging in some sort of Vulcan mind meld or telepathic communication.

Because that's only slightly less unbelievable.

"Huh. She *was* pretty good at multitasking, wasn't she?" Oliver allowed. Matt jabbed him in the ribs again. "But if you do that again, my fist is going to multitask on your face."

No fighting at your brother's wedding.

"Go ask your wife to dance," Matt said.

What Mattie said.

His brother snorted a laugh again.

"I think I will. But don't follow me."

"Wasn't planning to," Matt replied.

"Wasn't talking to you."

WHEN CHARLOTTE TREVOR got pulled onto the dance floor, Serena was left standing alone with a flute of champagne she was only pretending to drink. She searched the ballroom for Oliver. They hadn't spent much time together at the wedding so far. Since Oliver was part of the wedding party, he'd been seated at the head table for the meal. Mason and Cam got assigned to a special kids' table, which had left Serena sitting with Jackie's Ohio grandparents and two other couples she didn't know.

She spotted Oliver standing with Matt, the two of them apparently deep in conversation. Oliver was frowning. Not a good sign. *Now what? Where else was I spotted with Ben?* Oliver turned away from Matt, looked around, locked eyes with her, and began heading her way. She watched him warily and set the champagne flute down on the table next to her.

"Hey there." He leaned in and dropped a kiss on her lips. "Watching the boys?"

She nodded, though she hadn't been. She lifted Cam's shoes up for him to see. "I'm the keeper of the shoes."

They watched the boys dancing for several minutes before Oliver spoke again.

"Do you remember when we talked about hearing exactly what my mom would say? In our heads?"

The question caught her off guard. "Um … well … kind of? I mean, I can often imagine what she would say in a given situation."

"Jack and Matt think she's, like, haunting us."

"Hmm. Well, it does sound like something she would do. She worried about how you guys were going to manage without her."

"You remember that?"

Serena nodded, thoughtfully. "Although I think she was most worried about your dad."

Oliver gazed out over the ballroom, searching for his father. Serena followed his gaze.

"There he is," she said, nodding toward the dance floor. "On the other side from the boys."

Tim Wolfe was dancing with a tall, willowy blonde wearing glasses. The music was a dance-style pop song, and her father-in-law had a surprising sense of rhythm. Better than Oliver did.

"Oh shoot," he said and took a step toward the dance floor.

Serena grabbed his arm. "What are you doing?"

"Dad. He's dancing with some woman, and mom is here."

"What?"

Surely he didn't believe that Angie was really haunting them? But the expression on his face said that he most definitely did. She tugged him back. "How much have you had to drink?"

There was an open bar along the back of the room, and the waiters were rather liberally handing out flutes of champagne. She'd caught Mason angling for one, just in time. But Ollie was never much of a drinker. He'd seen the aftermath of drunk driving too many times.

"Nothing! I didn't even finish the champagne after the toast. But dad needs to know that she's—"

"Ollie. If your mom is haunting you and your brothers, she's probably haunting your dad, as well." Serena didn't really believe Angie was running around as a ghost. But if it prevented her husband from making an embarrassing scene at his brother's wedding, she'd say it. Not to mention, Oliver would regret the whole thing. He was not a scene-making kind of man. "Besides, he's just dancing with a guest. It's not like he brought a date," she added.

Oliver seemed to relax a little at that idea.

"But who *is* she?" he asked.

Serena shrugged. "I don't know. I don't recognize her." Which, of course, did not preclude her from being a lifelong resident of St. Caroline.

"Maybe she crashed the wedding."

"Ollie. When was the last time someone crashed a wedding in St. Caroline?"

"It could happen."

"And your mother haunting you could happen, too. But probably not."

"No, she really is—"

She took Oliver's hand firmly in hers. "Dance with me." She felt like she was with Mason and Cam, redirecting their attention from something she didn't want them to see.

Just as they stepped onto the parquet floor, the deejay cued up a slow song. *Perfect.* She slipped her arms around Oliver's waist. She would hold him in place, keep him from bothering his father. Oliver pulled her in close, even as she sensed his attention was still elsewhere. In any case, Tim Wolfe and the woman parted with the opening notes of the slower song. It looked like they thanked each other for the dance and went their separate ways. She felt the tension in Oliver's body lift.

Disaster averted. Inwardly Serena rolled her eyes, then let herself sink into the warmth of Oliver's arms. This was the closest, physically, they'd been to each other in weeks. Oliver was still working long hours … still avoiding her.

She took a quiet, calming breath and tried to focus on the pleasantness of being in her husband's strong arms, the comforting warmth of his hand against the small of her back, the scent of his cologne seeping through his white dress shirt.

"Who sings this song?" he asked.

She listened to a few more bars. The lyrics and the voice sounded vaguely familiar, but she couldn't place them. Most people had that problem with songs, though. For once not being able to remember something was not concerning.

"I don't know," she answered.

"Hmm. Maybe it'll come to me."

She didn't care whether she ever correctly identified this particular song. She could imagine that this situation would have bugged her to no end in the past. But now? It seemed trivial. No, it *was* trivial. Absolutely trivial. Unless she went on a game show someday, identifying the singer of this song was of no importance to her life.

What did concern her though—and seemed rather nontrivial, actually—was the idea that Oliver believed his mother was a ghost. She "got" the appeal of believing something like that, especially in the lead up to a wedding. It was too awful to contemplate all the things Angie was going to miss. Not just weddings, but grandchildren, graduations, family holidays. Quilts she never got to make.

The song was winding down. The singer—whoever he was—was ooh-ooh-oohing his way toward the end.

If it were Cam or Mason who believed their nana was speaking to them, Serena wouldn't be bothered. But for Ollie, it was just another way to pretend that his mother wasn't gone. Another way to avoid dealing with his feelings. She even wondered whether his fixation with Ben Wardman was just another way of avoiding his grief.

Yup.

And if Angie really was haunting her sons, surely she would have pointed this out to Oliver by now.

CHAPTER 32

The Monday after the wedding dawned grey and gloomy. Raindrops bounced like jumping beans off the hood of Oliver's SUV as he drove into work. He rolled down the window a tiny crack so he could hear the thunder rolling in. Every few minutes, the dark sky lit up with a slash of lightning.

He hoped Mattie hadn't told anyone at the station about the whole thing with their mother at the wedding. He could just hear Matt now. "Guys, you are not going to believe this. I had Oliver believing our mother talks to us from the Great Beyond!"

His brother got him good—Oliver had to give him props for that. Leave it to Matt to learn how to throw his voice.

You give your brother way too much credit.

People didn't give Matt enough credit sometimes. He was street smart. Wily. If anyone in St. Caroline was going to pick up some ventriloquism tricks, it would be Matt.

He pulled his car into the station's parking lot. His dad's car was already parked in the reserved spot for the fire chief. As the deputy chief, Oliver did not merit a special spot. *But hey ... at the new station?* He'd add that to his wish list for Finn Brody. With a sign and everything. *Reserved for O. Wolfe.*

Inside, he flipped on the overhead fluorescent light in his shoebox of an office. Without a window, the room never looked entirely lit up. That was another thing for his wish list. A bigger office. And a window.

Was that it? Had his station in life just not risen enough for Serena? He was the deputy fire chief, for pete's sake—didn't that compare favorably with being a high school science teacher? It had, in fact, involved quite a bit of training—and ongoing training. He had to get recertified as a paramedic every two years.

Yeah, he knew some people thought he had this job thanks to nepotism. But anyone who knew Tim Wolfe knew that wasn't the case. If anything, Oliver had to be better than any other candidate because his father expected more of him. More from Jack and Matt, too.

Serena knew how much training he did, how skilled he was, how hard he worked. The hours he put in at the gym after his shifts were over. She knew all that. But did she remember it? Was he going to have to prove himself to her all over again?

Maybe?

Well, he would. He would get the new fire station built, staff it, and run it just as well as his father ran this one. He would lower response times and get the summer residents—and the state government—off the town's case. Twenty years from now, the new fire station would still be around, proof of Oliver's industriousness. Twenty years from now, who would still remember a high school science teacher who had lived here all of five years?

He sat down at his desk and pulled out a legal pad to continue sketching out floor plan ideas. Yeah yeah, that was Finn Brody's job but Oliver had always found that he thought better with a pencil in his hand. Like his body had to be moving in order for his brain to work. Plus, he hated waiting around for other people to do their jobs.

He carried the legal pad upstairs to the second floor and the community room, where Cam's birthday party was held. His father had suggested not having a community room in the new station.

"Does the town really need more than one?" Tim Wolfe had asked.

Oliver looked around the current one. The town needed a nicer one. This room had undergone no renovation or redecoration since the fifties, except for the yearly addition of Firefighter of the Year plaques. Otherwise, the original linoleum flooring and faux wood paneling was still here. The ceiling consisted of weird textured tiles that Oliver assumed had been bright white at some point, and not their current dingy color.

It just wasn't a friendly place—okay for kids' parties and Halloween, but really no one else rented the room much anymore. If the new station had a nicer space, it could be used for family reunions or meetings. Maybe even wedding receptions. The town did need rental space for those kinds of events—rental space that was cheaper than the Chesapeake Inn and larger than a restaurant's private dining room.

The way Oliver saw it, it was part of the fire department's community service mission. He jotted down some notes. A nicer room would probably pay for itself in a few years' time. But it definitely needed to be further away from the main bay. He sniffed the air. Even with the door closed, the smell of motor oil from the trucks and the unmistakable odor of sweaty men managed to make its way up the stairwell.

His thoughts of hardwood flooring and recessed lighting were interrupted by a sudden commotion downstairs. A call was coming in. There was no flashing light stack on the wall in the community room, but Oliver knew the sounds. Boots hitting the floor. Metal locker doors clanging open. The whine of the bay doors lifting. It was a well-rehearsed dance. By the time the dispatcher's voice came on over the P.A. system, he'd already tossed his legal pad onto a table and pulled out his phone to check the app the fire department used to communicate the location of emergency calls.

His heart stopped.

It was the elementary school.

He sprinted for the stairs.

~

WHEN HE PULLED the fire engine into the circular driveway of the school, the storm was still going strong. The rain was coming down faster than the storm sewers could drain it, and the single file line of kids splashed through puddles on the wide sidewalk. Oliver forced himself not to look for Mason and Cam as he pushed open the truck's door and jumped out. His kids weren't any more important than anyone else's.

In the distance, a crack of lightning lit up the dark sky. This was not a good situation. Fire inside, lightning outside. He looked across the parking lot and spotted the yellow school buses lined up at the far end. He waved at a custodian who was directing the kids.

"Get the kids onto those buses!" he yelled and pointed toward the parking lot. The custodian nodded in understanding, then Oliver pulled his mask and helmet down over his head and face, and sprinted toward the school. His partner, Heath, ran next to him. He spotted Jack ahead of him, disappearing into the building. Matt wasn't on shift, but was on the way in. Even a small school like St. Caroline's elementary school was still a large building, and had to be cleared quickly.

Inside, Oliver and Heath headed down the hall on the right. The heat-activated sprinklers weren't going off on this side of the school yet—a good sign. Up ahead a small figure ran toward them. A kid separated from their class? Oliver picked up his pace. As he got closer, though, he saw it wasn't a child. It was Serena.

What the hell? His entire family was here? *Stay calm.* He slowed to a stop when he reached her and waved Heath on.

"I'll catch up in a sec." He turned back to Serena. "What are you doing here?"

"Today was one of my volunteer days."

"I get that. But why aren't you outside?"

"Cammy went to the bathroom. He wasn't back when the fire alarm went off. I told his teacher I would go get him."

"We'll find Cam. You get outside."

"I can help!"

He grabbed her shoulder to stop her stride and spun her around to face him. "No. Get outside now. Now!"

He saw the flash of fear in her eyes. Probably he had grabbed her shoulder a little harder than he intended. But this was important! *Stay calm.*

"Serena, I don't have time for this right now. I need you to exit the building. We will find Cam."

He was on the verge of giving her a little shove in the direction of the front door, when she turned and began walking quickly—but not running—away. He took a deep breath. *This is not the time to assert your independence, Serena.* He wanted to pick her up and bodily remove her from the building. *But my wife is no more important than any other person in this building.*

He rounded the slight corner into the second and third grade hallway and caught up with his partner. *Damn it.* He forgot to tell Serena to get in her car when she got outside, to protect herself from the lightning. He hoped she'd figure it out.

He began searching the second grade classrooms. There was no time to wonder which room Mason was assigned to. Jack's team was looking for the fire and the source. It was eleven o'clock. Normally, he'd guess a kitchen fire but who knew where the lightning had struck? According to dispatch, the principal hadn't exactly been calm. People generally weren't with lightning strikes.

He checked under desks, beneath the teacher's desk, behind the bookshelf that defined a quiet reading area. Each room looked like Pompeii—everything left right where it was. Jackets on hooks. Worksheets on desks. Other papers scattered on the floor.

But no Cam. His son knew what to do in the event of a fire, though. He was probably outside with the other kids. Serena just didn't realize it.

The sky outside lit up with another streak of lightning. He hoped the kids were all on the buses by now.

"Has the fire been located?" he barked into his voice port. "Has the gym been cleared?"

Back out in the hall, Heath gave him a thumbs up for the third grade classrooms.

"Classrooms on alpha delta all clear," Oliver relayed to the rest of the team.

Another voice came back. "Gym and office all clear."

There was a set of restrooms up ahead. He'd gone to this school as a child. He knew it inside and out, even without the training the department did here every summer. He had yet to see any smoke. A good sign, but the building was one story, flat and sprawling. Smoke in one wing of the building might not be noticeable in another. He sent Heath ahead to start on the back hallway, where the kindergarten and first grade classrooms were.

He pushed open the door to the girls' bathroom.

"Anyone in here?"

He opened every stall. Empty. Relief flooded his veins and he bolted from the room and into the boys' restroom next door.

"Anyone in here?

He pushed open the first stall door. Empty. Second and third, empty too. When he pushed on the wider handicapped door, he found it locked. A frightened squeak sounded from inside. He got down on his hands and knees, and poked his head beneath the door. Cam was huddled on top of the toilet, his face white, cheeks streaked with tears.

Serena was right.

"Cammy! It's dad! Come here!" He lifted his mask. "It's daddy, see? Come on, bud, we gotta get you out of here." *Please don't be too scared to move.*

Oliver started to shove his body beneath the door when Cam jumped off the toilet and fell onto Oliver's outstretched arms.

"Atta boy!" He pulled Cam under the door, picked him up and ran into the hall. "Alpha delta bathrooms cleared! Evacuating one child."

Oliver ran him outside, where it was still raining cats and dogs. He wanted to ask Cam why he was hiding in the bathroom, when he—of all kids—should know what to do in a fire. But there was no time for that now. He handed off Cam to a custodian whose clothing was soaked clean through. Cam would be in a similar state by the time they reached the buses.

Oliver headed back into the school. "Where's the fire?" he radioed as he ran to find Heath.

Jack's voice sounded in his helmet. "Source found. Kitchen."

"Kitchen?"

"Yeah, there was a lightning strike too, but the lightning protection system worked. Just a coincidence that the kitchen fire happened at the same time."

"Is the fire out?" Oliver found Heath waiting at the end of the kindergarten-first grade hallway.

"Just about."

Other voices cut in with rooms and building areas that were searched and cleared. Apparently, Oliver's son was the only child who hadn't made it outside with the rest of his classmates. Some remedial fire safety training might be in order after dinner that night.

Or you could maybe wait until he's less traumatized.

Dad wouldn't have.

Oliver's eyes darted around the hall. He was hearing the voice again, but Matt was nowhere to be seen.

Occam's Razor? The simplest explanation is usually the correct one?

Yeah, the simplest explanation was that his brother was pulling his leg and now the power of suggestion had kicked in.

CHAPTER 33

"Wait—what?" Mason's head snapped up so fast he nearly toppled off the dining room chair.

Serena returned her phone to the kitchen. When she came back, she repeated what she had just said a minute earlier. "That was a message from the superintendent. The elementary school is going to be closed for the rest of the week." She wasn't surprised by the superintendent's decision. If anything, she was surprised that it took five hours for them to make it.

"Yes!" Mason was up and out of the chair now, fist-pumping the air.

"Why?" Cam's voice was plaintive.

"Well buddy, they've got to clean up the kitchen. And they want to inspect the building just to make extra sure that it's safe," Oliver explained.

"That loud noise?" Mason added. "That was the school getting struck by lightning. It was so cool."

From the expression on Cam's face, Serena could tell he did not share his brother's opinion. Poor Cam had failed some sort of Wolfe family manhood test—panicking in a fire.

"The whole place was buzzing!" Mason continued.

Mason, on the other hand, loved anything that caught on fire, exploded, or just plain self-destructed.

"Yeah well, the school has a lightning protection system," Oliver said "But they want to test all the electrical and mechanical systems before they open the school again."

"So no school tomorrow?" Cam asked, clearly still disappointed.

"I thought you'd be happy about that news," Oliver said, catching Serena's eye.

"Cammy has a girlfriend," Mason supplied.

"Do not!"

"We'll find something fun to do tomorrow. I promise." There was already an idea taking shape in her head. "If everyone's done with dinner, let's get the table cleared. You guys can go upstairs and read for a little while before bath time. I need to talk to your dad."

When the boys were safely out of earshot in their bedroom, Serena turned to Oliver as he loaded the dishwasher in the kitchen.

"I'm thinking of taking the boys to New York this week." She leaned against the countertop for moral support.

"New York?"

She nodded.

"Why?"

"Why not? They have the rest of the week off. I can take the boys to the natural history museum."

Oliver closed the dishwasher. For a moment, he looked like he was about to speak. She waited, but instead he pressed his lips shut.

"Cam is pretty upset about what happened today," she said.

"Obviously."

She could tell that "obviously" Oliver was upset, too.

"I'm sorry about not evacuating the school right away."

She wasn't, actually. Not really. What mother would leave a

burning building with one of her kids unaccounted for inside? There were rules, and Oliver was a stickler for the rules. She got that. In his line of work, you had to be a stickler.

But she was a mother, not a firefighter. And being the wife of a firefighter took a back seat to her responsibilities as a mother. It just did.

Oliver shrugged off her apology. In any case, the fire turned out to be contained to the kitchen.

"I think Cam could use a few days away," she added.

Oliver pushed himself away from the dishwasher. "Or is it that you need a few days away?"

She gathered her thoughts. Oliver's pushback didn't surprise her. "I think you need a few days away from me," she said finally. "I love you, Ollie. But you're holding something against me that I don't remember doing. And can't imagine doing. To you or to Ashley."

She waited for him to say something. When he didn't, she went on. *Might as well speak my piece all at once.*

"If you have concrete evidence, now would be a good time to produce it. Otherwise, I don't know what to say to you anymore."

"Where there's smoke, there's usually fire."

"I'm not a firefighter so I don't see things that way. Tomorrow morning, I'm taking the boys to New York for a few days. You're welcome to join us."

"I have to work this week. You know that."

"Then the boys and I will be back this weekend."

"I thought we had talked about maybe doing this over the summer."

"We can go twice. It's not possible to see all of New York in one trip." She should probably end this conversation now. But in for a dime, in for a dollar and all that. "I'd like to show the boys where I grew up."

"Are you driving?"

"I thought I'd drive to Union Station in DC and then we'd take the train up. The boys would love riding the train."

His eyes caught hers and then he looked beyond her, at some non-specific point over her left shoulder. This was a special talent of Oliver's—being able to just stand there and say next to nothing. It drove her nuts. *It's always driven me nuts.* Yes, she remembered *that* with absolute certainty.

"Fine," he said. "I'm sure the boys will have a good time."

"You know what, Ollie?" There were more pieces to the piece she wanted to speak. They were here. Might as well get it all out on the table. "I think you could use a week alone, too. Take some time to think."

"Think about what?"

"Your mom." She caught the sudden flash of wariness in his eyes, but it disappeared behind his poker face just as quickly.

"I think about her all the time."

She took a deep breath. This also drove her nuts, this tendency for arguments with Oliver to go round and round. "I misspoke. You don't need to *think.* You need to let yourself *feel,* Ollie. I know you had a lot on your plate last fall, but—"

"Understatement of the century?"

She inhaled, then let it back out. "Whatever." She couldn't force Oliver to think about his feelings, to be a little less "Oliver."

"I'm taking the boys to the city for the week. We'll be home next weekend. If you need someone to talk to, Dr. Trevor has the name of a psychologist you can call."

"Great! You're talking about me to other people?"

"Dr. Trevor broached the subject when Cam was in for his appointment. I'm not the only person to notice that you're struggling."

"I'm not *struggling.*"

His voice rose on that last word. She lifted her eyes to the ceiling, where the sound of the boys playing was growing louder. Apparently, they were finished reading.

Oliver lowered his voice. "You don't know what it's like to lose a parent." He backtracked when he saw the look on her face. "Not lose one permanently. I mean, here you are, going to visit your parents tomorrow."

"You're right, Ollie. I don't know what that's like. I don't even know what it's like to lose a *friend*. I woke up one day and discovered that your mom was gone. I didn't get a chance to say goodbye or go to her funeral."

She bit back tears. She hadn't gotten to say goodbye to Ben, either. That felt like a loss, like more of a loss than it should, and doubt reared its ugly head again.

"Maybe *you* need to spend a week feeling, too." Oliver brushed past her on his way to the stairs.

AS THE TRAIN sped through the cities along the eastern seaboard —Washington, Baltimore, Philadelphia—Mason and Cam were equal parts pumped and awed. Every other minute, some new scenery lit them up. Bridges! Skylines! A dark tunnel as they entered a new station!

The boys had seen precious little of the world outside St. Caroline. Their trip to the museum in Virginia. Summer visits to Ocean City, Maryland. She knew they'd been there because there were photographs scattered around the house. But where else might they have been? *Probably nowhere.*

Their suitcases were stacked on the metal rack overhead. Just packing had sent them over the moon. You'd think they were actually *going* to the moon. And then the thing that had really galled their father: they were excited by the prospect of seeing their grandparents again.

Her boys were going to be innocents like her husband. Once upon a time, that quality had charmed her about Oliver. That mix of strength and guilelessness. The fact that he was so firmly rooted in one place. But rooted could also mean "stuck." And Oliver certainly seemed stuck in his way of thinking these days.

She looked out the window blankly, not seeing the exciting things her sons were seeing. She was replaying the argument she and Oliver had, lying in bed the night before.

"You're leaving me, aren't you?" His words had hung there in the dark for long seconds. "You're taking the boys and not coming back."

The words dropped and crushed her. She was speechless. Not that it hadn't occurred to her that this was where their marriage might be heading. A separation. But she'd worried it would be Oliver leaving her.

"Your silence answers my question."

She had rolled to face him but he stubbornly remained on his back, staring up at the ceiling. Angie's wedding quilt covered his chest.

"I'm not leaving you. Unless you want me to leave."

"That's why your parents were here last month. To talk you into leaving me. Is that what you had to give up to get your trust fund back? Me?"

"What? I don't even know yet whether my father is going to do that. My mother said she'd talk to him, that's all."

She had ached to roll closer to him, to wrap her arms around his body the way she had done hundreds—maybe thousands—of times before. So many times, even a person without a head injury wouldn't remember them all. But her body remembered. Oliver's body was one that pulled people from fires, rescued cats from trees, taught kids how to stop-drop-and-roll. But it was a body that seemed unable to save their relationship now.

"The only reason I'm taking the boys to New York is because they have the rest of the week off from school." She rolled onto her back again. "I wish I knew what I need to say to convince you that I didn't have an affair."

"And I wish I could get past the fact that your first memory after four months of being in a coma was of another man."

"That's it? That's why you think I cheated on you?"

"That, combined with the other things. You meeting him for coffee. Shadowing him at the high school. Him arranging for you to receive mail after he was gone. That's not *normal*, Serena."

Tears stung her eyes, and she closed them for a moment. She was determined not to cry. She was not going to bring tears into the equation. When she felt sufficiently under control, she spoke again.

"I'm sorry, Ollie. I don't know why I remembered Ben Wardman first. I don't have an answer for that." She pushed herself up onto her elbow. She wanted to look at him when she said this. She reached her fingers toward him.

"Don't touch me."

She pulled her hand back, as if she'd been burned. Maybe going to New York wasn't just for the boys. She needed a break from this, from Oliver's mood swings. Some days, everything seemed fine. Then the next, he acted like he couldn't stand to be around her. She'd thought the wedding was a turning point, that he was just stressed over the prospect of an important family event happening without his mother there to witness it. They had slow danced together, made love that night after the boys finally came down from their excitement and fell asleep.

She thought wrong, though. If anything, Ollie was even moodier since Jack and Becca's wedding. She inched closer to him. She wouldn't touch him if he didn't want to be touched, but he was going to hear her out.

"But you want to know why *you* weren't my first memory?" She paused, and waited. After a moment, his eyes darted over to her. She locked her gaze hard onto his. "Because I never forgot you, Ollie. I forgot Ben. I forgot Ashley. Hell, I even forgot my own kids." She took a deep breath, even more determined not to cry in front of him. "But I never forgot you. *You* were the first thing I thought of when I woke up."

"Wish I could believe that."

She sat bolt upright. "I wish you could believe it, too! I wish you'd believe me for once—your *wife*—instead of everyone else!"

She stood and yanked the wedding quilt off the bed. Oliver yanked back for a second, then let go. She dragged it down the stairs and spent the night on the basement sofa.

Oliver had sullenly waved them off that morning. In retrospect, it wasn't even much of an argument. Oliver had his position and he wasn't budging. Last night was the first time that the idea of anyone leaving had been broached, and it stung. She loved Oliver. She could remember that love. There was plenty she still couldn't recall, but she could remember how much she loved Oliver Wolfe. Her husband. Father of her sons. Lover. It was like muscle memory. She didn't have to think about that love. It was just there.

But she wasn't sure Oliver's muscles were still feeling it.

She leaned her forehead against the coolness of the window. Maybe he was right. Oliver usually was. He was a smart guy. Quiet, but he noticed everything. He picked up on things other people would never notice. Maybe she did have an affair. All these years, she had worried about becoming her mother. But maybe she had become her father, instead. She had to be honest —she wasn't happy with the way her life was right now. That's why she wanted to go back to school and get a teaching certification.

"And what if there are no openings in St. Caroline? What then?" Oliver had pointed out last week.

"Eventually there will be some openings."

"And what if they fill those openings with someone else?"

What then? That was a valid question. What if she invested the time and spent the money—which was no small amount— and then couldn't get a job?

If only Angie were still here. She could talk this out with her. She was headed to her hometown, but her own mother would be of no use on something like this.

She shook her head. And Ollie thought his mother was talking to him. *At least I got an actual letter from beyond the grave. That wasn't my imagination.*

What would Angie say in this situation? Probably that there was no knowing the future. Or something like that. It struck Serena as so obviously, sadly, true. She had no idea whether she'd land a teaching job someday. She just had to trust in herself and put herself in a position where it was possible.

She looked across at Mason and Cam, their hands pressed up against the window, intent on not missing a single thing flying by at sixty miles an hour. The pain in her heart was sharp and severe. Would their parents still be married a year from now? She wanted to trust in love, trust the vows they had made to each other. But it was getting harder and harder to muster. She trusted herself that she did not cheat on her husband—she just didn't have any way of knowing whether or not that was *true*.

The landscape outside the train disappeared suddenly as they entered another tunnel. The boys peeled off the window and looked across at her with slightly crazed eyes.

"Having fun yet?" she joked.

Before they could answer, a voice sounded overhead. "Penn Station. Now arriving at Penn Station."

"We're here."

"In New York? Already?" Mason looked skeptical.

She laughed. "Already? We've been on the train for hours."

CHAPTER 34

*T*he cab ride from the train station to the Upper East Side illustrated the difference between her two sons perfectly. Mason had his nose practically pressed to the cab's window, straining to look up at block after block of skyscrapers. Cam, on the other hand, was white-knuckling it as the cab swerved in and out of traffic, hitting the brakes, then accelerating between stoplights. Serena put her arm around her younger son's shoulders, hoping her touch would relax his tense muscles.

It didn't seem to help, but soon enough the cab pulled up to her parents' building. She paid the fare and managed to get both boys and their suitcases onto the sidewalk without incident.

"Well, guys, this is where I grew up." The three of them looked up at the stately limestone mansion, the brass trim on the double front doors gleaming in the mid-afternoon sun. Her parents' home looked both utterly familiar and utterly strange at the same time. After not seeing it for years, the building looked over the top to her—the ornately carved stone above the door that echoed the brass trim, the huge patinaed lamps, the five stories of grey limestone stretching up toward the sky.

Five stories. What did we do with all that space? She knew the answer to that, sadly. *We did nothing with most of it.* The formal rooms got used when her parents entertained. She and her brother rarely went into those rooms.

"Mom, this isn't a *house*." Cam said.

"Well ..." She searched her brain for the right way to explain things. *I should have maybe prepared them more for this.* "It's not like a house you'd see in St. Caroline."

"Where's the yard?" Mason wrinkled his nose, and tried to peer through the narrow space separating her parents' home from its neighbors.

"Well, it doesn't have a *yard,* exactly. There's a courtyard in the back."

"With a playset?"

"I don't think so, sweetie," she answered Cam's question. "But there are lots of other fun things to do in New York." She texted her mother to let her know they were outside, then hoisted one of the suitcases up the four wide steps to the door. Just as she was about to go back to the sidewalk for the other suitcase, the doors opened.

"Miss Serena!"

She looked up to see Mr. Delacroix, the Irving family's long-time butler, standing in the doorway.

"Let me," he said.

He hurried past her and the open-mouthed boys to retrieve the second suitcase. Then he picked up the first one and carried them both inside.

"Mason! Cam!"

Her mother appeared in the doorway. She was impeccably dressed, as usual. Cream-colored slacks, brown suede boots in a low heel, and a silk blouse in a pale shade of tan or grey or blue. It was a completely impractical outfit for most people. But then, Georgia Irving was not "most people."

"How was the train?" she asked the boys, taking their hands to lead them inside. Cam looked back at Serena, the expression on his face saying that he still wasn't a hundred percent certain this was a real house.

Just wait until they see—

"Whoa."

The boys stopped cold in the foyer, their brains unable to process everything they were seeing. Just as Serena expected. The intricately tiled floor. The giant fireplace along one wall, with its elaborate marble mantel. The wide, sweeping staircase, also marble, that gently curved up to the second floor. In the corner stood a round table topped with a giant arrangement of fresh flowers. Even in the dead of winter, there were always fresh flowers there.

Mason turned back to look at his mother, in curiosity and wonderment. "You grew up here?"

She nodded. Well, here and at boarding school. But that was a concept to explain another time. She had the feeling that Cam would be quite alarmed at the news that some kids go away to attend school. She and the boys followed her mother up the staircase to the large kitchen and casual dining room.

"Anyone hungry?" her mother asked.

Serena knew the boys were. They had wolfed down the snacks she packed for the train ride. She led them over to the table, set with platters of chicken fingers, french fries, and crudités. Bowls filled with dipping sauces were artfully arranged between the platters.

"Thank you," she mouthed to her mother as the boys seated themselves. Serena was pretty certain that chicken fingers had never darkened the doorway of this house until today. The boys watched, befuddled, as the housekeeper brought out glasses of lemonade for everyone. Serena could almost see the gears turning in their heads. *Who is that?* She dipped a chicken finger into the bowl of barbeque sauce and popped it into her mouth. There was so much she would have to explain to the boys later.

"These are good, mom." She dipped another one into honey mustard dipping sauce. She waved at the boys to follow suit.

"They're delicious," Mason added.

Serena smiled. The boys seemed to intuitively understand that a house like this required their best behavior. She scanned the kitchen.

"Are those new cabinets?"

Her mother's face lit up. "Yes! They are. Aren't they lovely?"

"Gorgeous." Truth be told, they looked as lovely as the old cabinets. Her mother had traded in white cabinets for a soft grey, but otherwise the styling and hardware looked the same.

Georgia sat down across from the boys. "For dinner, we're going to the Chinese restaurant that was your mom's favorite restaurant when she was a little girl."

"That's still around?"

"It is. Same ownership, even. Your father made reservations this morning."

Color me impressed. Her *father* made the reservations. Maybe her mother was right—a brush with mortality can change a person's outlook on life.

"We haven't had Chinese food in a long time," Mason offered solemnly.

"Oh? Why not?" Georgia inquired.

"The Chinese restaurant at home closed."

"It did?" Serena asked. She couldn't recall there ever being a Chinese restaurant in St. Caroline. "When?"

"Last summ—" Cam started to answer, then—realizing that his mouth was full—stopped.

"Last summer?" Serena finished his statement.

"Right after your accident, mom," Mason explained.

"Ahh. Well then, this will be a treat for all of us." The idea of Chinese food hadn't crossed her mind in—well, she couldn't remember how long, obviously—but now a craving was starting to build.

"But before then," Georgia said. "I have another treat for you."

Uh oh. Serena was beginning to worry that the boys were going to get used to all-you-can-eat ice cream and other sweets. Oliver would not be happy about that. On the other hand ... *Oliver's not here.*

"We have a pool now."

"You do? Since when? On the roof?"

Georgia shook her head. "In the basement. The doctor told your father he needed to get more exercise and at his age, swimming is easier on the joints."

"Oh. That must have been quite the renovation project."

Georgia smiled wryly. "It was a bit of a disruption for awhile there. But it's all ready now. Do you boys like to swim?"

Serena watched with dismay as their faces lit up. "Um, I didn't bring swimsuits." It was early May—she wasn't thinking about swimming yet.

"No problem. I had some sent over from Bloomies."

"There's a pool here in the *house?*" Mason's voice was drenched in amazement.

"*Is* this a house?" Cam was evidently still not convinced.

Her mother's laugh burst forth like she was ... *happy.* Serena tried to remember how often she had ever seen her mother truly happy. *Not often enough.* Mason and Cam had the magic touch.

When the boys finished their chicken and fries, Serena took them up to her brother's old bedroom to change into the swimsuits. In the elevator, the boys' conversation ping-ponged between just the mere fact of an elevator in a *house* and the sheer awesomeness of a pool in the basement.

"How many people will be at the pool?" Cam asked, pulling his sweater over his head and tossing it onto the bed.

"Well, you and Mason. Me."

"That's it?" Cam looked dubiously at the swim trunks the personal shopper had chosen. They sported skinny orange and blue stripes. Mason's were purple and green.

"The pool belongs to Grandma and Grandpa Irving," Mason explained.

"Grandma will be there, if she decides to get in," she added.

Personally, Serena couldn't imagine her mother in a pool. But sure enough, when she pushed open the door to the steamy, chlorine-scented pool room, there was her mother in a black one-piece, bobbing in the water.

"You're not getting in?" Her mother frowned at the jeans and sweater she was still wearing.

Serena shook her head. "The boys can swim. Don't worry. They're country kids."

As the boys talked their grandmother into a rousing game of Marco Polo, she surveyed the pool room. Chaise longues were lined up precisely along one side of the pool, a thick navy blue towel folded and placed at the foot of each chair. There was a 99.9 percent chance that the towels were monogrammed. Halfway down the length of the side wall stood a bottled water dispenser on spindly legs.

"Mom! Mom!"

Mason was waving at her.

"Can you toss us some pool noodles?"

She was about to reply that there probably weren't any pool noodles here when she spotted a large teak box at the far end of the room. Of course, her parents would have had their interior designer fully outfit the pool. She pulled three spongy noodles from the box and dropped them into the water. Then she took a seat on one of the chaise longues and held up her phone, recording ten seconds of the boys and her mother playing in the pool.

She texted it to Oliver. Without waiting for an acknowledgement or a reply, she laid the phone on the folded towel and stood up. She waved to her mother and the boys.

"I changed my mind. I'm getting in, after all."

OLIVER'S PHONE vibrated with a text. He pushed his scribbled drawings of the new station aside and tapped his phone. Serena. Finally. He'd been waiting all day for confirmation that she and the boys made it to New York okay.

The text was a video. He tapped it, then frowned as he watched the clip of Mason and Cam in a swimming pool with Georgia Irving. He texted back: *Where are you? YMCA?*

It was another five minutes before he got a response. *Lol. My parents have a pool in the basement now.* The next text came through quicker. *Boys are having fun. I'm about to jump in.*

He leaned back in his chair. *Great.* He was worried about the wrong thing, apparently. Serena not wanting to come back? The *boys* might not want to come back. St. Caroline could hardly compete with Manhattan, especially when their grandparents were richer than sin. His mom used to say that all the time.

I never even met the Irvings. But they can't be all bad, if they produced Serena.

Yeah well, if anyone was richer than sin it would be his in-laws, who were plotting to take his children away from him. He was certain of it. He spent the rest of the afternoon vacillating between anguish and an anger so fierce his legs were shaking beneath the cover of his desk.

"Hey." Matt stuck his head into Oliver's office. "Your shift's over."

Oliver looked up from the paperwork he was supposed to be filling out. "Yeah. Thanks." He shut down his computer, filed the paperwork away, and locked the filing cabinet.

On the drive home, he did not think about New York or the Irvings. He forced his mind to think of absolutely nothing … right up to the moment he drove into his garage. No, make that drove into his garage *door.*

"What the—!" He slammed on his brakes, his brain snapping

out of its thinking-about-nothing mode. Fortunately, he was going slow at that point, but …???

What the hell.

How did he just drive into a closed garage door? He looked around to see whether any neighbors were out to witness it. Blessedly, the street was empty. He put the car into reverse and backed it away from the garage door. He got out to inspect the damage.

Yeah, it was dented alright. But not enough to prevent it from working. He sighed, running his hand through his hair. *How did I just run into it?* There was a garage door opener clipped to the sun visor. Why didn't he push that button like he always did? For that matter, why didn't he notice that the garage door was closed? *I was looking right at it.*

He trudged back to the car and was about to push the button on the garage door opener when he changed his mind. Instead he put the car in reverse and slowly—carefully this time!—backed down the driveway.

$\mathcal{S}$erena sat at the long marble-topped breakfast bar in the kitchen while her mother expertly pulled two espressos from an espresso machine that would be right at home in most coffee shops. The boys were chilling with a movie and popcorn in the home theater. If you lived here, there was almost no reason to ever leave the place, she thought, as her mother frothed milk for their lattes.

I did live here. Well, part of the time. Thinking back, her boarding school in Connecticut had felt more like home than here. And now that she'd been away for years—living the way normal people do—her parents' home seemed almost unbelievable. Who needed a kitchen this large? Or a grand marble foyer? Or a shower big enough to accommodate six people? Even so, there were plenty of homes in the city that were more over the top than this one.

She shook her head gently. *It's a wonder I turned out okay.* Her mother slipped a foamy latte in front of her. *Or maybe I didn't?* A tiny sigh escaped her chest, but not tiny enough to avoid notice.

"What's the matter?" Her mother sat down next to her.

"Oh, nothing."

"Serena. Why do I get the sense that this visit involves you running away from something?"

"I just needed to get away for a few days." She took a tentative sip of her drink. "Recovering from the accident has been harder than I expected. And more exhausting, some days."

"Harder in what ways?"

"Just … I feel like I did that first year in St. Caroline. When I didn't know many people and Ollie and I were still getting to know each other. Only now everyone else knows me—and knows things about me that I can't remember. Or even think are true anymore."

Her mother sipped at her coffee, thoughtfully. "You remember your grandmother in Atlanta?"

Serena nodded. "Of course."

"Well, she was fond of saying, 'start where you are.'" She reached over and lightly touched Serena's forearm. "Dear, maybe you need to think less about remembering your old life and think about the life you have. Do you like it? Is it what you want? What you want *now*—not necessarily what you wanted before."

"But Oliver wants our old life. And I'm the one who's changed, not him."

"Oliver can't have your old life, sweetheart. Life threw the two of you a curveball. The question is whether you want the life you have today."

When did her mother get so wise? Or had Serena been so overly sure of herself when she was younger that she hadn't noticed? On the other hand …

"Is that what you and dad are doing? Starting where you are?" She held her breath. She had never, ever broached the topic of her parents' relationship with her mother.

Her mother was unfazed. "Yes, we are. His heart attack last fall was a real wake-up call for him. He's stopped drinking. He's exercising the way he should have been before. He's eating better. We're seeing a marriage counselor."

"But after everything he did—"

Her mother shook her head. "All I have is this life today. I can leave and start over. Or I can stay with the new and improved version of your father. The past doesn't change with either option."

Serena had to admit—she liked this new and improved version of her mother. But she also worried that her mother was being more optimistic than the situation warranted.

"What if dad goes back to his old ways?"

"He's been put on notice that if he does, then I *will* leave."

Part of Serena hoped her mother would follow through on her declaration, if things got to that. Another part had grave doubts. She glanced at the giant clock on the wall. "We should get going soon if we're going to meet dad at the restaurant."

MASON LOOKED around the restaurant as they followed the hostess. He liked to know where the emergency exits were, as well as the location of any fire alarms. He spotted one on the wall just before the room narrowed into a back hallway. He hoped the kitchen was well equipped with fire extinguishers. If a building like this caught on fire? He couldn't imagine how the firefighters would attack it. There wasn't exactly a lot of room out on the street for the engines. And every building was right up against the one next door. How could they keep a fire from spreading?

He'd have to ask dad when they got home.

On the inside, though, the restaurant looked pretty much like the Chinese restaurant that had closed in St. Caroline. There were gold dragon statues on the bar. The walls were hung with giant paintings of the Great Wall of China.

The hostess seated them at a table smack in the middle of the room. He wondered whether it was because his new grandparents were rich. Or as Olivia J. in his class had said, "they're stinkin' rich." That's what her father told her.

He fiddled with the paper-wrapped chopsticks next to the placemats containing the Chinese horoscope animals. Mason was a rabbit. Cam was a snake, a fact his younger brother did not like to be reminded of. ("I'm not *afraid* of snakes! I just don't *like* them!") Then a waitress arrived with a stack of big fancy menus.

"I can't believe this place is still around," his mom said after the waitress took their drink orders (water for him and Cam).

But at least his mom remembered the place. Actually, she was remembering more things lately. Mason noticed that. Dad had told him and Cam not to make her feel bad by helping her too much. Mason mostly ignored that idea. A lot of what his mom forgot wasn't that important. Like what drawer something was in. Who cared about that stuff?

Besides Dad, obviously.

He opened his big fancy menu, turned to the page for main dishes, and ran his eyes down the long list. Yep. They had pretty much the same stuff as the Chinese restaurant at home. He liked to mix it up a little. Beef and snow peas one time, shrimp in garlic sauce another. Cam always ordered sweet and sour chicken. He leaned over to show his brother where that dish was on the menu. Cam was pretty smart, but he was still in kindergarten. He couldn't read restaurant menus yet.

Truth be told, Mason couldn't either. Not normally. But he knew Chinese dishes. The junk drawer in the kitchen had a couple of takeout menus in it. When his mom was in the hospital, lots of stuff got put in the junk drawer because he and Dad didn't know where it belonged.

No wonder she can't find things.

I know, right?

His eyes skimmed down the page of dishes again. "On-trays," his father always called them. He was getting a little worried. He wasn't seeing his mom's favorite dish. They had to have her favorite dish if this was her favorite restaurant, right? He turned the page and scanned the lines of tiny letters. He let out a little whoosh of breath. There it was—pineapple fried rice with a choice of chicken, shrimp or vegetables. She always got it with the shrimp.

Nana? Can you make sure she knows that's the one?

He was surprised to see his grandmother here in New York. His *other* grandmother, that is. He had assumed she couldn't leave St. Caroline. But "assume" makes an ass out of you and me. That's what Uncle Mattie always said.

Oh dear lord. I really fell down on the job with my middle child.

Mason held back a snort of laughter. He didn't want to let on that Nana was here. Most people couldn't see her. Cammy couldn't, and Mason didn't want to tell him. It would scare the bejeezus out of him. Even Mason couldn't see her all the time. Mostly just at night, when his mom turned the bedroom light out. It was right in that second before his eyes adjusted—he would see her leaning against the wall, blowing a kiss at him and Cam.

He could always hear her, though. She was around a lot.

Got nowhere else pressing to be.

Heaven?

Isn't that where the good people went when they died? Nana was a good person.

Haven't run across that place yet.

The waitress was back, interrupting their silent conversation. His new grandmother ordered wonton soup and a salad. Grandfather Irving looked at his mom. *Nana! Make sure she knows.*

One of those things that's not important, sweetie.

Mason held his breath anyway. Your favorite Chinese food was kind of important. Because what if you ordered something you didn't like?

"I'd like the pineapple fried rice, please." His mother closed her menu and Mason quietly let his lungs empty. "With chicken," she added.

Chicken! It was the shrimp she liked. He watched her to see if she would realize her mistake.

Shrimp, it's the chicken of the sea.

That's tuna, Nana.

You sure?

Google it.

He could swear he felt a soft squeeze on his shoulder just then. Sometimes he wanted to jump up and shout, "she's still here!" But he was old enough to know he'd probably get carted off to the funny farm if he did.

You're not old enough for the funny farm.

Next to him, Cam blurted out his order. "Sweet sour chicken. Please."

Mason ordered his beef and snow peas next, then his grandfather ordered last. The waitress finished writing on her little pad of paper and left.

"Who wants to go to the Empire State Building tomorrow?" Grandpa Irving asked.

"Me!" Cam bounced in his chair.

"Well, that's good because I got you guys tickets. Express Entry so you won't even have to wait in line."

That's good.

You've been there?

Your Grandpa Wolfe and I went years ago. Stood in line for hours.

Are you going with us tomorrow?

No, I need to go check on your dad.

Okay.

He doubted his dad wanted to be checked on. Lately it seemed like he mostly just wanted to be left alone. Mason, on the other hand, liked that his nana checked in on him. She refused to help him with his homework (Uncle Mattie said it couldn't hurt to ask), but it helped just that she was around.

"Mason, what do you think about that?"

He heard his mother's voice and became aware that everyone at the table was looking directly at him.

"Umm …"

His mom's forehead creased into little lines. "Pay attention, sweetie. Your grandfather was telling us what to look for in the natural history museum tomorrow."

"Sorry. I was thinking about Dad." That was mostly true, right? They couldn't be mad at him for thinking about Dad.

"We'll see Dad in a few days, okay?"

He felt a ticklish sensation on his cheek. *Have fun tomorrow. Keep an eye on your brother.*

Will do, Nana.

CHAPTER 36

Oliver parked his SUV in the main parking lot at the cemetery. It was possible to park closer to the gravestones, but he needed a chance to walk and think. To clear his mind. He had just driven his car straight into a garage door. *How the hell does anyone do that?* He hadn't fallen asleep. He was 99.99 percent certain of that—he very clearly remembered making the final turn onto his street and thinking that Mrs. Macintyre's azaleas were huge this year.

But then the next thing he knew, the white garage door was right in front of the hood and he was slamming on the brakes. Just in time, too. Another second and he would have made more than just a dent.

He got out and took a deep breath of early evening air. He liked that about St. Caroline. The breezes off the bay kept the air clean. He couldn't understand how people lived in DC or Baltimore or … New York. That smell of car exhaust, especially in the summer when the heat baked everything into your skin … if he had to move to New York to be near the boys, he didn't know what he would do.

"I would hate it there."

He spoke out loud, not caring whether anyone was around to hear. Everyone would know soon enough, if they didn't already—

"Serena Wolfe left Oliver! And took the boys to the city!"

"I heard her parents gave her back the trust fund."

"Trust fund? She had a trust fund?"

"Smart boy, that Oliver, for marrying her."

"Yeah, but he couldn't hold onto her, could he?"

"No worries, plenty of women in town would kill to marry one of the Wolfe boys."

That was true, if Oliver could say so himself. He would have no trouble getting married again. In St. Caroline he was a catch. Deputy fire chief! Father of two adorable boys! Not bad looking —if he could say so himself. He had his father's hairline so he was going to end up bald at some point. But some women found bald to be sexy. That's what people said, right?

Only ... he didn't want to remarry. Even after everything, he wanted to be married to Serena. The old Serena, the one before the accident. The one before ... Ben.

He wondered what the gossip around town was on that. How many people knew? Everyone? That was probably a good bet. News travels fast in a small town. Maybe people had been whispering behind his back for years. If Matt had seen them together at Two Beans, then other people had also.

Maybe I'm the last to know.

After twenty minutes of walking aimlessly on the cemetery's winding path, he ended up at Ben's grave. Even Oliver wasn't surprised by that. He started to walk on by, but then stopped. He turned toward the pale marble stone.

Ben Ezra Wardman. Born 1987. Died 2017.

"Everyone says you're such a great guy. And that you'd never cheat on your wife. Nor would I." Oliver let out a bitter laugh. "I guess that's one thing we have in common." He walked around to the back of the headstone, as if expecting something else to be carved into the back. Some pithy quote or secret message. There was nothing, of course.

"Another thing we have in common—we both got extraordinary women to move to St. Caroline." He returned to the front. "We both clipped the wings of women who would have had bigger lives, if not for us. Quite the fraternity we're in, huh?"

He leaned over and yanked up a few weeds, tossed them into the grass beyond. "Well, Serena has her trust fund back." Another bitter laugh escaped. "She gave that up for me. How stupid was that? Would *you* have given up a trust fund for a woman?"

Oliver wasn't sure he would have. And what did that say about him?

"She wants to go back to school. She should, too. I'm a firefighter. What if something happens to me? I mean, look at my Uncle Jack. Died on a call. Hell, look at you. You died young and left a widow. And you didn't even have a dangerous job."

A breeze whistled through the leaves overhead. Oliver sensed someone behind him, his firefighter's situational awareness kicking in. He turned around to see a stocky bald figure walking on the path and headed his way. His father, dressed in his standard navy chinos and St. Caroline Fire Department windbreaker. Oliver stood and watched as his father approached.

"Hey son. Thought that was your car in the lot back there." His father glanced down at the headstone. "Paying your respects?"

"I was on my way to mom's. Noticed Ben's here."

"I'm on my way to your mother's, as well. We can walk together."

Tim Wolfe was a good three inches shorter than Oliver, but he seemed to take up more space. He had presence. Confidence. A groundedness that Oliver had always hoped he'd one day grow into. Clearly, that day wasn't here yet.

"Heard from Serena and the boys?"

"Yeah. The boys are enjoying the Irvings' indoor pool."

"Oh yeah? Well, who wouldn't?"

A cellophane-wrapped bouquet of flowers was cradled in his dad's arms. Why hadn't he noticed that until just now?

"You've never been to their house, have you?" His father seemed determined to add insult to injury.

"Never been invited."

"Hmm. I hope Serena doesn't feel she has to wait for an invitation to come to my house."

"I'm sure she doesn't. But the Irvings are different. They cut their daughter out of their life for eight years."

"So what's changed?"

"Her father had a heart attack or something. Rethinking his priorities, apparently." Oliver really did not want to discuss his in-laws with his father. Or with anyone, for that matter.

"Better late than never, I suppose."

Angela Wolfe's headstone came into view. With his father next to him, the empty expanse of grass next to her stone appeared more obvious. His parents had purchased side-by-side final resting spots. He stopped to let his father go ahead and place the flowers.

"Do you want me to leave?" Oliver asked. "Do you want to be alone?"

His father made an adjustment to the bouquet, then stood. He shook his head. "No. I don't think your mom would mind if we're both here."

"Do you ever hear mom's voice, like, talking to you?"

"No."

"Huh."

"I think she probably said everything she had to say to me when she was alive."

"Maybe she thinks you wouldn't listen anyway."

His father lightly socked him in the shoulder. "She always thought none of us listened. But that wasn't true."

"So what's the secret, dad?"

"Secret to what?"

"A long and happy marriage."

"Hell if I know. Love? Luck? Lack of better options?"

"That's helpful."

An insistent buzz sounded between them, and they pulled their respective phones from their jackets. Oliver hoped for a text from the boys. But it turned out to be his father's phone that had buzzed. His father glanced at the text, then returned his phone to his pocket.

"Who was that?" Oliver asked.

"Mattie. He agreed to take your shift for tomorrow. Heath is willing to trade with you for next week."

"Why are you changing my schedule?"

"So you can go join your family."

"Serena doesn't want me there." In fact, she had told him exactly that, told him he needed a few days by himself to think. Or feel. Or something.

His father turned to look at him, one eyebrow lifted. "What's going on with you two?"

"Serena had an affair."

"She did? With whom?"

"Ben Wardman."

His father frowned. "Honestly, Ollie, I doubt that. If for no other reason than that Serena is smart enough not to pick someone who lives in town."

"Thanks, dad. That's just what I needed to hear."

His father clapped a hand between Oliver's shoulder blades and gave him a gentle nudge back toward the paved pathway.

"She's not the same person she was before the accident," Oliver added.

"Spouses change over the course of a marriage. Even without head injuries."

"I think I was just a youthful rebellion on her part and now she wants the life she was born to."

"Love is always kind of a rebellion, I'd say."

Oliver didn't agree with that idea, but he kept his disagreement to himself as they walked back to the parking lot. He had never needed rebellion in his life. Rebel against what? His parents, who'd had exactly the life he wanted for himself? And now that life had gone all to hell. His mother was dead. His wife was like a person he didn't know anymore. His boys were two hundred miles away, getting their heads turned by their rich grandparents.

His father walked him right up to his car. "You know, Oliver, your mother made me a better person. And I like to think I made her a better person, too. Maybe that was our secret. We were better together than apart."

CHAPTER 37

*O*liver gazed down at the street, fifty-two stories below. The distance looked much greater from up here. In fact, everything looked different now that he was actually standing in the reception area of the company where Peter Irving worked. Every decision he made in the past twenty-four hours was beginning to look suspect—even the decisions that were made, reversed, and then reversed again.

But here he was. Behind him sat a well-dressed young woman who had quietly picked up a phone and relayed the news of his arrival to Serena's father. Oliver hadn't expected his father-in-law to agree to see him this morning, especially not on such short notice and in his office. He still had no idea what he was going to say to the man, despite wracking his brain for words on the train ride up from Washington. But if he was going to lose his family, he wasn't doing it silently, without even a word in his own defense.

That's all he had ever wanted. A family, a decent life in St. Caroline. Hell, to hear Mattie talk, that was all every single woman on the planet wanted. A decent man who wanted to get married, make babies, and live happily ever after. Maybe that wasn't enough for the Serena Irvings of the world, but that was what Oliver could offer. That, and great sex.

Might want to leave that off the table.

Yeah, he wasn't going to mention that to her father.

Just be yourself.

Yup. He glanced down at his pressed khakis and his boat shoes. When the Irvings came to visit over Easter, Peter Irving had seemed disappointed that Oliver didn't have his boat out of winter storage yet. Not that he owned a yacht or anything, but years ago he purchased a used Chris-Craft that had seen better days from a guy on Kent Island and fixed it up.

He fiddled with the braided leather belt Serena had given him one year for his birthday, then tucked in his shirt some more. He'd worn a navy tee shirt emblazoned with the St. Caroline Fire Department logo on the chest. Maybe he should have gone with a dress shirt.

But this is who I am.

This was who Peter Irving's daughter was married to. A man who taught kids how to stop-drop-and-roll. A man who stood on street corners with his boot in hand, raising money for the fire department. A man who could find his way through a smoke-filled building. A man who knew how to restart a heart on a side-walk. A man who would run into a skyscraper, like this one, to save someone like Peter Irving.

Oliver turned back from the floor-to-ceiling windows just in time to see his father-in-law, in his expensive suit and silk tie, headed across the grey carpet toward him. Oliver met him halfway in a firm handshake.

The realization emboldened him as he accompanied Peter Irving back to his office—which was spacious and elegantly decorated. He sat in the chair that the other man waved at. Peter sunk into his own large leather chair, one that seemed to dwarf him rather than make him look important. He appeared marginally better than he had in March, but his age was clearly catching up to him. Serena's parents were older than his.

"Glad you could join us here in the city," Peter Irving said. "Serena took the boys to the Empire State Building this morning." He checked the heavy gold watch on his wrist. "They're probably heading over to the museum of natural history about now." He looked directly at Oliver. "But I'm guessing that's not why you're here."

"No, it's not." He was not going to let this man intimidate him. "I never formally asked for Serena's hand in marriage."

Peter laughed. "Doubt she would have let you do that."

"No. I'm certain she would not. She seems to have been raised to make her own decisions." He held his father-in-law's gaze. "I will never be a rich man. But I love your daughter and I have been good to her." Peter Irving opened his mouth to speak. Oliver cut him off. "She could do better than me, I'm sure. But she could do a lot worse, too."

He watched as the other man struggled to maintain his poker face. He imagined that not many people challenged Peter Irving.

"She waited until the absolute last minute to begin our wedding ceremony because even at that point she was still holding out hope that you had changed your mind and would be there," Oliver continued.

His father-in-law took a deep breath. "You know, you were both young. She was always a little impetuous. Leap before you look. That sort of thing. We wanted the best for her. You have kids now, so I'm sure you understand that feeling."

Oliver nodded to concede the point.

Peter continued. "We didn't think rushing into marriage with a man she'd met less than six months earlier was a good idea— emotionally or financially. It was our expectation that the two of you would split up within the year." His eyes darted toward the heavy gold watch on his wrist again.

Oliver knew the time allotted for this appointment was dwindling.

"Obviously, we were wrong."

That was about as close to an apology as Oliver imagined he would ever get. Not that he had come here for an apology. He had come to ... what? Draw a line in the sand? Stake a flag in the ground? He had spent mile after mile on the train, staring sightlessly through the window, knowing that he had to make this trip but not quite knowing exactly why.

He wasn't here to antagonize his father-in-law. He was here to ... then it hit him. He was here to assert his place in Serena's life, something he should have done years ago—and something that was more necessary now, if the Irvings were going to be part of their lives from here on out. He was here to set the ground rules. *For my family.*

He stood. "My boat's coming out of winter storage next week. If you can make some time this summer, you're welcome to come down and sail with me and the boys."

He was here to be the better man.

OLIVER FOUND his family by the triceratops. Mason and Cam were counting the fossil skeleton's rib bones, while Serena pored over the museum's foldout map. He watched them through the crowd for a few minutes, his heart aching with love at the sight of his sons in their best khaki shorts and polo collared shirts. He couldn't help himself—his mind sketched into the picture a little girl wearing a sundress and Converse sneakers.

Converse sneakers?

He'd seen Jack's daughter wearing them with a dress. *It was a cute look.* Girly but tomboy. Exactly the way he had always pictured a daughter of his own.

When Serena was pregnant last year, he had convinced

himself that their daughter would have her mother's wild, curly hair and infectious laugh. Of course, who knew? She could just as easily have ended up with straight hair and Mason's more guarded disposition.

Either would be fine—or perhaps even some completely new-to-the-family personality. Something to dilute all the testosterone.

He sensed his mother rolling her eyes about now.

He moved with the crowd to keep his wife and sons in view. He was a man of modest ambition, beyond providing for his family and making his hometown a better place. But if he didn't do those things, who would? Certainly not the "masters of the universe" like his father-in-law.

All of a sudden, Mason and Cam lost interest in the triceratops and rushed over to their mother. Oliver's heart skipped a beat. Was something happening? A vision of Cassidy in Boston flashed through his head. He glanced around the dinosaur hall, but saw nothing out of the ordinary. Families clustering about, tired kids, bored parents. Cam was patting Serena's hand and it was then that Oliver noticed the vibration in her shoulders. She wiped her cheek with her other hand.

She was crying! He threaded his way through the crowd of tired kids and bored parents, resisting the urge to push people out of the way. What was going on? Did something happen that morning at her parents' house?

"Dad!" Cam's voice rang out over the low-level buzz of the dinosaur hall. Mason and Serena turned to look Oliver's way.

"Babe." He wrapped his arms around his wife and cradled her dark head against his chest. "What's the matter?"

"Mom's sad." Mason patted her hand.

Oliver peeled the museum map from Serena's fingers and handed it to his older son. "Why's that?" Beneath his arms, Serena's sobs had stilled.

"The dinosaurs remind her of her nana."

"They do?"

Serena's head bobbed up and down against his chest. She leaned back to look up at him.

"My grandmother in Atlanta used to take me and Peter to the Fernbank museum when we visited in the summer. They had dinosaur fossils there."

"Ah." He looked over her head at Mason and Cam, expecting to see bemused expressions on their faces. But it appeared that bursting into tears over old bones made complete sense to them.

"I'll explain later," she said. "What are you doing here?"

"Dad gave me a few days off." He ran his thumbs beneath her eyes to wipe away the tears. "Hope you don't mind."

"Dad! Come check out the triceratops!"

Oliver lifted his eyebrows, silently asking the question.

"It's fine," she mouthed back.

Oliver slid his hand down to hers, laced their fingers together, and turned to their boys.

"Okay, so what do I need to know about this fearsome dinosaur here?"

AFTER AN EXHAUSTIVE TOUR of the prehistoric era and a late lunch at Shake Shack, the four of them tumbled out of a cab in front of the Irvings' limestone mansion. It was four in the afternoon, and even Oliver needed to get off his feet and rest.

But ... he looked up and down the block, then squinted at the house number on the "house" they were standing in front of. Could you call this a house? The building looked like something you'd see in a movie. A movie about extremely rich people. It was —he counted the rows of windows—five stories. Ahh, it was an apartment building! That made sense. City people lived in apartments.

"Dad!" Cam headed for the wide grey steps. "This is where Grandma and Grandpa Irving live!"

"Cam, wait up," Oliver cautioned.

But it was too late. Mason was bounding up the steps, as well. Then things got weird. The wide double doors to the building opened and an older, uniformed man stepped out.

"Mr. Delacroix!"

Wait … his boys were on a first name basis with the doorman? Well, not "first name" but clearly past the "stranger danger" admonitions he had drilled into their heads.

"You must be Oliver," the man looked at him. *Okay, so the doorman is on a first name basis with me.* "Mr. Irving rang to let us know you were in the city."

Serena tugged at Oliver's arm and led him toward the steps. "Ollie, this is Mr. Delacroix. He's been with my parents for years."

With her parents? Oliver's head was spinning now. Then Mr. Delacroix stepped aside to allow them all to enter and … Oliver's head nearly exploded. He was expecting the usual apartment building lobby—nicer than any he'd ever seen, naturally—but one with a front desk, a bank of metal mailboxes set into a wall, an elevator or two …

"This is your *house?*" he whispered to Serena as the boys ran up a staircase that looked to be made of … marble?

She looped her arm through his. "Take a deep breath." She smiled at Mr. Delacroix, who hovered for a moment and then discreetly disappeared up the staircase behind Mason and Cam. "I know it's a bit much."

"I guess when you said your parents had a pool in the basement, I thought it was like a communal pool. For the whole building. But …" He looked around at the foyer and shook his head. "Granted, I've only been in them when they're on fire but the mansions around St. Caroline aren't anything like *this.*"

"Just one of the many things I like about your hometown."

She gave his hand a gentle squeeze, a simple gesture but a

familiar one that calmed the blur of agitation in his chest. It had been awhile since he felt calm. Maybe Serena hadn't been able to magically turn him into a better man all by herself, but he certainly *felt* better when she was around.

"So why are you here, really?" she added. "And how did my father know about it?"

Footsteps sounded on the staircase, then Mason's voice. "Dad? You guys coming up?"

"Be right up, bud!" He looked at Serena, badly wanting to take her in his arms but also not wanting to make a fool out of himself if she'd already made up her mind.

To leave him.

"I went to his office first."

"Why?"

"I should have stood up for myself eight years ago, when we got married. I should have stood up for *us*. I told him that I know you could have done a lot better than me. But that you also could have done a lot worse."

Her expression was unreadable, another thing that was different about Serena these days. She no longer wore her feelings on her sleeve. The accident had taken away more than just her memory—it also wiped away some of her exuberance, that devil-may-care approach to life that had led her to marry a man she'd known for mere months.

She was a little more like him now. Cautious. Prudent. Burdened by the understanding that everything could disappear in a heartbeat. He was going to have to shoulder more of the emotional weight of their relationship. He knew that now. If their marriage was going to survive the accident, it couldn't just coast along on her energy alone.

He took a deep breath. Talking about relationship stuff had always been akin to running into a burning building for him. Get in, locate the fire, extinguish it, and then get the hell out. That wasn't the right analogy, though. A relationship wasn't a fire to put out. It was a fire to keep going. For a firefighter, this was scary territory.

Losing her was an even scarier prospect.

"But I didn't come here to talk to your father." He pulled her closer. "I came because we need to talk about … stuff. About everything. About us." He tucked a dark curl behind her ear.

"It couldn't wait until the boys and I got home?"

"I was afraid that might be too late. And I know that I totally and completely suck at talking about … you know, stuff. Feelings. But I know I need to try. Try a little harder."

He held his breath while her eyes searched his, studied his face, took his measure. He wasn't used to not knowing what she was thinking just from looking at her face or her body language. *I must have driven her nuts all these years.* Probably he was lucky they were still married.

Her small hands reached up and cupped his jaw, tugged his face down toward hers. Her lips were about to brush his, when Mason's voice sounded again from the top of the staircase.

"Guys?"

She let her hands slip from his cheeks.

I love my kids. I really do, but … Mason had terrible timing.

Serena took a step back, then turned toward the stairs. "Boys, please ask your grandmother to give you some milk. Then why don't the two of you go up to Uncle Peter's room and rest before dinner?"

"Cam's already asleep at the table," Mason answered.

She sighed. "Okay. We'll be right up." She looked over her shoulder at Oliver. "We'll have to talk later tonight, okay?"

"Sure thing." He followed her up the marble stairs to the rest of the Irvings' ridiculous house.

CHAPTER 38

Serena quietly closed the door to her childhood bedroom behind her. Surprisingly, the room looked mostly the way it had when she was a teenager. She wondered why her mother had never redecorated it.

"So this was your room?" Oliver said from beneath the covers of her childhood bed.

She nodded. "Well, when I was home from boarding school, that is. I spent more time at school than I did here."

"It doesn't really seem like you."

"No. It's probably not how I would have done the room."

The walls were covered in a pale, textured wallpaper. A large Persian rug was centered on the dark hardwood floor. An upholstered loveseat sat in front of the heavy chintz drapes that shielded the windows. There really wasn't anything in the room that had been chosen by Serena herself.

Which was fine.

This wasn't her home anymore. She tried to give Mason and Cam more autonomy in their lives than she'd had in hers as a child. But her childhood was water under the bridge now. She was trying to accept her parents as the people they were right now. Today.

She turned off the bedside lamp and crawled into bed. Oliver opened his arms and she snuggled into them. The fact that he had gotten on a train and come to New York made her cautiously optimistic.

But not completely optimistic.

"Now where were we?" he asked.

"You were going to demonstrate your new talking skills, I believe."

"Oh. Right. I guess I was thinking about what almost happened after that."

She pressed her lips lightly to his. "There. If you want more, you're going to have to dish." There was just enough light in the room to see Oliver's mock pout.

"I dented the garage door."

"Okay. That's technically not a feeling, but ... how on earth did you do that?" She imagined him kicking it out of frustration.

"I ran into it with the car."

"You didn't open the door first?"

The mattress vibrated with his shrug. "I don't know what happened. I wasn't paying attention, I guess."

"Well, now there are two unexplained accidents in the family."

"I think I can hammer out the dent."

"Or we can have it replaced. My parents are definitely releasing my trust fund. And we will pay back your dad for my medical expenses."

"Oh. Can I ask how much that is?"

She hesitated. They had never discussed this in great detail. It hadn't mattered since she didn't have the money anyway. But now Ollie had a right to know.

"It's a little over two." She flattened her palms against his chest, feeling his heartbeat beneath the skin. "Million." She glanced up at the stunned expression on his face.

It took Ollie a few more moments before he could speak. "You gave up two million dollars to marry me?"

"Mmm. I must have really loved you."

"Either that, or you're a complete idiot. If I had known how much it was, I wouldn't have let you marry me."

"Good thing I didn't tell you, then."

"Seriously, Serena, what were you thinking?"

"I was thinking that I loved you, Ollie. And I loved your family, how close you all are." She lifted a hand from his chest and waved it at the room surrounding them. "That's what upset me in the museum today. I was remembering my grandmother and how close I was to her. And it hit me that Mason and Cam won't have that kind of relationship with a grandmother. My mother is trying, but … it won't be the way it was with your mom."

She felt tears stinging at her eyes again. Ollie pulled her closer until there wasn't even a centimeter of space between them.

"No, they won't have that," he said. "But they'll have aunts and uncles, their cousin Jackie, really cool trips to New York. They'll have other things."

"Those things can't replace—" A hiccup escaped her chest. "—your mom."

"There's nothing to be done about that." He pressed a kiss into her hair. "But their children can have those grandparents. *We* can be those grandparents someday."

She tilted her head back so she could look him in the eye. If he was talking about them as grandparents, then maybe he hadn't completely given up on their marriage.

"I don't remember being anything more than just friends with Ben. But if there was, I am sorry, Ollie. Sorrier than words can express. I want you. Only you. I can't picture the rest of my life without Oliver Wolfe in it."

"Would you ever tell me if you remembered?"

"Would you want me to?"

He was silent for a good long while.

"Probably not," he said at last.

"I'm not the sort of person to sleep with my best friend's husband. I know I'm not." She traced her finger along his jaw. "All I can offer as evidence is my character, Ollie. What you know of me as a person." She grazed his lower lip with the pad of her thumb. "And you know me better than anyone else ever has. You know that's true."

"And you know me better than anyone. Hell, better than I know myself. And you're right. I haven't let myself grieve for my mom."

"You bottle things up."

"I have to or I'd be useless on a call. I can't afford to *feel* everything I see."

He paused and Serena allowed him the time to think.

"I lost it that day, the day of the accident. Dad and Mattie had to physically restrain me to keep me from tearing you out of that car with my bare hands."

She felt his arms twitch and she knew he wanted to cross them in front of his chest, assume that protective, closed off posture he did so frequently. She took his hands in hers and kissed his knuckles, one by one.

He spoke again, his voice low. "You've always made me feel out of control, Serena. Ever since I met you. I find myself doing things I wouldn't normally do. Like hopping on a train to New York and asking some rich man who's never particularly liked me to come visit so I can take him sailing."

"You invited my dad to go sailing?" She touched his forehead, like she was checking one of the boys for a fever. "Why? I mean, that's nice of you but if you'd rather not …"

"I was trying to be the better man."

She let her hand slip from his forehead to his cheek, holding it there, lightly. "Oh Ollie. You were always the better man. I knew that the night we met." She giggled softly. "We went skinny-dipping and you didn't even *try* to sleep with me."

"See?" He smiled in the dark. "You make me do ridiculous things." Then his face grew serious again. "You also make me feel things I don't always want to feel."

"Like what?"

"Like sheer, unmitigated terror. That I'm going to lose you. Lose the boys. That one day you'll wake up and realize that you could have a bigger life than I can give you."

"So you know how I feel every time you go to work. That today will be the day you don't come home from a call."

"How do you do that?" He rose suddenly, pushing himself into a seated position against the silk-covered headboard of her bed.

He was putting distance between them, the way he always did when a conversation got into uncomfortable territory. Normally, she'd allow him to do it, let him stay in his comfort zone. But not tonight. If they didn't finish this conversation, he might not be willing to go this far again.

"I pretend I'm not afraid," she answered. "I hope that you'll be like your dad and not your Uncle Jack." She pulled herself up off the mattress and crawled toward Ollie. She straddled his outstretched thighs, staying on her knees so they could be face to face. "I trust in your training to protect you."

"I don't worry about my safety that much. I have some measure of control over what happens when I'm working. Or my response to it, at any rate."

"But I don't have any control over it. I just have to trust that the universe will deliver you home to me and the boys, day after day." She leaned in and flattened her palms on his chest. "If you love something, it's going to hurt if you lose it. You can't have love without that fear."

"Sometimes you sound just like mom."

"I loved your mom. And to wake up and discover that she was

gone … and to see that you and your dad and your brothers are all just flailing around …"

Suddenly Oliver's arms were open and reaching around her, pulling her into his chest. "I know you loved her. That the two of you were so close always made me …"

His words hung there, unfinished, but she didn't push him on this. He was being more open than she'd ever seen him—it was progress and she'd take it. She kissed the warm skin of his chest.

"We never told her about your accident," he added. "She passed a few days later. We didn't want to upset her any further. Dad, especially, was worried that she'd try to hang on if she knew you were in the hospital and she was in so much pain by that point …"

She watched Oliver's face crumple and tears begin to stream down his cheeks. She'd seen him cry a few times before—at Mason's birth, after a particularly difficult call with the fire department—but not often. But now the bottle that his emotions were normally stuffed into had popped its cap.

She held his shaking body as he cried into her chest, soaking the front of her pajama top with his tears. As she held him, something nudged at her brain. She closed her eyes to focus on it, try to pull it closer before it could slip away. For every memory she managed to lasso, two others disappeared as quickly as they came.

But she had this. A husband whose faithfulness she'd never had reason to doubt. Two sons. Enough time to try and have more children. A truce, finally, with her parents. So what if she couldn't remember everything that came before—maybe this was enough. It *had* to be enough.

Live in the present.

Right. The here and now. That's what was most important. It was a cliché, but no one was guaranteed a tomorrow. She was given a second chance when she woke from her coma. *They* had been given a second chance, when so many other people weren't. What more could they ask?

It would have to be enough for Ollie, too. She couldn't give him back the past. He would have to be content with what they had right now.

She held him until every last emotion had been cried out.

CHAPTER 39

Serena took a deep breath and pushed open the door to the education and health sciences building at Talbot College. It was the evening of the education program Open House. Oliver was at work, but Becca was watching the boys for a few hours. They had barely noticed her leaving, so excited they were at the prospect of Facetiming with their cousin, Jackie.

She stepped into the air-conditioned lobby, where tables were lined up around the perimeter. Check-in, Admissions, Curriculum, Financial Aid, Career Services. The soft light of a summer evening washed everything in the soaring windowed atrium with a shimmery gold.

She headed for the Check-in table, where two women sat behind laptop computers and tent cards that read "A—M" and "N—Z." She walked up to the "N—Z" woman.

"Last name?" the woman asked.

"Wolfe. Serena Wolfe."

She waited as the woman clicked and scrolled, then paused. Nodded. Looked up at Serena.

"This is your second Open House?" the woman said.

Serena shook her head. "No. My name's *Serena* Wolfe. I registered back in March."

The woman leaned in and squinted at the computer screen. "Right. Serena Wolfe. It says here that you attended an Open House last August, as well. No, wait." The woman squinted harder. "You were registered for the August session but it looks like you didn't check in. So I guess you didn't come." She looked up from the screen and smiled. "It happens. Life gets in the way, right? But you're here now."

She tapped a key, then slid a sheet of blank labels toward Serena. "Make a name tag and you're all set."

Serena printed her name on a label, peeled it off, and stuck it to her twill summer blazer. She walked to the Admissions table and got in line. With a degree from Princeton, she wasn't worried about her academic credentials but her work experience was a little thin. She was stretching the concept of switching careers, since she'd barely had a career before marrying Oliver.

And what was all that about her registering for an earlier Open House? They must have her mixed up with someone else in their records. As she gazed up at the atrium's ceiling, a dizzying sense of déjà vu slammed into her. She took a deep breath to clear her mind, then returned to the Check-in table.

"Excuse me," she said to the woman she'd left just a moment earlier. "What day was the August Open House?"

The woman smiled brightly at her. "August 12th. But you never checked in."

"Right. But I was registered?"

The woman nodded.

"Thank you." Serena turned away from the table, thunderstruck. August 12th. *The day of the accident.* She was driving here that day. *Only I never made it.*

She hadn't been driving to see Ben. Or to see Angie in the hospital—even her own theory was wrong. *And I didn't tell Ollie about it because I didn't want to upset him if I changed my mind.* It was all coming back to her now.

She dug in her purse for her phone, and tapped Oliver's name in her contact list. Predictably, he didn't pick up. He was at work. She didn't leave a message.

The line at the Admissions table had cleared, so she approached the older gentleman standing behind it. She introduced herself, explained her academic background and volunteer experience. They discussed application deadlines for a moment, then Serena moved on to the Curriculum table. She was juggling an armful of brochures and course planning worksheets, when she heard her phone ring deep in her purse. She hurried to a bench by the back wall to answer it.

"Babe? I saw you called. What's up? Are you at the Open House?"

"I am. And guess what? I was registered to come to an Open House here last year. On August 12th."

She waited for that information to sink in, then heard a sharp intake of breath on the other end.

"On the day of the accident? You were at the college?"

"No. I never made it here. I must have had the accident on the way. They have me in their system as being registered, but not checked in for that date."

"But I don't remember that—"

"I didn't tell you, Ollie, because I wasn't sure I really wanted to do this."

"And that's why you left the kids with Charlotte that day."

"Yes."

"Wow."

"I know, right?"

She leaned into the hard back of the bench. For the first time in months, she felt relaxed. There was no looming secret hovering just out of view, ready to drop and crush her entire life.

"I'm glad I remembered that," she added.

"Me too. When will you be home?"

She glanced at the other tables she still needed to visit, and the lines moving slowly by each one. "I think I'll be here another half hour. Then half an hour to drive home."

"I'll try to be home before the boys go to bed."

"Love you, Ollie."

"Love you, too."

An hour later, she was pulling the minivan out of the parking lot, a folder stuffed with class descriptions and schedules on the passenger seat beside her. She opened the window on her side to enjoy the warm evening air and cranked up the radio a bit. It felt so damn good to have that mystery behind her. She was looking forward to going back to school. It would be difficult, with the boys still so young and Oliver's crazy schedule at the station. But she was up for the challenge. Speaking to the professors at the Open House had only reinforced that. For the first time, she could imagine her own classroom with her own students.

But there was still one mystery left.

On her way to the college, she had driven past the accident site but not stopped. On the way home, she braked the minivan onto the shoulder of the road and cut the ignition. The big white oak tree stood on the other side. She checked for traffic, then got out of the car. She ran across the road to stand in front of the tree.

What had happened here?

"I was on my way to the college," she thought out loud. "Why didn't I make it?"

She trailed her fingers down the bark of the tree. She knew the answers didn't lie behind it. They were stuck deep inside her brain—too deep for her to reach. After a few more minutes, she gave the tree a friendly pat.

"Not your fault."

She darted back across the road to the minivan. She was about to put the car into drive when her phone rang. The bluetooth screen displayed her mother's number. She stared at the numerals and listened to the distorted ringing coming through the car's speakers … and couldn't move.

This is what happened.

Her mother's call rolled over to voice mail.

My phone rang.

But it hadn't been her mother calling on August 12th as she drove to the college. It was Angie Wolfe, calling from the hospital. And Serena had answered, hands-free. Earlier, she had thought about stopping by the hospital to see her mother-in-law, if there was enough time after the Open House. Charlotte wasn't available to babysit the entire afternoon.

But she had ended up in a different hospital instead, airlifted to Baltimore, because Angie had called to say "goodbye." *Just in case.*

Angie's condition had been recently downgraded but, like the rest of the family, Serena was in denial about it. They were all going to wake up one day and discover that Angie's illness was just a bad dream. Angie was healthy. She was going to be around for years to come, for all the future weddings and grandkids, retirement and old age. All of that would still happen.

Angie wasn't in denial, though. She was the sort of person to try and put every last affair in order before shuffling off the mortal coil. Of course, she would make her goodbyes.

"Take care of those boys of yours," were her final words, "and that boy of mine, too."

Tears were streaming down Serena's face—then and now. She had stretched her arm to reach her purse, digging around for that small package of tissues. The car drifted into the other lane, just for a moment. She dropped the tissues and grabbed the steering wheel with both hands. She swerved back into the right lane.

But she overcorrected and lost control of the car.

That's where the memory ended. But she knew what happened next—the car collided with the white oak tree.

She leaned her forehead against the steering wheel of the new minivan, her body shaking uncontrollably. *Thank god no one told Angie about the accident.*

FOR A NIGHT with no calls so far, the station was barely-controlled mayhem. The department's "committees"—Oliver always used that term loosely—were meeting to finalize plans for the annual Fireman's Carnival at the end of the month. For St. Caroline residents, the carnival marked the official start of the summer season.

"Just put me wherever you need me," Oliver shouted, then closed his father's office door behind him.

"You have plans from the architect already?" His father looked up from his computer screen.

"Well, not final plans. There's a process here. So what we have now is the program." Oliver put air quotes around the word. "It's a preliminary list of proposed spaces and sizes." Oliver dropped the printout in front of his father.

"Oh, okay."

"It's based on the meeting we had with him and some additional input I gave him."

His father flipped through the pages. "I see the community room is on here."

"We need one, Dad. Come on. If we have a nicer one in the new facility, you could repurpose the old one here."

Tim Wolfe toggled his head back and forth, considering the idea. "Maybe."

Oliver bit back an exasperated sigh. *You're dealing with a Wolfe here. Stubborn to the bone.*

"Mom always said you were stubborn to the bone."

"Your mother was occasionally right."

Always right.

Oliver had no intention of getting in the middle of an argument between his mother and father right now. His head was still reeling from the news that Serena had been headed to Talbot College when the accident occurred.

"Well, take a look at it and give me your feedback." His phone buzzed in the pocket of his black pants. He pulled it out. It was Serena.

"Hey there," he answered as he backed out of his father's office.

"Ollie?" Her voice was faint and shaky.

"Serena? What's wrong? Where are you?"

Thoughts of everything that could possibly be wrong rushed his head. His father looked up from the architect's program, a worried expression on his face.

"I'm at the accident site."

"Why?" His hand trembled.

"I was on my way home from the Open House. It's on the way."

"I know, but … are you okay?"

"I'm fine. But I need someone to come pick me up. I don't think I should drive the rest of the way home."

"You didn't have another accident, did you?" Oliver started to pace back and forth.

"No. But I remembered the accident. I know what happened, Ollie."

She remembered the accident. That was good! Or wait … how *much* did she remember?

"I'm okay, Ollie. I'm just too shaken to drive home."

"I'll be right there, babe. Don't move." He leaned back into his father's office. "Dad, is Jack home tonight?"

"Is everything alright?"

"Serena remembers the accident. Is Jack home?"

"I assume so. Becca is babysitting your kids."

Oliver ran from the station, leaving its carnival mayhem

behind. He was headed toward his own mayhem—the thing he had wanted to happen. And the thing he had dreaded happening.

Jack was waiting in the driveway when he got to his father's house. His brother and new bride were still living there, for the time being. The official reason was for them to save money. The unofficial reason was to keep their dad from coming home to an empty house each night.

"Dad called." Jack opened the door and hopped into the passenger seat of Oliver's SUV. "Why's Serena at the accident site?"

"She was driving home from the college. It's on the way. I don't know the whole story yet. But she said she remembers what happened. And she knows where she was headed that day. To an earlier Open House at the school." Oliver backed the car down the driveway. "She didn't have an affair with Ben Wardman." Even he could hear the note of defensiveness in his voice.

Jack held up his hands. "Hey, man. I never thought she did."

Right. No one else thought she did. *It was only ever me.*

Oliver drove faster than the speed limit and hoped no one recognized him and Jack. EMTs speeding—not a good look. But he needed to get to Serena quickly.

He spotted the minivan immediately, even in the fading light of dusk. It was stopped on the other side of the road, well away from that damn tree. Gravel on the shoulder sprayed as he pulled an expert U turn and slammed on the brakes.

A million memories marched through his mind—that moment when he recognized the crumpled car as his own, the heart-stopping fear that the boys were in the back seat, the utter helplessness he'd felt while other men cut his wife from the vehicle.

The memories were fighting with what he was seeing right now. The car intact. Upright. On the other side of the road from the tree, which would always look menacing to him. This time, he knew the boys weren't in the car. They were safe at home with Becca.

He got out and ran to the minivan—and this time, no one held him back. This time, his lovely wife stepped down from the driver's seat before he even got there. He lifted her up off her feet and swung her around once before setting her back down. He heard Jack driving away.

"That was quite the driving maneuver there," she said.

"You make me do crazy things. Crazy, idiotic things." He cupped her cheeks in his palms, amazed still—after all these years —that she had consented to marry him.

"I would never cheat on you, Oliver. I love you. I love the life we have together."

He leaned down to kiss her, but stopped himself at the last moment. He needed to do something else, first.

Apologize.

"I'm sorry that I doubted you. I was scared and feeling like nothing was under my control after the accident. After mom's passing."

Now he could kiss her—kiss her the way he should have been kissing her these past months. Her lips were warm and soft, and her body melted into his. Just the way it had before they were married. Before they had kids and a house to take care of and … sorrows to share. "I needed an explanation for what happened."

"Now I can give you one. But it might upset you, so we should drive home first."

Normal Oliver knew they should do exactly that. Go home, relieve Becca of her babysitting duties (untie her, if necessary), put the boys to bed. Load the dishwasher, take out the recycling, turn out the lights.

He locked Normal Oliver in the backseat.

"I have a better idea." He turned and knelt. "Climb on."

"Your better idea is a piggyback ride?" But she looped her

arms around his neck and her legs around his waist. "I *do* make you do crazy things."

He jostled her a moment. "This is just the transportation."

He looked both ways up and down the road, then jogged with her over to the other side. He let her slide down to the ground, then led her to the base of the white oak. He sat down and pulled her down with him, wrapped his arms around her.

"So tell me what happened."

And then he listened, holding Serena as she began to cry again, biting his lip to keep his own emotions under control, hugging her tighter.

"So my mother called you to say 'goodbye?'"

She nodded. "I was so upset, Ollie. It wasn't real until that moment, that she was going to die."

"I know, babe. I know."

"It wasn't her fault. She didn't know I was in the car."

"She didn't know you were headed to the college?"

"No. I didn't tell anyone. I guess I should have."

Headlights appeared in the distance, tiny spots of light that grew until the car neared the tree, going too fast for the road. A car full of teenagers. One boy leaned his head out of the window and yelled, "Get a room!"

"I think that's our cue," she said. "Are you okay to drive?"

"Yes." He stood and helped her to her feet. "And babe? You're going to be a terrific teacher. St. Caroline is lucky that I convinced you to move to town."

She jabbed an elbow playfully into his side. "You're incorrigible, Oliver Wolfe."

Out of the corner of his eye, he saw her smile.

CHAPTER 40

"*I*'m going to be in the dunk tank someday," Mason said apropos of nothing and through a mouthful of funnel cake. He sported a powdered sugar mustache and Serena's mind flash-forwarded to a time in the future when Mason would be able to grow real facial hair.

Not ready for that yet.

She handed him the rest of her own funnel cake. The oil it was fried in was making her stomach queasy. "I don't doubt that." If he ended up in the St. Caroline Fire Department, he probably would do a few rounds in the dunk tank every year.

It was the last weekend in May, and the opening night of the annual Fireman's Carnival. Oliver was off somewhere, working. She spotted Jack up ahead, dressed in the department's Sparky the Fire Dog costume and handing out red plastic fire hats to kids. And a few adults.

This was where she and Oliver met, at a silly game she'd been completely inept at. He'd given her a prize anyway. She still had that black and white stuffed dalmatian. She'd given him her room number. Room 222. She would long ago have forgotten that, if it weren't for the fact that Oliver remembered it.

She smiled. Exactly none of her life before that night had been leading her here. Yet here she was.

And she was happy.

"Mom?" Cam tugged at her elbow. "Is Dad in the dunk tank yet?"

"I don't know, bud. We'll go check."

The boys needed a break from the rides anyway. After funnel cake, french fries, milkshakes … yeah, they needed some time to let their stomachs settle. She held their hands—Mason on the left, Cam on the right—as she made her way through the crowds.

"Mom! Mom! He's in there! Hurry!" Mason tugged at her left hand.

"Slow down," she said. "I need to buy some tickets."

She shepherded them into a line at the ticket booth, wondering whether the dunk tank still required three tickets or whether the "price" had gone up since she had dunked Oliver that first night. Behind them, the cheering grew louder, culminating in a distinct splash.

"Dad got dunked!" Cam shouted.

At the window, Serena squinted at the sign and then requested six tickets. The price was the same. It was probably three tickets back when Oliver, Matt, and Jack were kids.

"No charge for you, Mrs. Wolfe," the young firefighter inside the booth said as he slid over a strip of tickets.

"Really?" She had her wallet out. "I don't mind paying."

He shook his head. "Kids get to dunk their parents for free." He leaned forward to speak to the boys. "Guys, the secret is to keep your eye on the metal target, not your dad. Okay?"

Serena doubted the boys would even remember that advice by the time they got to the front of the line at the dunk tank. Or that either of them had a strong enough arm to dunk their father. She hadn't, at the ripe old age of twenty-two. Oliver had cheated at that game for her, too. Those were quite possibly the only two times that straight arrow Oliver Wolfe had ever cheated at anything.

When they got to the head of the line, Mason went first. He handed over his tickets in exchange for the first ball. He hefted the white ball in his hands, while the crowd chanted, "Mason. Mason. Mason."

Serena looked up at Oliver, wondering whether he would cheat for his sons.

Mason's first throw went wide, missing the metal target entirely.

"Keep your eye on the target," Cam advised.

"I *know.*"

Serena could hear the frustration in her older son's voice. His second and third throws merely clipped the edge of the target, not with enough force to drop his dad into the water.

Mason stepped dejectedly back as Cam took his place. Serena again met Oliver's eyes. She could tell he was rethinking his parenting at the moment. His hand flirted with the release lever she knew to be beneath the narrow seat. She shook her head at him. If he didn't do it for Mason, he shouldn't for Cam.

"Cam-my, Cam-my," the crowd chanted.

Cam looked at the ball in his hand, then looked up and squinted his eyes, his concentration fierce. Serena held her breath. The crowd's chanting died down and she could hear Cam's quiet voice.

"Eye on the target."

Then Cam let loose with a beautiful line drive. Oliver was laughing as the seat gave way beneath him.

"ARE YOU SURE YOU'RE OKAY?" Oliver touched Serena's shoulder. She was looking a little green around the gills.

She smiled wanly. "I'm fine. Just a little … too much junk food tonight. You two go on." She waved at the ferris wheel. "I'll wait here with Cam."

Cam was still floating on cloud nine from his dunk tank triumph. But he wasn't fond of heights. He had inherited that from the Irving side of the family.

"Do you think ... maybe?" Oliver lowered his voice so the boys couldn't hear.

She gave a little shrug. "I'll go to the drugstore in the morning."

As he climbed into the ferris wheel seat with Mason, he tried to tamp down his hopes. The metal car swayed gently in the night air as it rose.

"You okay, bud?"

"Fine, dad."

This was the first year that Mason was tall enough to ride. The car stopped near the top as more people got on below. He glanced over at Mason, whose expression was a mix of wonder and peace. Oliver knew that feeling well. He could still remember riding the ferris wheel when he was a kid. Tonight, he enjoyed the shared moment with his son as the two of them took in the view. Out beyond the lights of the carnival and the edges of town, the countryside was dark.

The carnival was a place to test your luck. He'd gotten *very* lucky the year he met Serena Irving. He had known pretty quickly that he wanted to marry her. His was not an impulsive nature, but falling in love with Serena had never felt like a decision at all—much less an impulsive one. It felt more like he had been waiting for a woman like her—so when she showed up, there was really no decision to be made.

He peered down at the ground. Cam was engrossed in a nearby game of chance that some older kids were playing. But Serena's face was lifted toward the sky. She waved. He waved back.

He had almost lost her. Twice. Once to an accident and once to his own stupidity.

"Your mom is a good woman," he said to Mason, as the car began to move again.

"I know." In Mason's voice, Oliver could hear that his son was only half paying attention to him. In fairness, it was hard to compete with the view.

"One day, you'll meet a good woman too."

"Whatever, dad."

*M*ason felt older.

Well, it was his birthday so—*duh.* He was now officially eight years old. It was July 7th, also his dad's birthday. He wasn't quite clear on how old *he* was. *Old.* Maybe older than his mom? He wasn't sure on that, either.

But no matter. He was eight and going into the third grade in the fall. It just seemed older than seven. *A lot older.* Second grade was still kind of young. Like kindergarten, first grade, and second grade were the baby years of school. But third grade? *That's almost fourth grade.*

He glanced over at his younger brother, strapped into the minivan next to him. It wasn't fair that Cam was basically as tall as he was. Although Mason was pretty sure he was growing too. He wiggled his new Converse high tops. If he concentrated really hard, he could almost feel his leg bones stretching.

Two plastic-wrapped bunches of flowers lay across Cam's lap. They were driving to Ocean City for a week's vacation. The beach! Cotton candy! Saltwater taffy! He couldn't believe Cam didn't remember what saltwater taffy was.

But first, they were stopping at the cemetery to put flowers on Nana's grave. Cam was nervous about going to the cemetery, because they hadn't been before. Mason had the impression, though, that his parents were going on a regular basis. Of course, they had to if they wanted to talk to Nana.

Mason could talk to her almost every night. So he wasn't the least bit nervous, not even when his dad pulled the minivan through the fancy iron gates and row after row of gravestones came into view.

Okay, well maybe that made him a teeny bit nervous. There were an awful lot of gravestones. That meant an awful lot of dead people who were probably hanging around downtown, talking to their grandkids.

They walked along a path, and Mason eyed the stones as they passed. Some of them were so old you could barely make out the names and dates. But if he squinted, he could see 1792. Then 1845. 1871. 1923. Man, he knew St. Caroline was old, but …

"When are we gonna get there?" Cam's voice interrupted the scenery.

"Almost there, bud," his dad answered.

After a few more minutes, his parents stopped in front of a grave that looked newer. "Angela Jane Wolfe," it said. That was Nana.

"Is this it?" Cam asked.

"Yes, this is it." His dad unwrapped the flowers and handed one bunch to Cam and the other to Mason. "You guys put the flowers on."

"Where?" Cam looked from the flowers to the grave and back again.

"Just right there. On the ground." His dad pointed at the grass.

"How will Nana know they're here?"

Even Mason was beginning to get a little exasperated with Cam now. "She'll know." They carefully placed the flowers on the grass. Mason made sure his were touching Nana's stone.

"Is there something you wanted to tell Nana?" their dad prompted.

Mason could practically see the light bulb go off over his brother's head, like they show in the cartoons.

"Oh! Nana! We're getting a sister!" Cam blurted out. "We're going to have Jackie *and* a sister!"

Mason listened for his grandmother's response. But the air was silent. How could she not be here? *I told her we were coming.* Maybe she forgot?

"But we haven't picked out a name yet!"

Cam was on a roll now. Once you got him started, he could be a real motormouth. Besides, Mason knew his parents were already discussing names. Sometimes when he got out of bed to use the bathroom, he could hear them downstairs in the kitchen, talking. And sometimes he would stand at the top of the stairs for a few minutes, listening.

That's how he knew their mom had almost died in the accident. And that dad had totally flipped out at the scene, which you're not supposed to do when you're a firefighter. (Uncle Mattie confirmed the dad freakout.)

"Hey guys, we should hit the road so we get ahead of the beach traffic coming from the city."

His parents and Cam turned to leave. Mason kept staring at Nana's name on the stone. *Why wasn't she here?*

"Bud? You ready to go? The beach awaits," his dad said.

"I'll be there in a minute."

His dad gave him a weird look and for a second, Mason thought he wasn't going to leave. Then he did.

Nana? Are you here?

I'm always here, sweetie.

Oh. Did you hear though? We're getting a sister.

I heard. That's wonderful.

I'll look out for her.

I know you will.

Will you look out for her, too? Even though you never met her?

There was a long silence and, for a moment, he thought she was gone.

I'll look out for her, too.

Are you ever going away?

No. Not yet. Why do you ask?

Because I think Paps is still sad. He pretends he isn't but I think he is.

Yes, he is. I'll watch out for him. Now you go catch up to your brother and have fun at the beach.

We will, Nana. He waited a moment, to see if she'd say anything else. But it seemed that she was really, truly gone this time—probably off to take care of Paps.

"Ma-a-a-son!"

He turned to see his younger brother waving his long arms at him. He wouldn't tell Cam about Nana. Just like he had promised not to tell Cam yet about Santa. Uncle Mattie had made him pinky swear. Said it was part of the firefighter code of honor.

Yeah right.

He already knew that Paps had to tell Uncle Mattie the truth about Santa when Uncle Mattie was almost ten. *That's seriously late, dude!* And Paps was the best firefighter he knew. Probably the best anyone knew.

Definitely the best.

He flashed his nana a discreet thumbs up and broke into a jog to catch up with his family.

∽

Thanks for reading THIS REMINDS ME OF US!

Stay tuned for Book 5 in the St. Caroline Series—*Once in a Lifetime* (hint: it's Ashley's story).

In the meantime, check out my other books ...

If you've ever fantasized about running off to Paris with a sexy Frenchman, THE SENATOR'S WIFE is the story for you! (Warning: it may melt your e-reader.)

Or if you're of the mind that the wealthy CEOs in a romance novel should occasionally be the *women,* my PHLOX BEAUTY SERIES is a must-read. (Bonus points if you also like Beauty and the Beast and damaged heroes.)

ABOUT THE AUTHOR

Julia Gabriel writes contemporary romance that is smart, sexy, and emotionally-intense (grab the tissues). Her books have been selected as "Top Picks" by RT Book Reviews, and critics at RT Book Reviews, Kirkus, and others have called her work "nuanced," "heart-wrenching and emotional," "well-crafted contemporary romance," and "deeply moving storytelling."

She lives in New England where she is a full-time mom to a teenager, as well as a sometime writing professor and obsessive quilter (is there any other kind?). If all goes well, she'll be a Parisienne in her next life.

Sign up for Julia's Coffee Break email for the chance to win Coffee Care Packages, learn about new releases and sales, and more!

Say "hello" on social media ...

www.ingramcontent.com/pod-product-compliance
Lightning Source LLC
Chambersburg PA
CBHW070649180626
46817CB00006B/2290